Death

on the

Derwent

A Murder Mystery set in Belper 1949

by

Narvel Annable

British Library Cataloguing in Publication Data.
A catalogue record for this book is available
from the British Library

ISBN 0 9530419 2 1

Published by

Narvel Annable and Terry Durand

44 Dovedale Crescent
Belper
Derbyshire
DE56 1HJ

CONTENTS

Introduction

Introduction to Second Edition of Death on the Derwent

Hello Readers,

Over 15 years since the publication of Death on the Derwent, many have expressed pleasure in this first novel. I've been delighted and greatly encouraged by your kind words.

Some of the characters were inspired by gay men I knew personally. Like me, they were deeply closeted in a mindset, a cloak concealing the continual anxiety of leading a double life. Just as I was in 1999, they were frightened isolated individuals trying to behave like confident heterosexuals on the outside. They had to look like citizens easily fitting in with the majority.

As with my quirky composited characters in Death on the Derwent, I succeeded in dodging disapproval and maintained a mask of po-faced respectability for nearly 20 years hiding inside my small bungalow in the ultra conservative colliery village of Clowne in north-east Derbyshire. Like most closeted gay men, I spoke little of myself and was constantly on guard. It became a way of life.

Re-reading this work, sadly, I now reflect on the last days of the 20th century when an author and his creations had to proceed with such cowardly caution, disguising their true nature. Today's people who share same-sex attraction have come a long way from the dark homophobic days of Belper in 1949.

Most of the men I knew are no longer with us. Events described in the following pages took place in real places, peopled by a fictitious cast of caricatured composites inspired by a selection of the types I met many years ago. However real flesh and blood the original model, characters depicted on these pages, after being processed through my brain, are far removed from any real person - alive or dead.

Death on the Derwent was well received by the local press as you will see below. Accordingly, I invite you to join the formidable schoolmistress Miss Florence Calder and her small, cantankerous, hunchbacked sister Miss Madge, as they detect and attempt to unmask a clever murderer in the leafy, ivy-clad, quaint and quieter Belper of 1949.

This entertaining blend of fact and fiction, set against the skilfully described background of spectacular Derbyshire scenery, is both an intriguing 'whodunit' and also a local history. Atmospheric narrative will take you around the nooks and crannies of the old mill town, in both bright sunshine and also in menacing thick fog.

It is complete with a body in a boat, psychic phenomena in the candle-lit haunted halls of the rambling old Bridge House School, a séance, a conjuring trick and all ending in a surprise.

Some hilarious, colourful and quirky characters spanning the social divide from the past poverty of Cowhill, to the opulence of Bridge Hill, combine with suspense and dramatic tension to produce a thoroughly enjoyable thriller.

https://linktr.ee/narvelannable

narvel@btinternet.com

Tel: 01 773 82 44 83

Chapter 1

A Difficult Day at Bridge House School

Even from the parlour, the voice of Miss Madge Calder could be heard rising to a crescendo! Not yet a scream, not yet at its maximum - but getting near. These were the gloomy thoughts of her elder sister Miss Florence Calder, as, with foreboding, she sadly contemplated the bad start to this Saturday morning, September 3rd 1949.

Maud the maid had taken continual abuse from Miss Madge Calder for the last four years, but of late Florence had started to notice small warning signs in the form of glowering looks that -

"...the worm may be about to turn!"

The frequent raucous reprimands were loud enough to reverberate all the way from Miss Madge's bedroom on the first floor, down to the simple, old fashioned, but tastefully furnished and decorated dignified parlour. In the grand old easy chair facing her pleasant well shaded, dank, deep green, fern garden, sat the redoubtable dame of Bridge House and Bridge House School. In strong contrast to the present, measured, quiet, soothing tick-tock of the long case clock, this large room had for the early years of this century, echoed with the chatter, the excitement and laughter of six sisters and their mother. All now silent; all now long dead, save for the once beautiful Florence and her crippled and cantankerous ugly sister, in their half of a mansion of 30 rooms.

The other east wing had been occupied by the Lewis family since 1867, when the great house was originally divided, giving 15 rooms to each half. Old Samuel Lewis was **the** unassailable physician of Belper. His son Philip joined the practice in 1882, and his son Paul had been a GP since the First World War, and principal doctor in Belper since the death of Philip Lewis in 1935. Belper had always had the trusted benefit and confidence of a Dr Lewis for the last 82 years. Bridge House itself dated from 1812, when it was built for the mill manager on to the south facing side of the five storey South Mill.

After 137 years, the great handsome ivy clad Georgian house was now like its inhabitants, slowly decaying under the vast canopy of the ancient giant plane tree. This immense lofty riot of foliage and tangle, had looked down on the development of the little town since medieval

6

days. The comings and goings of little people to the Dame School, were just as the winking of an eye to the memory of this old tree which would have seen the time long before old Jedediah and his eighteenth century mills. The Calders proudly boasted that it needed ten children, arms outstretched, hand to hand, to span the circumference of the massive trunk. Fortunately the venerable old giant was blithely ignorant of the fact that its life would be cut short, literally, within one decade.

It was also peacefully insouciant to the present drama being played out behind the solid door below, with its attractive classical portico.

It was the third sharp reprimand suffered by Maud Cooper that morning, and was destined to become one reprimand too many! First it was Miss Madge Calder's boiled egg at breakfast, boiled too long, and consequently was too hard. Then the great kitchen had been left in a good clean condition of orderliness by normal standards, but **not** up to the pristine standards required of Madge Calder. The last straw was the unacceptable corners of the bed clothes on Madge's bed. Maud knew well that neat hospital corners were expected, but suffering from a cold, and a little slower than normal, she had 'cut' a few corners to save time. And it was even worse than the usual telling off. Miss Madge Calder had actually **poked** Maud to make the point!

The furious retaliation which followed was not entirely spontaneous. Over the previous few months, Miss Cooper had carefully considered and discussed her deteriorating position with her only living relative - granny.

*"Don't ya be 'asty my girl! Ten bob a week int ta bad when its all spending mooney. Ya **may** get four pounds a week at t' mill - but 'ow mooch will ya be left with after expenses, board and lodging? And **will** you 'ave two big fine rooms to call ya own? In a big fine 'ouse we a nice garden ta enjoy? Think on my girl before ya give Miss Madge Calder a mouthful and leave with no reference!"*

But Maud had thought, and thought long and hard. This was the moment -

"You nasty ugly 'oomped foul 'ideous owd crone.
Pokin' ya bony claw in ta me ribs!

A similar outburst a year before including the word 'hag' had very nearly seen her out on the street, but the maddened maid knew that the term 'crone' and a direct reference to the hump - would never be forgiven. At that time Florence had pointed out to Madge that if a

7

humiliating abject apology were to be accepted, she would continue to enjoy her morning cup of tea in bed, have her bed made up daily, be able to use a clean bathroom and toilet; not have to sweep out, shake mats and clean out her bedroom, not have to sweep, clean and polish the ground floor parlour, not have to help Florence sweep, clean and polish the first floor drawing room, and not have to help Florence with fire laying, the shopping and cooking. This list of chores did not include the heavier schoolroom and laundry duties, and extra kitchen pan polishing of the reliable and valuable daily Mrs Tonks.

After Miss Florence Calder had painted this prospective dramatic and unwelcome change in the daily life of Miss Madge Calder, the latter was persuaded to receive a tearful cringing Maud begging forgiveness, promising to work harder, and pay heed respectfully to appropriate correction from her betters. The lesser sister did not need to be reminded that maids were an endangered species, and the ones who worked six and a half days for ten shillings per week were positively extinct.

In this emotional scene, Maud did not relish facing Miss Florence Calder with whom she had more respect and more fear. Nothing to be gained, she went straight to her rooms on the second floor. Choking back tears, she collected her few personal belongings into a sad cheap suitcase. Ten minutes after the fracas, the elder sister heard the ominous and final click of the school room door. Maud had gone for ever.

Some few minutes later a slow, bent and weary little old lady came into the great parlour and cast a miserable and anguished eye at her big sister who spoke her sarcasm with more sorrow than anger -

"Well done, Madge!" The other had moved to the window and was now contemplating the mottled effect of the sun on the lawn, and gazing into the deep shadows of damp corners formed by rocks and ferns. The senior mistress had intended to remonstrate and scald, but was stopped by the pathetic sight of the twisted woman before her.

Margaret Campbell Calder was the youngest sister of six, and in many ways the least blessed. The second daughter born to Frederick and Sara Calder, Mary Agnes (Miss Polly) 1873-1914 was equally malformed, but was extremely clever. Madge had been given few compensations in life. She taught music reasonably well - if savagely whacking erring fingers occasionally. Most humiliating - it was generally believed that she was **not** a good teacher. In so many ways Madge lived in the shadow of her more successful sister. Studying her grotesque profile against the window, Florence suddenly saw how generations of pupils had seen the grumpy hunched figure, which would not be out of place in a book of fairy tales. In that moment she suddenly realised how the repulsive cruel trick of nature had, over long years, forged the bitter and hateful character - after the style of Shakespeare's Richard III.

"I, that am rudely stamp'd.
Cheated of feature by dissembling nature,
....since I cannot prove a lover...
I am determined to prove a villain."

A wave of heartrending affection swept over the solicitous sister. She approached the window and put a comforting arm around the poor little woman.

"Don't worry, Madge. Something will turn up.
We'll manage. We always have - haven't we?"

At this sudden unexpected and unusual show of affection, the younger sister broke down and sobbed into the protective arms of her only friend and companion.

Something **did** turn up, just a few minutes later. Fortunately, the rarely weeping Madge had just composed herself. In the doorway stood a slightly scruffy slender wiry woman, showing all the signs of a hard life of labour. She spoke words which were polite, yet had a tone clearly telling the listener - *Don't cross me!* This was the one and only Mrs Tonks. In the presence of the prestigious educated Misses Calder, the charwoman was well aware of her subordinate place. Olive Tonks had obviously heard the embarrassing row from her scrubbing and polishing in the school rooms, one of which was actually under the South Mill.

"'Scuse me, Miss, if you'll pardon the liberty, but I might be
able to 'elp ya out. Not me of course, as ave got next door, Fern Glade,
an Mr 'Oadly, an me own family like - but 'av an idea. Will ya be takin'
ya Saturday walk, Miss Florence?

"Naturally!" replied Miss Florence Calder in her deep commanding voice, slightly bristling that such a lowly creature had stumbled onto a private family crisis.

"If ya 'll oblige me to honour arr little 'ome when passin', an
a might be able ta see me way ta a solution to ya troubles."

She disappeared after a slight courteous bob and nod, leaving the two women in a haze of speculation.

The customary Saturday walk took Florence south bound, down along side the river, across the meadows, over the pontoon bridge to the east side. Then crossing Derby Road, the railway line, up the steep jitty, across Becksitch Lane and on up steeper still, along a cobbled lane, into the precipitous poor area of a few mean cottages known as Cowhill. Further up into open parkland with occasional clusters of mainly holly and oak, known locally as The Parks, a remnant of ancient woodland and part of the mediaeval Royal Forest of Duffield Frith. From here, on a log at the summit, the foremost dame of Belper would take a temporary rest and enjoy her splendid views of rolling fields and woodland to the west.

Nearer she noticed a familiar landmark, now a sad indentation, which was all that was left of a once massive tree stump of her childhood memories. As a child at St Laurence's Convent, she and the other girls had chanted the T.C. Crofts poem lamenting the felling of the ancient and venerable Raven's Oak only a few years before her birth -

> *"This towering oak, that once to childhood eye*
> *Waved in the wind and seemed to touch the sky,*
> *Though but an acorn in thy humble birth*
> *Then fell a mighty oak to earth."*

At a very fit 73, fitter indeed than most Beaurepairians less than half her age, she occasionally wondered how much longer she would be able to scale the 200 foot climb from river level each week. It was indeed a 'beautiful retreat' - the meaning of the original 13th century settlement called 'Beaurepaire'. If the weather was kind, she would let her old bones soak up the warm sunshine and mouth the last few words of the old Herbert Strutt Grammar School song-

> *"...the spot so very fair,*
> *That it charmed the men who found it,*
> *And they called it Beaurepaire."*

Up and on, down past the holly trees, out of The Parks, in to Mill Lane, up to the Butts, down Lander Lane, across Chesterfield Road, cutting through the heavy shade of St Peter's Church yard from its splendid dense avenues of tall lime trees, sparklingly green under the clear bright sunshine. Then out into Green Lane, and down the quaint old cobbles of Long Row. A quick disapproving glance at the state school at the foot of the hill, and back home to Bridge House School at the Triangle.

Chapter 2

Low Life on Cowhill

Miss Florence Calder had now been invited to interrupt her walk and take rest with a visit to her daily charwoman. Thirty minutes before her arrival on Cowhill, which was usually around 4.00pm, there was much activity and strident scolding going on within a certain primitive and humble dwelling.

A naked boy was standing on a shallow stone sink beside a hand pumped bucket of tepid soapy water. Closer inspection would show that the 'boy' was in fact a delicate petite pretty man of 23 years, whose use of the chamois leather had slowed down to dream like proportions. The sharp tongued Mrs Olive Tonks, who was vigorously scrubbing the wooden kitchen table, grossly uneven after many years of such vigorous scrubbings, suddenly noticed the onset of these bovine ablutions.

"Get that chammy movin'! Gerrit round thee rude bits! A want thee smellin' nice fa Miss Calder. She's not use to it. She's a lady! And get movin'! She could coome in any second - an ad die o' shame!!"

The prospect of Miss Florence Calder abruptly walking through the rickety old door and being shocked by male nudity, had a dramatic effect on the speed of Simon's strip wash. The admonishment had also attracted the attention of his sister Sally, who was ironing next to the simple antiquated fireplace, the only means of heating the ancient iron. She looked over to her cowering, pathetic, bony, bare brother and shook her head with half amused sardonic sadness -

"Ee, arr Simon, nature's not bin generous ta thee!"

Before Mrs Tonks could give suitable censure to this cruel comment, the worst happened - a firm and authoritative knock at the door!

Miss Florence Calder was without, wishing to be within!

Panic! Poor Simon had already leaped down on to the cold stone flags, and was now speedily ascending the crude wooden stairs, ending with the fleeting sight of his milky white buttocks disappearing into the single bedroom of this primeval 'one up - one down' terraced cottage. The following was interspersed with frequent genuflections -

*"Oh **DO** coom in Miss Calder! Thank you for honouring our oomble...."*

"Yes, yes, Mrs Tonks, but please can we get to the point. As you well know, my time is precious."

Minutes later the VIP was seated with the family in front of a pile of cream cakes and a large brown tea pot. The children had no idea why this meeting had been called, and were all ears as mother started on a rather pained note -

"Am a disappointed woman, Miss, that I am. Jack Tonks took one look at 'im at birth..." She briefly gestured towards Simon, who (now fully dressed) was about to force a large cream bun into his small mouth. *"...an cleared out, never ta be seen agen!!"* She choked back a small sob. *"Yes, an av 'ad ta do it all me sen. Both on um, Miss"* At this point Olive nodded her head, as a further curtsy would have been impossible in the sitting position. *"Tonks av always bin proud of arr tough masculine men folk. Yes - **real** men they are! Look at 'm."* She pointed to sepia photographs prominently displayed around the timeworn yellowing walls. *"That were 'is granddad - a fine figure o'a man. Yes, that 'e was!*

Florence peered at the aggressive pose of an angry, pock marked, bent nosed brutal looking boxer, menacing the photographer with massive fists raised high. She looked in vain for a shred of similarity between the hard countenance of the grumpy grandfather, and the simple cartoon-like face of the weedy effeminate boy opposite. *"An that were 'is uncle Ron."* The fierce, sweaty, hairy, muscle bound Ron was clearly some kind of wrestler, triumphantly standing with one foot on his latest victim.

"An naw look at 'im! Messy chops there!" She brandished a furious finger at Simon, silent, wide eyed and innocent, still chomping on rich cakes, with the cream running down his jaw from a sugar caked mobile mouth. Sally was amused at this stark contrast and merciless character assassination, but Miss Florence Calder was uncomfortable and becoming impatient for the riled mother to state her business.

"Miss Florence. You an Miss Madge need a maid. Well - 'eres one as 'll do nicely!" All eyes turned to the elfin creature whose mouth was suddenly stilled with surprise.

In the moments which followed a rush of mixed thoughts raced across Florence's mind. The dangerous screwed up visage, well known to generations of Beaurepairians, shot a withering icy stare at both mother

12

and son. Her immediate impulse was to say - *"OUTRAGEOUS!!*
Absolutely not!"

There had been too many 'unsavoury incidents' in the life of
Simon Tonks. Only two weeks ago she had come across him on the
Parks, tied and trussed up like a chicken, suspended under a tree,
pendulum like, being swung back and forth with shrieks of merriment
from a group of rough wayward lads. Before giving one final
contemptuous twist, they quickly scattered as the redoubtable Dame of
Bridge House School approached and put the obvious question in her
autocratic boom -

*"SIMON! How on **earth** have you got yourself in this*
undignified and disgraceful predicament?"
In a falsetto voice, the dizzy response came in a haze of shame and
embarrassment -

"Oh, Miss Calder! Don't ask!!"
The strict schoolmarm, now busy cutting bonds with her nail file, took
the wise view that this was probably very good advice.

Another recent unsavoury incident occurred one midday when a giggly
mill girl whispered a message into the ear of Mrs Tonks, who was
shaking rugs outside of Bridge House. The enraged harridan sprung
into immediate action and made a determined march under the ivy
covered mill bridge, past a group of amused mill girls enjoying the last
few sunny minutes of their lunch time. She strode forth over the
Derwent Bridge, quickening her pace, directly to the quaint old French
style convoluted cast iron gentleman's urinal, which had stood at Bridge
Foot for as long as any one could remember. Ignoring all conventions
of propriety, she dived in and rudely dragged out her naughty Simon,
who had been in there much longer than nature would have normally
required. With a sharp quick slap to the back of his head -

"Get thee sen 'om ya dotty little bogga!!"
This humiliating, but hilarious and entertaining scene, was played out in
front of a now larger audience of delighted laughing, nudging, common
raucous young women.

Not to mention the tarot card reading, deeply disapproved of by the
devoutly Anglican Miss Florence Calder. She briefly recalled Mavis
Fig who sat in the River Gardens every day for a fortnight because
Simon had told her -

"You'll meet ya future 'usband by water."

13

But the old teacher remembered that help was urgently required at Bridge House School, and these critical thoughts were mitigated by more positive considerations. Simon was young. On the occasions when he helped his mum at Bridge House School, he worked very hard and always did a good job. He was strong enough to attend to the needs of two elderly ladies. Like all the Tonks family, he never missed church. Even Madge once said -

"In spite of all his faults, there is something rather nice about Simon."

As if to underline this fleeting thought, at that moment the family tom cat affectionately jumped onto Simon's lap. The creature was caressed, and the boy instinctively buried his face into the warm cuddly black fur and gave it several loving kisses. This glimpse of simple but sincere tenderness, drew from the formal spinster, for just a moment, an almost unwilling smile. It passed when the voice of Olive Tonks broke into her cogitations -

"...not to mention that 'e can make a nice job o' ya pans an sweep leaves. An a lad o' is age could do we' a bit more privacy. That 'e could. Am sick o' 'im rattlin' that bed! Coz it tint nice we me an Sally..."

"Yes - yes, Mrs Tonks. If your proposal is agreeable, after discussion with my sister, and due consideration; Simon will be entitled to the two rooms on the second floor."

At this word, the daunting dame was on her feet, politely followed by all Tonks (they knew their manners) with curtsies all round. She fixed the boy with a momentary pained closure of the eyes -

"I think a slight inclination of the head will do, Simon!"

Completing her walk up the Parks, she suddenly realised that Simon, the principal subject of the proposal, had never actually said a word!

Miss Madge Calder was lost for words! Slightly dazzled by the sun glinting off one of the many bright, highly polished copper pans hanging in the great kitchen, she blinked at her sister and struggled to express her vague fears.

"Will he be referred to as 'the maid'?"

"Of course not, Madge! He'll be a servant."

*"People will **talk**, Florence!"*

14

*"Yes, but not about **us**! Let me remind you that we have little choice in this situation. The children arrive on Monday. These days since the War, girls will simply **not** do this kind of work. They'll go over the road, where no doubt Maud has gone. Simon will be grateful for his ten shillings and two rooms after that appalling hovel. Under the watchful eyes of **two** disciplinarians, his conduct and character **will** improve. Heaven help him if **I** have to march to Bridge Foot! In this Christian house, rules will be clearly laid down. Naturally he'll have to be trained, and I doubt he'll ever become the butler at Fern Glade, but he could.."*

Affectionately, she looked across at her small crumpled sad looking sister behind the large Victorian table.

"We're a couple of tired old women, Madge, relics of a past age. I suppose... if... if we were better off?

She sighed, and briefly considered if more money would buy better quality. *"Anyway we must be thankful and make the best of what has been provided. And at the present moment, Simon Tonks has been provided!"*

The two women looked at each other.

The Calders had never been rich, but for the most part, enjoyed a comfortable living. Frederick Calder, was a prosperous Derby lawyer when he moved his large female family, with the three year old Florence, to the substantial Albion House, on Green Lane in Belper in 1879. They all lived well with two maids until Frederick Calder suddenly died at the age of 40. With help from the benevolent Strutt family, the younger girls were educated, and a small school was started on Albert Street. Eventually Bridge House and the school under the South Mill was provided for a 'peppercorn rent' in 1902.

The fee for each term had been one guinea (£1.05) per pupil since the beginning of the century - until recently when Miss Florence Calder reluctantly increased it to twenty seven shillings (£1.35). With just two classes giving a total of about forty pupils, the annual income was modest indeed -

1.35 x 40 = £54.00 / term x 3 = £162 per year, or £81 per teacher. This at a time when young teachers were earning over £400 per year in the state system, and average earnings were creeping up to £500. The Calder sisters may have increased their minuscule income by about £100 from renting their house on Albert Street.

Chapter 3

A Disastrous Dinner Party on Bridge Hill

Thoughts of money had reminded Florence that she and Madge were expected to attend a dinner party that evening up Bridge Hill at Fern Glade, home of the wealthy Burgesses. Both women were dreading it! Of course they would enjoy the company of the charming and delightful Oliver, but his obnoxious spiteful wife Sarah would be a trial - she always was. Thirteen years before, Sarah Burgess (nee Grindle) had been an unpleasant, difficult and disruptive pupil at Bridge House School. An intelligent girl, she had gone on to the Herbert Strutt Grammar School where she grew into an unpleasant difficult and disruptive adolescent. The present odious young woman of 24, now the Lady of Fern Glade, was no different - unpleasant, spoilt and difficult.

Florence reflected on how two, so very different people, separated by a quarter of a century, could have come together into what, after two years, all of Belper knew to be a disastrous marriage. For Sarah and her working class parents, Billy and Gladys Grindle, the advantages were clear. They had struggled, scrimped, saved and sacrificed to give their only daughter a good education at the private school of Bridge House. Not easy on the pay of an honest coal miner, but Sarah took full advantage of the social uplift and alas, came to regard her good parents with contempt. Outwardly her moral qualifications were impeccable. Every Sunday she attended Christ Church where she first met, and gradually became friendly with, her future husband, the wealthy Oliver Burgess. It is unlikely that the initial liking of this pleasant, soft and slightly plump man, old enough to be her father, ever turned to love.

At the moment of proposal, Sarah saw a list of major improvements to her life which would come in to fruition if she simply said 'yes'. She saw herself on a luxury liner in tropical waters drinking champagne, a pleasant change from a day in Skegness sharing a jug of tea with Sally Tonks. She saw herself eating at a large immaculately laid table, complete with candles and flowers, looking out on to the beautiful rhododendron garden of Fern Glade. A 'no' to the round spongy industrialist, would have condemned her to meals at the usual miserable little kitchen table, with the only view being a milk bottle and a few tea soaked crumbs. Sarah Grindle had no intention of staying at the tiny terraced cottage at the far eastern end of Belper in an area known as 'The Gutter'. Here was an opportunity to be waited on hand and foot, morning to night, at the impressive house on Bridge Hill - the better part of Belper, west of the River Derwent. The relatively intelligent conversations with the articulate, well spoken, Mr Burgess, was a much better prospect than the continued company of her coarse taciturn father and the inanities of the ever chattering Gladys Grindle. Months of expensive elocution lessons with Mr Claud Hoadley had finally added necessary H's, lengthened the flat A, and most important, opened up the low, common sounding, closed Derbyshire U.

*"Now Sarah, let us try that again, remember it is - 'We will **h**ike across the b**a**tter t**a**bs in the a**rr**fternoon'."*
"That's wot a keep sayin', Mr 'Oadly!"
*"**NO**, Sarah, it is definitely **not** what you keep saying! You **keep** saying - 'We'll 'ike over b**oo**ter t**oo**bs in' t' **a**fternoon.' In so speaking you reveal your humble and lowly origins and will always go **down** in the estimation of others. I suggest more time should be spent with your new friend, the Reverend Mother Helen; and definitely less time with your old friend, the dreadful and vulgar Sally Tonks!"*

But Sarah had no intention of giving up the fun and companionship of her friend Sally, with whom she had spent many happy disruptive days at the Herbert Strutt Grammar School.

"Why would Oliver Burgess marry so far beneath himself, and to such an ill-natured creature?" continued the thoughts of Miss Florence Calder. She had to admit that Sarah was young and beautiful. Lust would have played its part. Also the girl would have brought an enticing lively and gay presence into his rather staid life. The old spinster could appreciate these matters. Then there were more noble considerations. In spite of regular church attendance, and lip service to Christian principles, Sarah was generally disliked. She had treated boyfriends badly, had offended almost everybody she met with malevolent skill and a sadistic tendency to find the weak spot and thrust the dagger home - with a twist!

Had Oliver seen this and been challenged to 'save' this lost soul? A chance to mend a damaged character? Mr and Mrs Grindle were in high hopes that Sarah would improve under the influence of the older,

17

kindly, gentle and much respected maker of bicycles. This man, fast approaching 50, was beginning to realise that he may not have too many more opportunities to pass on his good name and empire to a son and heir.

Oliver was the successful businessman, **not** the engineer. Indeed it was rumoured that he had never been on a bicycle in his life! Albert Burgess was the father of Oliver, and the father of the factory down on Derwent Street. Over several years of refinement, a very reliable, well finished, sporty looking, all purpose tourist bicycle had been efficiently produced in volume **and** at a competitive price. The 'Beaurepairian' soon became the envy of all British cycle manufacturers, and made Albert Burgess a wealthy man in the 1920's. The shy and modest Oliver inherited the lot when his father, at a very fit 72, died suddenly in 1931.

Burgess II was not the proverbial son who would spend the life savings of the careful father. Under the skilful stewardship of the prudent Oliver, 'Beaurepairian Cycles Ltd', continued to prosper. But Oliver dreamed bigger dreams with regard to a lifestyle befitting the Burgess name, which he intended would rival the very name of Strutt! At the outbreak of the Second World War, he had broken into the American market, and built a magnificent modern house on the south side of Bridge Hill, overlooking the Derwent Valley. As a young man he had been much impressed and influenced by a trip to the 1925 Exposition Internationale des Arts Decoratifs in Paris, which gave rise to the term Art Deco, a critical reaction to the old world of Victoriana. The imaginative and radical work of the American architect, Frank Lloyd Wright was also an inspiration. Fern Glade was partly born out of his love of these new clean cut angular shapes and geometric curves which promised a bright and better future.

No expense was spared for all modern convenience and up to the minute gadgetry. To the delight of guests, plush drapes opened at the touch of an electric button to reveal, through a giant window, a panoramic view of the far hills and verdant valley sweeping to the north, including the meadows, the river, the beautiful River Gardens, and the mills sheltering his old dame school. The eye travelled upwards to the distant east over a tangle of myriad rows of humble cottages, before coming to rest on the near two acres of blazing and riotous colour.

But not now, not in September. Oliver had taken full advantage of the acid soil and planted mostly rhododendrons and azaleas, at their best in spring, interspersed with conifers and deciduous trees. A small fortune had been spent in completing the garden with a series of fish ponds at different levels creating dancing splashing waterfalls, and one large fountain near the house. Everywhere rocks, rocks large and small, rocks picturesque and rocks grotesque, in islets and alcoves covered in spongy lush deep green moss. And with the rocks the ubiquitous fern, for after more than ten years, this maturing magnificent garden was living up to its name - Fern Glade.

At Fern Glade the guests were beginning to arrive. First and rather too early was young Robin Kirkland. His invitation was at the insistence of Mrs Burgess. Their friendship was ostensibly excused and tolerated on the grounds that the 18 year old boy and young wife of 24 were separated by six years only. But six years in these circumstances was a chasm, and a chasm which drew whispered comment. Robin would never be far from Sarah in church and they usually spoke afterwards. In these short meetings, it had been noted that the teenager wore a doting, pining expression, and went away miserable, in contrast to the gloating, triumphant and sardonic cheerfulness of his tormentor.

But there was worse still. On several occasions during the last year, and increasingly during the last few weeks, they had been seen walking together. Not in the River Gardens under the public gaze, but in parts of Belper where observations would be few and far between. Miss Madge Calder, walking the school dogs, had seen them down on the meadows and reported the matter to her sister with considerable acidity. Claud Hoadley had once seen them emerging from a clump of holly trees on the Parks. At the next elocution lesson, with some passion, he challenged the boy, reminding him of the fact that Sarah was now **Mrs** Burgess, and no longer Miss Grindle. Resenting the implication of the reprimand, Robin was unwilling to give much away -
*"We were only walking...that's all.....it..it was **her** idea, not mine."*

The firm fine Hoadley features held tight and were unmoved. Sour, disapproving thin lips remained pressed together in an icy silence, which was born of a deep frustration 'which dared not speak its name' - certainly not to the pious, pristine and pretentious Claud Hoadley.

Two guests were puffing and panting up the hill. Not so much Julian as his mother, who was gasping out her apprehensions -

*"On the rocks I say...about to hit the final rock by the evidence of the last few Sundays. He won't look at her - and she just sneers. Odious vile creature...and **still** in tow with that bitch Tonks. Poor Mr Burgess can't stand her..and who can blame him! One can hardly refuse an invitation to Fern Glade, so I can only hope and pray we escape an appalling scene."*

She looked at her son who seemed fairly indifferent to these predicted horrors.

"It's you I'm thinking of, Julian. Such a sensitive child. You could be unsettled by the unpleasantness and your work may suffer!"

"It could be improved, mother! A flaming row would unravel all the careful 'Hoadley crafted' affected enunciation's! You'll recall the time outside Christ Church when she called him a 'fat b<u>a</u>stard', in her agitation she forgot to say 'ba<u>rr</u>stard'!"

*"**Julian! Really!** Language! Please try to remember that the Misses Calder will be present tonight!"*

"Indeed, mother. I was simply reflecting that my work was getting a little sugary, perhaps too sentimental and Victorian. Some bile may just be the right amount of corrective inspiration."

Before a response could be given, a slug shaped car shot out a strident and startling 'toot' 'toot', and roared past them up Bridge Hill. The shapeless driver, with toad-like head jutting aggressively up to the windscreen, seemed huddled over the wheel determined to reach his destination. The pedestrian mother and son looked at each other and - groaned.

Inside the large living room of Fern Glade was a capacious settee of modern design with simple clean lines. It could hold twelve, having three four seater segments, arranged at right-angles in front of a rough fireplace, crafted from big chunks of Derbyshire gritstone in warm colours. Being a cool evening, several logs were cheerfully crackling and burning as Sarah and Robin were close together in conspiratorial conversation. They both heard a familiar 'toot' 'toot', and looked out of one of the three massive plate glass windows to see a frenetic toad like creature spring out of an odd looking car. Aubrey Pod, ever eager to get to the next item on the list of life, was rushing to the door, little podgy arms flapping up at shoulder height, aiming for the electric door bell. With a sense of urgency, like his car horn, it continued to ring until the serene and stately butler opened the door.

"Which is more ugly?" mused the lady of the house.. *"The creature or the car?"*
Her young friend took a more benevolent view.
"He'll be fun, Sarah! I can't help but like him."
"You're the only one who does."
Robin was mischievously enjoying his mock defence of the little man he found endlessly fascinating and most entertaining.
"Poor Mr Pod! He can't help being ugly."
"No, but he could at least stop at home."

Before Alex Haigh, looking down his nose, could finish his regal announcement - *"Mr .."* The silken tones trailed away, since there was no point competing with the explosive spittle strewn gaggle, which erupted as Aubrey Pod raced past the butler, and across to the first people he saw within -
"Am I too early or too late? Oh hello, Robin." Pushing his repulsive face too close, and into the boy's private space - *"I've not seen that suit before. Is it new?"* Before Robin could answer, he spun round, and delivered a suitable stock line to his hostess - *"You're looking very grown up these days, Sarah!"* She darted her head back partly to reclaim personal space, but mainly to escape an appalling exhalation of foul breath. The door bell caused the excited child-like little man to prance over to attack Tatiana and Julian Lawrence. Savouring the relative calm, Sarah said -
"My God! It was worse than rotten eggs!"

Ten minutes later the last two guests arrived. Haughtily, but with more approval than some of the others, the tall black butler called out
"The Misses Calder." As they entered to join the gathering, Florence's eye was drawn first to the man who usually commanded and held court at any social gathering. The immaculately dressed, bolt upright, clean as a pin, (and as sharp) - no less - Mr Claud Hoadley. His circle of seeming obedient disciples were hanging on to every word....
"... and as Lady Britomart said - 'Nobody can say a word against Greek: it stamps a man at once as an educated gentleman'. Ah! The redoubtable Dames of Bridge House! A warm welcome to the west bank, Dear Ladies!

Ignoring these theatricals, Florence guided her sister to greet the real host, Oliver Burgess.

"Who is Lady Britomart?" whispered the less well read Madge.

"A foolish woman from one of Shaw's more socialist plays, 'Major Barbara'. Florence was tempted to add, *"and about as daft as Hoadley!"*

Oliver Burgess was looking pale, tired and old, but struggled up a thin smile, and spoke with grateful and genuine affection

"So glad you could both come." He warmly looked down to the diminutive hunched and lesser sister. *"How are you, Madge?"* This wealthy and respected 'King on the Hill', was one of the very few privileged Beaurepairians who were permitted to address the Calders without a title. It had been forty years since a quiet and obedient little Oliver, had sat in the classroom of the all powerful Miss Margaret Campbell Calder, in the early years of the century. She had then been firm and unyielding, but now was melting and twittering under the effect of kind words from a prestigious industrialist and personal friend. Clearly the atmosphere held strain and tension. The host had been deeply unhappy for some time. He had lost the bounce, energy and enthusiasm of fifteen years back, when he was the envy of Belper and had triumphantly completed Fern Glade. Commonplace pleasantries were spoken, but his sad eyes were appealing to the wise women, his former teachers -

"Please help me! It's been a disaster!
She's destroying me... I can't go on."

The trio wandered over to the main group, now on edge, as Sarah was verbally stalking a victim, Julian the poet -

"I bought your latest slim volume, Julian!"

"Really!"

"Oh yes, there was a prominent display at Pickering's down on Bridge Street. We went straight to the Memorial Gardens to savour every poetic word, didn't we, Sally." The two mischievous friends exchanged an insincere smirk which warned all present that cruelty was afoot.

"We particularly enjoyed the one called 'The Kind Little Kitten'. So sweet and sentimental. Quite tender and very touching. It made us really weepy at the bit where she let the mouse go, didn't it, Sally?"
Julian appeared stoic and composed, but Mrs Lawrence wore a face of

thunder. In the same light lilting but mocking tone, she manoeuvred for the kill.

"Sally and me...well... we're pretty ordinary folk, but I'm afraid Mr Hoadley who knows all about these things took a more critical view didn't you?" A look of horror came to the sharp sour features.

"Indeed! I really don't recall.."

"Oh yes! Yes you said it was juvenile... something, and then... 'birthday card poetry'. And then there was something about...yes! Yes that was it. About you wanting to be a Catholic priest, Julian. How did it go?" Here Sarah affected the manner and artificial accent of Claud Hoadley -

*"Julian **has** talent, but it is neither literary nor liturgical!"*

A sudden firm female voice broke from the group, loud and deep enough to have an air of reproof, yet the content of words could have bore a casual interpretation.

*"Perhaps you **should** be telling us about your own developing talents, Sarah. Tell us about Wednesday, when you can demonstrate your flower arranging skills for us all to enjoy."*

This authoritative interruption had the desired effect. Julian had been spared and Mrs Burgess was now inviting everybody to visit the Flower Festival at the Convent of Cranmer at the top of Belper Lane. The speaker of these words of rescue was the Reverend Mother Helen, who had started life as Evelyn Lewis, sister of Doctor Paul Lewis. Her unquestioned standing was backed by an unspoken sartorial command. An imposing figure! The crow black habit had a medieval aspect, but the active sisterhood up Belper Lane was open, cheerful and welcoming having a non-cloistered life style. The Cranmer Open Day, an established annual event, had took on a new lease of life under the imaginative and energetic new leadership of the relatively young Helen. It was planned for the following Saturday September 10th.

In hushed tones as an aside, her closest friend Florence Calder unburdened her feeling of guilt -

*"Thank you, Helen, but you've made me feel ashamed! **I** should have interceded and stilled her evil tongue before she hurt that boy. After all, it is expected of me."*

*"Not at all Florence. She **is** our hostess, and I had to wait for just the right opportunity."*

She gave a single 'tut', and cast her eyes to heaven in despair.

"There's the most appalling atmosphere in this house. You could cut it with a knife. A mixture of misery pain and hate. Sarah is so immature - and I fear damaged."

"She'd be 'damaged' if I could lay my hands on her!" This from Madge who had just joined this whispered exchange. The head nun continued.

"Before you arrived she made poor Mr Pod look such a fool. It seems he taught his music class in the Strutt School Hall standing and conducting on the stage behind the curtain line. One day when Sally and Sarah were being impossible, he ordered them out into the corridor."

"Quite right too!" said Madge. *"Sarah Grindle was more often standing **outside** my room than in it. A confounded nuisance!"*

Helen looked down into the haggard lines etched into the old schoolmarm's face and felt grateful she had resisted a girlhood inclination to teach.

"Anyway, Mr Pod had to endure the story of how they found and wound the curtain mechanism closing him off from the other pupils!" In spite of herself, Florence had to smile at the scene of the excited toad like Aubrey Pod, puffed up and full of self importance, knees bent, arms wide in exaggerated sweeping motions, beating time high on the platform. This ridiculous spectacle only to be extinguished by eclipsing drapes. The other boys and girls would have been in an uproar of ecstatic hilarity. Helen noticed the twinkle of amusement before continuing -

*"Yes, Sarah tells a good story, and I'm afraid most of us **were** laughing. Events about ten or eleven years ago, but her guest was deeply embarrassed and annoyed to be hearing this in front of his friends. With great enthusiasm Sally took up the tale and said that the irate teacher chased them along the corridor. They escaped into the girls lavatory, where he banged on the door, demanding that they come out at once!*

"Hardly the best way to regain his professional dignity!" observed Florence, but at that very moment she was horrified to see the subject of their conversation fast approaching. She skilfully managed to alert the other women, and smooth over any embarrassment, by eagerly seizing on a neutral subject.

*"Good evening, **Mr Pod**. Just the man! I especially wanted to ask you about the bird watching."* Explaining to her companions - *"Mr Pod has invested in expensive binoculars. He's studying ornithology."*

*"Good evening, ladies. Yes that's right. An absorbing hobby, **most** satisfying. I've already filled up two notebooks!"*

"It must be wonderful to have such an extensive knowledge, and be able to name all of our feathered friends." said the Reverend Mother Helen.

"I expect it's useful in other ways." said Madge looking at his soft plump body. He gave her a sharp look, and she added quickly - *"I was thinking of the very useful exercise, up and down the hills of Belper. I'm afraid I take the easy option and just keep to river level with the dogs. Florence has noticed you in The Parks."*

"You must come and observe our little garden and give us a report. I'm so ignorant on the subject. Perhaps you'll give me a list of the birds who inhabit our dear old Plane Tree?"

*"It would be a **privilege**, Miss Florence. I could provide you with neatly written full details. It would be just like being back at Bridge House School!"* He thrust out his face and beamed.

"I've noticed a lone starling, or is it a blackbird? So difficult to tell them apart. Anyway it's a very quiet bird."

*"In that case it's **definitely** a starling, Miss Florence."*

*"It would be **so** nice to have a blackbird in one's garden. There **is** one in the meadows. I often see it hovering for minutes on end, high in the air, warbling his little heart out."*

"You see they'd sooner hunt near water.." replied the bird watcher, with confidence and authority.

The doctor was suddenly by their side.

"Sorry to but-in, ladies, but your musical knowledge is needed back here, Aubrey." With quick apologies he flew back to the main group. Madge was puzzled.

"Florence! Why are you speaking such utter nonsense? Starlings are gregarious, hundreds of them in spectacular flying formations!"

"Indeed, Madge. We've also been teaching the children for the last fifty years that they are very noisy birds, have beautiful iridescent green and purple feathers, and that blackbirds are just that - soot black!"

"And the hovering warbling bird you described over the meadows, is, I believe - a 'skylark'?" added the nun.

*"It's just as well that Aubrey is now talking about music where he's sure of his ground, and **not** ornithology!"*

Madge was still flustered and mystified -

"Well then, why the new binoculars and hours of surveillance down the meadows and up at The Parks? Why the ... Good Heavens! It's disgusting!" The penny had now dropped, and she looked up at her two companions who were nodding sagely. Miss Florence Calder simply said - *"Quite!"*

At this convenient moment, and with professional dignity, Haigh the pristine butler, stood to attention and announced - *"Dinner is served".*

They did not have far to go. The long modern dining table was at the eastern end of the vast living room. It was a work of art and a joy to behold. Expensive clear plain crystal glasses reflected the glinting special electric spot lamps from above. The centre was a generous tasteful arrangement of late summer flowers and candles, and all the immaculate place settings had been laid with precision. Alex Haigh took his work very seriously, and was justifiably proud of this exquisite presentation. Doctor Paul Lewis spoke the thoughts of most as they sat down -

"This is wonderful, Oliver! Where did you find this man of such talent?"

"In Detroit last summer, when I was selling cycles to the Midwest. To start with, he's not a butler. He was teaching English Literature in a private Catholic high school, and accepted my offer to double his salary, play the part of Jeeves, and experience the culture he's been studying all his life. A capital fellow and first rate cook!"

Recounting this single success gave Mr Burgess a momentary sparkle. But if the master of the house enjoyed a brief 'up', Robin Kirkland was about to endure a brief 'down'.

Just as he had most feared, in clear view, he sat opposite the disdainful disapproving countenance of the high and mighty Hoadley, away from the kind protection of summer flowers. The punctilious pedant would be watching his every move, and publicly comment at any opportunity - as he had done at the dinner table on numerous previous occasions. A simple knife and fork job would not be so bad, but the first course was mackerel pate and Melba toast, which disintegrated into a hundred pieces at the slightest touch! Robin struggled, but his heart sank as the expected supercilious smug voice rang over the table -

"May I suggest, Robin, that you take a little of the pate...."

Only last week, after an elocution lesson, at odds with the usual procedure, an apple was offered to the pupil from the teacher. Robin was relaxed as surely he could not possibly go wrong with the eating of a common apple! Or could he? The fruit was served with a knife, tea plate and serviette! Carefully avoiding the natural instinct of giving it a simple bite with the teeth, he gave it his best effort. Cutting the item into quarters, he began to consume the first segment with hope. Then it came!

"Oh! I see you are eating your apple arrfter the style of the labourer in the field! It will demonstrate much better breeding, Robin, to take the knife thus and..."

One time he had been reprimanded for cutting up his hot boiled potatoes to allow them to cool. *"That is very rude, Robin!"* Then there was cutting comment about the wide and too generous distribution of brown sauce over his steak at Ramsdens in Derby.

"May I suggest that a small soupcon on the side of your plate to be applied to each portion of cut meat. The done thing with most people of quality..." not to mention the very first correction at the breakfast table in a Youth Hostel at Castleton, when the overweening master actually became physical! He knocked a knife out of Robin's hand before it was about to be thrust into butter. Apparently it was the wrong knife.

Miss Florence Calder sitting next to the boy was sensitive to his hurt, brooding discomfort, and casually mentioned -

"We all have difficulty with thin brittle toast, just enjoy your food, Robin."

She reflected over the years that this odd friendship had progressed. Man and boy separated by 43 years and different classes, yet joined by Robin's idolatry of the higher gentleman, and Claud's need to bully and demean. Not of course the interpretation he once gave.

"I feel I can offer so much to the boy, Miss Florence. The child says he wants to be just like me and become a teacher!" Here he gave a sad condescending and slightly reptilian smile. *"Alas! Not impossible but certainly, improbable. Junior management at the bank is a realistic target. Socially he can be greatly improved. I've already rid him of that appalling habit of referring to a relative as 'our'. One can still*

27

hear the odd split infinitive, but his grammar is already much better than it was. I've instructed him to read Horace fifteen minutes a day. Always an unimpeachable sign of high learning to be able to quote Horace!! Do you not think so, Miss Florence?
Miss Florence Calder, who was not very familiar with Latin poets, gave him a cool empty stare.

Robin had been a favourite pupil when Mr Claud Hoadley was the classics master at the Herbert Strutt Grammar School, and was flattered by the interest and attention of such a perceived well bred gentleman. When free elocution lessons were offered, Charlie Kirkland was overjoyed. Lessons were followed by tea and scholarly readings.
  "Observe, Robin! We read Milton in the a__rr__fternoon. Chaucer is always better heard in the forenoon, and any house of culture will only tolerate Shakespeare a__rr__fter dinner."

The pupil - teacher relationship gradually developed into an unequal friendship, when Robin had been invited to join his former schoolmaster on long walks into Derbyshire at the weekends.

  "Come, Robin. Stride out smartly! Quick step! Brisk exercise is as good for the brain as Plato is for the mind. You don't want to end up looking like Mr Pod do you?"

A good deal of contempt was held for the slug shaped church organist who despised and conscientiously avoided any form of physical exercise. The latter was often maliciously gratified when he heard that Mr Hoadley had walked too far and aggravated an old ankle injury which resulted in several days of pain.

In the lovely Derbyshire dales and high on the moors, man and boy both enjoyed educative conversations which stimulated the ex-pupil's innate intelligence. A rough Belper lad had now been transformed into a more thoughtful and knowledgeable young man.
  This much Florence admitted - he **had** been improved, but she was continually irritated by the young man's adulation and distorted assessment of Hoadley's social position and influence -
  *"But do you not think, Miss Calder, that an atmosphere of **awe** descends upon a gathering when **Mr Hoadley** enters a room? An aura*

of quality which commands respect. It's beyond description... It's almost as though.... as though they **bow** *to him!"*

Looking sadly at the misty eyed hero-worshipping boy, Florence reflected that at **no** time had **SHE** been moved to drop Mr Claud Hoadley a curtsy! Robin continued with the slightly affected enunciation which always seized him when exalting his glorified master.

"He's wonderful! He seems to hold invisible power over the lesser mortals in the room. His perfect command of the English language, his erudition, his natural authority, his beautiful royal 'Rolls Royce' accent, his vast experience! No one **dares** *to contradict him, Miss Calder! No one at all! Mr Hoadley is everything I would ever want to be!"*

Her attention came back to the table when Oliver was once more commending his new butler.

"Alex is a treasure. He chooses the wines with expert precision, and this one is a winner." The graceful servant graciously inclined his head and continued to fill glasses. Mr Hoadley passed his drink several times in front of the snooty nose, before taking a sip.

"Indeed! This claret is very fine. It comes from a particularly rich area of Burgundy." The tall Negro displayed a momentary flicker of surprise, but correctly remained silent and continued to his duty. The Reverend Mother Helen gave Miss Florence Calder a mischievous glance, but the latter could not resist the tempting opportunity, and in a voice slightly louder than was necessary -

"How very interesting, Mr Hoadley! One learns something new every day. **I** *was always under the impression that claret came from Bordeaux!"*

The prissy pedant took some comfort in the fact that half the assembly would have missed this howler, and skilfully disguised his embarrassment by a quick comment on the flower border -

"I notice your Aster novi-belgii and Callistephus are well advanced this year. They do one's heart good."

Florence leaned close to her puzzled sister and whispered -

"Michaelmas daisies". That prompted a short private discussion about the need to decide on spring bulbs in the Calder garden.

After a few minutes both women noticed with some alarm, that Sarah Burgess, with evil glint and derisive tone, was putting questions to Mr Hoadley about model railways!

*"But you **must** remember! Me dad...**my** dad, said what a big display it was. 'Cost a fortune' he said. All laid out in your big attic. Tiny people, trees, cows, bridges, roads and motor cars. Yards of track and lots of trains. He was fascinated, and what a lovely time you both had. Years and years ago. Is it still there?"* She caught Sally's eye with a mocking nod, which was returned with a leering sneer.

Claud Hoadley was visibly disturbed and had gone quite pale. He avoided all eyes, looked through the great window and focused on a point on a remote distant hill. His response, when it finally came was low, controlled and dangerous.

"I don't recall the visit."

In an effort to break the icy silence and biting ambience, Oliver Burgess said in a cheery upbeat manner -

"Sounds like a splendid set, Hoadley! Must be worth a lot of money now. I had no idea you were an enthusiast. I'd like to see it sometime."

But Mr Hoadley said very little after that incident,
and left at the earliest opportunity.

Chapter 4

Psychic Simon

A happy high pitched musical voice of a common slattern rang out into the cool clear blue sky of early autumn -

> *"I love my home, my dear old home,*
> *That stands at the top of the hill,*
> *And I oft times sit and sigh,*
> *For I long to be on Cowhill, once again...."*

Listeners forty years on would have been reminded of Hilda Ogden bursting into song, but this was the familiar sound of a contented Olive Tonks, sweeping out her kitchen. The residents of the other adjoining small cottages were comforted by the local reassuring strains, as they drifted down the hill, and dissipated into the special peaceful atmosphere which was a fine Sunday morning in Belper. So it was for the little fat man, next door but one, sitting on the dustbin, piggling his smelly toes.

Olive Tonks took a moment from her labours and looked at her ancient and grossly inaccurate yellow faced clock. It indicated some minutes after the hour of nine. *"Late enough!"* she thought, and leaped up the old creaking stairs, three steps at a time, broom still in hand, into the only other room in her little Spartan cottage. There was only just enough room for the three sad, shabby, narrow single beds. Two were already made up. Sally had been dispatched to buy the Sunday paper, and Olive had been up working at least an hour. In the third bed was tucked up, warm snug cosy and comfy - little Simon Tonks. She paused for a moment, and looked at his pretty young face; a picture of contentment with the deep slow breathing of peaceful sleep, enjoying his late morning dreams of happy eroticism, without social cost. But not for long. Grasping the broom handle, she aimed and gave his back side a sharp poke -

> *"Gerrup ya idle bogga!"*

Indeed she was hoping this would be the last night for Simon on Cowhill, if her proposition were to be accepted by the Misses Calder. Minutes later, Simon was mincing past the unshaven little fat man, still on his dustbin. Very casual in a once white, collarless, soup stained shirt and braces, hauling up at near nipple level ancient baggy trousers; still attending grubby toes -

"Mornin', 'Arry."
"Ow doo, yoong un. Ay, in tit grand!"

He toddled on down the hill, down Gibfield Lane, past the Herbert Strutt Swimming Baths, where he had been banned for *"Inappropriate conduct towards other bathers"*. Turned right at the bottom, into Chapel Street, into Bridge Street, on to the Triangle and up to the school entrance of Bridge House. Miss Florence Calder opened the door and looked at the silent baby faced Simon, expressionless, with his head slightly cocked on one side. He was a pathetic sight, having only the clothes he stood in, together with a paper carrier bag containing a few mean possessions. These turned out to include a soggy Dandy comic, some weeks old, a half sucked sweet, a scratched bent photograph of Roy Rodgers and his dirty, tatty, dog-eared, fourth hand, tarot cards.

On Sunday September 4th, 1949, Miss Florence and
Miss Madge Calder took delivery of Simon Tonks.

Not the most convenient time to start training a new member of staff. For these strict Anglican sisters, the Sabbath was packed with commitments for Sunday School and church. By the day's end, Simon had been thoroughly briefed on strict house rules, all the do's and don'ts - especially the don'ts. As he was sent scuttling up stairs to bed, Florence turned to her sister and said -

"Give him every chance to make good.
*And, Madge...please, **please** - be patient!"*

The following morning was the busiest, hectic and most stressful morning of the year for the elderly Misses Calder. This was the time when the children would arrive. It was the first day of the new autumn term at Bridge House School, and the first day of the new academic year. The cave-like entrance corridor, dimly lit, cold stone flagged, was full of bemused benumbed little girls and boys - at best. Some of the new pupils, hardly into their fifth summer, were in floods of tears, devastated by the stark reality of a sudden end to their erstwhile idyllic freedom. In the middle of this heart-rending tragic drama stood whittling twittering mothers, unwilling to leave, being consoled and reassured by two competent professional sisters who had seen almost fifty such anguished Mondays before.

32

Simon was well out of sight, upstairs, trying to recall instructions and struggling with the hospital corners of Miss Madge's bed, now on the third attempt.

Wednesday afternoon was his designated time off, but during this 'honeymoon' period, he was permitted two hours after lunch to honour a previous engagement on Becksitch Lane.

Simon was, according to his own claims, a psychic. Denied to others, he had special powers to see the future, communicate with the dead, read the cards and give advice. On this subject Miss Florence Calder, a true and constant daughter of the Church of England, had made herself perfectly clear.

"Under no circumstances are you to engage in these un-Christian, dubious and superstitious activities under this roof. Let that sink in well, and let it be clearly understood! Do you understand, Simon?"

The old grey bullet eyes, shot out menacingly from wizened sockets and into the fresh boyish face. Simon noted the wrinkled lips, tightly pursed with disapproval, and was cowed into silent submission. He mustered a look of innocent surprise, and gave a slight nod of assent.

The strict schoolmarm wisely stopped short of a complete ban. She knew the young man had achieved very little in life with which to commend himself. Throughout history there had always been within the ranks of the poor and ignorant, soothsayers and necromancers. To compensate for their low status, they would conjure up the spirits of the dead and astound neighbours with paranormal abilities. So it was with poor little Simon, the butt of Belper jokes. If that buffoon Aubrey Pod was gullible enough to be duped by such rubbish, more fool him! Her frosty features softened to a slight smile when she recalled accounts of Aubrey in the gypsy's tent at the local fair.

"Ahh thee crystal, ees dim, she ees misty...I no longer see..."

When the silly music master produced his second half crown, it had a miraculous effect of clearing away the fog.

Inside 'Crow's Hole', the Pod residence up high on Becksitch Lane, Aubrey was engaged in his favourite pastime - talking about himself.

*"Do you know, Mavis, when I'm gone and they read my will, they'll all be surprised to see how generous your share is. They'll be wondering just what **sort** of services you were giving me!"*

33

Mavis was languorously drying a plate, not looking at him, totally unimpressed by this comment.

"Wills can be changed, Mr Pod!"

The will of Aubrey Pod was a constant source of amusement in Belper. Altered at regular intervals, depending on who was in, and out of favour, and frequently used as a tool of influence. But one group always had a good portion - animals. Within this majority, the British Hedgehog Society hogged the big piece. It was well known in the town that a day would come when many happy wealthy hedgehogs would be wandering around The Parks. Mr Pod loved animals, and found them much less prickly than people. He informed his housekeeper that a visitor was due any moment.

"Simon Tonks is coming to sit in mother's chair!"

Aubrey explained the procedure that by coming into contact with a familiar object of the departed, the clairvoyant can subsume the spirit and effect a brief communication. Mavis was not impressed. Why anybody would want to bring back such an old battle-axe as the odious and unpleasant Mrs Pod, she could not fathom. Least of all the son she had nagged, bullied and warped in her lifetime. Mavis Fig had suffered abuse from her deceased employer over many years, but continued to faithfully serve her current employer from the early morning emptying of his smelly chamber pot, to the greasy bacon sandwich he gobbled down last thing at night.

The mere mention of Mrs Pod had irritated her. Bitter memories flooded back. How she would stand in the kitchen and put up with humiliating, barked, bad tempered orders. Always trying (in vain) to please her -

"Yes, Mrs Pod. No, Mrs Pod. Certainly, Mrs Pod.
I'll do that, Mrs Pod."

Then to have to endure her constant habit of that contemptuous final -

"See that ya do!" or "See that it is!"

The sound of a light knock sent Mr Pod racing to the door, where he all but grabbed Simon, and put him into an old worn easy chair. Eagerly bending over him and pushing his ill formed face close, too close, he studied closely the boy's features while he tried to go into a trance. Simon had considerable difficulty concentrating, having to look into the hovering blob of blubber. He recalled a comment once made by Sarah Burgess - *"His mouth is like a crack in a pie!"*

34

The mystic closed his eyes and began to moan. The ardent piggy eyes pushed closer -

"What are you getting, Simon?"

Suddenly the seer opened wide his eyes, and then his mouth -

"Nowt!!"

*"I'm not surprised, this is **not** her chair. That was a test!"*

The process was repeated in the correct chair, and Simon's features began to screw up into a cantankerous scowl, before a gravely thick croaky voice let forth growls and grumbles attacking son and servant -

"Don't be gettin' greasy fat on ya bed sheets! Make Mavis ponch ya whiffy kegs regular, an scrub ya po, an watch t' shoppin' list. She'll nick a shillin' if she can!"

*"**Ooh!** Evil, nasty owd cow!!"* This last ejaculation from the irate char seemed to disturb the seance, and Nelly Pod drifted back into the ether from whence she came. Simon was again moaning and gradually returning to Belper.

Minutes later a miffed Mavis served tea and a few soft old biscuits. Simon was talking about his dreams of premonition and the one he had last night.

"Oow it were odd! A fast train, puffin' away we that stuck up Mr 'Oadley - only young, an Sarah's dad, an 'e were young, joost a lad. There were a mighty crash an both choocked out! Mr 'Oadley were all oopset an ran over, 'sterical like, ta young Billy Grindle, bent, twisted an bloody!" He paused.

"Well?" said the impatient host.

"Ooo it were rate queer! It wont 'is friend!"

In the best words available to the illiterate Simon Tonks, he described a nightmarish transformation. An unconscious teenage William Grindle had been face down in the wreckage. When turned over, he became the future beautiful daughter Sarah, who opened her eyes to give the horror stricken Claud a malevolent wicked grin!!

"I wonder what it means?" said the eager, excited Aubrey Pod.

"Don't know." replied the rather smug augur, who simply sat wide eyed and innocent, head slightly on one side, nibbling at an eighth soft chocolate biscuit, and sipping at his fifth cup of tea.

Back at the Bridge House great kitchen, a furious Olive Tonks was raising her voice and brandishing her duster to the bread woman who, not being the object of her fury, was listening with rapt attention.

35

*"Owe'll get me bloody fist in't middle o' her bloody gob 'ole, spreadin' dotty lies. **SLANDER!** That's wot Reverend Mother called it! An I'll 'ave her oop for it. That a will. Owe'll get me knuckles down 'er throat if she....."*

*"**MRS TONKS!!** There are children near by! Please remember my school rules!"*

With the appearance of the headmistress and sudden high drama, the bread woman, who had been there too long anyway, took this tactful opportunity to slide away.

*"Am **rate** sorry, Miss Calder, but am **that** mad! Its that rich bitch, lady muck oop 'ill. Arr Sally sez she's bin on about arr Simon at 'baths, wen 'e were choocked out. 'E canna afford to drop money. Not 'is fault if pennies roll under other cubicles! 'E's got ta gerrum back. That lyin' slut..."*

*"**That** will do, Mrs Tonks. Calm yourself."*

Florence was beginning to get a clearer picture of the recent incident of his removal from the Gibfield Lane Swimming Baths.

"All guests present last Saturday evening were perfectly aware of the malicious character of their hostess. They, and indeed most Beaurepairians, are familiar with her iniquitous tongue and her habit of drawing depraved interpretations from any misunderstanding."

Olive was not too sure what all this meant, but gathered Miss Calder was on the side of her Simon.

"However, to avoid further embarrassment, it will be much better if he abides by the current ban and keeps away from that particular pastime.

Think of all those pennies he will save!"

This was not to be the only reference to the acid and scandalous dinner party, whose reverberations were spreading through the whole mill town.

After a fractious and exhausting long first school day, the two spinsters were enjoying a well earned relaxation taking afternoon tea, nicely served up on a silver tray with flowers, by Simon who was working hard to make a good impression. The front door bell could be heard distantly tinkling in the kitchen, followed shortly by Simon's funny little face poking round the door.

"It's Jasper the gardener. 'An will the Miss Florence be kind enough to bring 'er self to the door, as me boots 'r mucky'."

*"**Mr** Wormall to you, Simon! That gentleman is older than any of us, and has been tending our garden for as long as we can remember. I'll see what he wants."*

Framed in the wide Georgian doorway, was a small gnarled craggy man who could have been related to the Raven's Oak, and looked about as old. His goblinesque face appeared to be dominated by ugly and interesting protuberances, the largest of which was a hawk nose, far forward of the deep set grizzled, leering eyes. But these were the kind eyes of a kind man, once described by old Mrs Sara Calder as -
"The nicest little chap in Belper".
Uncomfortably, he stood wringing a beaten up mediaeval felt cap, politely removed at the approach of his employer. To Jasper Wormall, the Calders were the Royalty of Belper, only to be disturbed and directly addressed on a matter of great importance. This was just such a matter.

"Beggin' ya pardon, Miss Florence, but av somethin' on me mind, n it's rate whittlin' me."

"What's the problem, Jasper?"

"Well..." He twisted his cap more tightly still. *"You were at t' big 'ouse oop 'ill, last Satdy?"*

"Oh I see!" She saw it all very clearly, felt wretched, and gave a deep sigh.

*"I'm so **very** sorry, Jasper. For you most of all. I **could** and **should** have stopped it. The Reverend Mother did at one point with another one of her unfortunate targets. Of course I was a guest and she the hostess, but that does not excuse my standing by and...."*
She looked at the injured and pained expression.

*"Perhaps there is something I **can** do in a practical way. She may well tell me to mind my own business, but if I asked for an appointment with Sarah and Mr Burgess together, and, in no uncertain terms, in the spirit of reprimand, spell out the distress these ribald anecdotes can cause..."*

"A was goin ta ask ya about goin' further than that, Miss Florence....a think its called... slander..er a solicitor?"
She paused and looked at him with great compassion.

"No, Jasper, I'm truly sorry, but very much doubt you'd have a case in law. Unless you've been seriously damaged financially, or can prove defamation of character....It could cost you a great deal of money for nothing!"

37

He stood looking miserable and hopeless. She continued -

"It's little comfort to you, I know, but a number of people on that evening were hurt by her spite and depravity. Some of those people were actually present! They were expected to be 'good sports' and share the 'joke'.

After a moment he said in a low defeated hoarse voice -

"Yes, Miss...Thank you, Miss." He turned slowly, put on his battered old hat, and plodded back to one of the island rock gardens in the lawn. For a moment she stood and looked, then closed the door and smartly marched back to the parlour and briefed Miss Madge Calder.

She became incandescent with rage at the appalling injustice.

"It would be better if that woman were dead!!"

"MADGE!!"

And then a little softer, observing the horror in her sisters face, realising the magnitude of such a hateful outburst -

"Madge..please..." This tense moment would seem to call for a retraction or an apology in a Christian house, but the deformed Madge Calder had too much empathy with the ugly Jasper, and recalled cruel similar humiliations. Fourteen years ago she had unexpectedly returned to her classroom, an uproar of laughing children, to find a young Sarah strutting and mimicking her teacher. That was bad enough, but it was the pillow stuffed up the girl's back - which was most excruciating. Madge looked sadly at Florence, and they both knew there would be no retraction and no apology.

In an effort to change tack, Florence returned to Saturday evening.

*"Of course, little credit is reflected on the mischievous culprit who **told** Jasper."*

"We live in a small town of wagging tongues." murmured the other. An effort was made to remember the grouping when 'Jasper stories' were producing shrieks of merriment after the dinner. It was Sarah's younger friends mainly, Sally, Robin and Julian who was with his mother Tatiana. Aubrey Pod, a keen listener, always enjoyed hearing about the misfortunes of others, and indeed, had himself happily recounted funny tales of the Wormalls before. Doctor Paul Lewis was also enjoying the fun. The school sisters took coffee on the other side of the large sofa nearer the fire, with Reverend Mother Helen, Claud Hoadley and Oliver Burgess making up the older quieter quintet. They clearly heard the buoyant banter of the larger audience nearby.

38

The talk started innocently enough. Mrs Burgess had an interest in local history, and the folklore surrounding the mysterious lives of the shadowy nightsoil men intrigued everyone. The Wormall family had lived up Shire Oaks for as long as anyone could remember and were 'Honey Dumpers' in the 1880's. This involved emptying privies at the bottom of gardens before the days of water toilets. During the hours of darkness, large buckets full of human excrement, 'jollop', were removed, tipped into a cart and returned empty to the privy. The appalling stench was overwhelming, but the malodorous Wormalls were accustomed to it. Jasper the boy was the 'limey-lad' for the cart team. This consisted of his brother known as 'Dirty Don', his father 'Smelly Old Sam', and the horse called 'Wiffy Willie'. Jasper had to hold a naked flame torch, walk after the cart and spread lime over any spillages to 'get shut at stink'. Sarah's favourite party piece was telling the story of the time that Sam dropped his teeth into the cart tank, and made Jasper dive in to retrieve them!

It was now more than 20 years since Don Wormall had died. Jasper had been alone in the primordial simple stone cottage of his birth, up the lonely, narrow, stony road on Shire Oaks Hill. He had a pleasant personality and was very popular. Many different friends called and enjoyed excellent tea from boiled well water in an ancient iron kettle suspended over an open fire. There was always freshly baked bread and cakes produced out of the mediaeval kitchen. Guests were seated at a solid thick oak table. On the wall a solitary ornamental brass plate, bearing words which seemed to sum up his kind and gentle personal philosophy -
'Make new friends but keep the old, one is silver, the other gold.'

Occasionally the Calders would trudge up the rough track and call in at the crude dwelling below the raucous rookery. He called it an honour, but Florence felt that **they** were honoured indeed to savour, if only for a short time, the high quality experience of good company, in a quaint setting, from a totally charming man of a past age.

Jasper was a first rate reliable gardener to several local properties, and had been requisitioned by Oliver Burgess for advice and service when he transformed the grassy hillside into a miniature paradise. When the marriage with Sarah Grindle had been announced in 1947, Jasper Wormall abruptly downed tools - and with good reason.

The invention of Thomas Crapper's 'water closet' in the Victorian period eventually had an adverse effect on the Wormall family business. As the 20th century dawned, Beaurepairians were increasingly unwilling to put up with a cold, dark, climb up to the unpleasant stinking privy at the end of the garden to answer the call of nature. Cisterns and sewers were being introduced, and the better off were able to install water flushing toilets **inside** the house. Understandably, Jasper was no friend of this form of 'progress'. He was proud to have one of the few earth closets left in the town, a two holer at that. He took the view that it was 'disgusting' to defecate dirty smelly stools inside the house, when such 'goings on' had always taken place as far from the living area as possible - *"at top o' garden"*. He steadfastly refused to 'sit over water' on such a new odd 'contraption'. He quoted a micro-biologist, who warned that each modern flush released an invisible germ-laden cloud in the aerosol spray, which was a menace to public health. He was proud of his privy at the end of his colourful old English garden.

Unfortunately his privy and past profession made him vulnerable to the nasty pranks of the depraved duo, Sarah Grindle and Sally Tonks. Funny stories of Jasper and Don sitting and chatting together on the two holer were recycled and exaggerated, but worse was to come. The girls when young, were fascinated by the remote crumbling cottage and folklore of the grotesque elfin creature within. After secretive exploration, they discovered the pongy little place at the back of the garden, occasionally visited by the old man. Mischief soon followed, made easy by the evil use of a little door at the back of the privy. On various occasions, by various means, they delighted themselves with the screams and shrieks he would utter. One time, long stemmed stinging nettles were applied to his bottom. Another time burning newspaper was thrust under him. Once one of his hens was introduced to give him a squawking shock.

Not every week, not even every month, but these outrageous attacks continued intermittently from about 1935 until well into the war years, when the girls were in their mid teens, and finally losing interest. Poor old Jasper never did get justice. The local 'bobby' questioned and cautioned parents, with little result. Sally received a sound thrashing from Olive on one occasion.

And so we come to Saturday evening, when the now adult duo were entertaining uncomfortable listeners with nasty narrations of their past

40

adventures tormenting the innocent and gentle Jasper Wormall. Just for an instant, Miss Florence Calder permitted herself a forbidden thought -

"Perhaps Madge has a point - she'd be better dead."

Chapter 5

A Wicked Wednesday

The same persistent autumnal high pressure which made Sunday such a beautiful crisp sunny day, had spoiled the Monday and Tuesday with high cloud. The cool Wednesday morning started with an intense sparkling deep blue sky. *"It is good to be alive!"* were the thoughts of Miss Madge Calder, as she first looked out of her bedroom window through the tangle of branches, and down Bridge Street beyond. The unpleasantness of Saturday evening was receding and, more than three full days later, she was feeling unusually cheerful, hopeful and decisive. The other inhabitants of Bridge House were equally buoyant and becoming busy preparing for another school day.

Next door, Doctor Paul Lewis also started the day taking some comfort from the sunshine, looking through his bedroom window, south west up to the distant Chevin Hills. He was less animated, his thoughts still mulling on the disturbing conversations of the dinner party. He felt threatened...he would have to think.

As was often the case, there was a stormy scolding atmosphere up on Cowhill. Mrs Tonks had been hearing all about the interesting bulges and shapely form of the handsome and well built butler of Fern Glade. In great alarm, the fearful mother was giving her fascinated daughter a belated but powerful lecture about the blackbirds and the bees. Olive Tonks lived many decades before the enlightened concept of a 'Multicultural Britain', and her xenophobia was fairly typical for an uneducated working class woman of her day. In agitation, and struggling to make her point, she grabbed at the old soot encrusted sturdy three legged stool by the fireplace. Brandishing a thick dark leg in Sally's face she warned -
"You keep away from 'im! Am tellin' ya!
Are ya listenin'? 'E'll ruin ya lass!!
Alas these dire admonitions only served to titillate the already tardy mill girl, who just said *"Oooh!"*, and like her lewd brother, was hungry to taste forbidden fruit! It would not have occurred to the ignorant woman that the sophisticated Alex Haigh had no interest whatsoever in her odious offspring. Eventually mother, and now giggly daughter, were launched down-hill to their separate places of work. Olive was quieter

than usual that day, brooding over the reported conversations of last Saturday evening.

Up Bridge Hill at the site of those conversations, there was also a brooding sleepy sad mood. At a little after eight, Oliver Burgess was dolefully eating his morning fresh fruit salad, hardly looking at, or speaking a word to, the indifferent and very correct respectful butler. His thoughts concerned an important meeting which would take place in the afternoon - a meeting which would make a big difference. Having just put an ornate German stein, full of hot tea, in front of his serious silent master, Alex Haigh was considering the relationship between money and happiness. This had been a deeply unhappy house for the short time of his stay. He liked his employer who had been generous, but was now, for the first time, having thoughts about the length and end of his contract.

A tray of coffee and toast was ceremoniously taken to the bedroom of his mistress. She was awake, sitting up and staring westwards down the lush verdant valley, through the large wide window which dominated the wall. The distant, dancing ripples on the river, picked up the morning sun like a ribbon of liquid gold. For the first time he felt sorry for her. An alluring beauty, socially trapped in her gilded cage, generally disliked and reviled by all. She was also imprisoned by her dysfunctional personality and inability to blend into her new position, new role, and adapt to her new status.

Depositing the tray, he was startled by an unexpected question -
"Are you happy, Alex?"
"I am reasonably content most of the time, madam.
I understand that some people call that happiness."
His deep purring cut-glass voice, which had only a trace of the expected western twang, was soothing and comfortable. She returned her gaze to the far off golden Derwent, and noted two tiny specks of humanity walking together along the bank.
"Will there be anything else, madam?"
She responded in a far away voice.
"There's only one person who really cares for me, who really likes me, and I'm going to help her today."
This pleasant thought gave her a small brief lift.
"I admire the Reverend Lady. Her gracious friendship must be a pleasurable and valuable asset."

He continued to stand to attention for a moment while she savoured his last comment.

> *"Will there be anything else, madam?"*
> *"No."*
> *"Very good, madam."*

At that moment another woman was looking out of a small Gothic heavily mullioned window, up high on Belper Lane, which had an equally impressive and more extensive view of the Derwent Valley to the north. The eye went towards Ambergate, and the sea of deep green woods beyond. She was absently admiring the lovely morning, but her gladness was tempered by the thought of a busy day ahead, and a certain visitor expected in the afternoon.

Reverend Mother Helen had held her position for only two years at the Convent of Cranmer. She took the opportunity of returning to Belper from a small convent in Northumberland, after an absence of 32 years, to fill a vacancy left by the sudden death of the previous Reverend Mother. It was an 18 year old Evelyn Lewis who abruptly decided to go north and become a nun in 1915. The departure surprised everybody, except her older brother Paul Lewis, who at that time was a 26 year old newly qualified doctor. From all accounts he had seen the religious fervour coming on for some time, but had considerable difficulty explaining this to his parents when they returned from an extended holiday in Canada, to find their only daughter absent. In those days there was a general belief that once a girl entered a nunnery to become a 'Bride of Christ', she would never be seen again! In fact long-distant visits, both ways, did take place after a few years. Evelyn eventually managed to persuade Dr Philip and Enid Lewis that 'she had been called', and that 'a window of opportunity' had been opened for a limited time only. She **had** to go. She could not delay months for the return of her parents - as much as she loved them.

Like the other guests, Reverend Mother Helen had frequently recounted to herself the ugly events of last Saturday evening. Like the Lawrences, she took the view that the frustrations of a 26 month marathon of misery was about to erupt into - what? Both parties, albeit of different social backgrounds, had been raised under the influence and protection of Holy Mother Church. Divorce was unthinkable - but the situation was untenable and increasingly unbearable.

"Poor Oliver!" She looked down at the small sepia photograph he had given her over three decades ago. A plain spongy 16 year old, clearly nervous of the camera with wide appealing eyes. Inclined to puppy fat, he was indeed in 1915, a besotted puppy, who followed her about everywhere. A girl of 18 tends to view a boy of 16 as a child. So it was that Evelyn Lewis saw Oliver Burgess as a kind thoughtful boy. She liked his company and enjoyed walking with him. He was hoping there would be more, but there **was** no more, and he was broken hearted when she disappeared one day. His status as a bachelor for over thirty years was attributed to the loss of his teenage dream. That same school of thought concluded that he had definitely grasped at the wrong straw.

"If things had been different?" She tried, and failed, to imagine herself as the Lady of Fern Glade. On the few occasions they met, there was a certain tension. Tension which was smoothly covered by mutual charm and impeccable courtesy. Oliver Burgess displayed admiration and high regard for her top position, yet at the same time boyish eyes showed the old affection. Evelyn Lewis was no more, but the Reverend Mother Helen had an extraordinary magical quality of making everybody love her. After minutes, perfect strangers were telling her all their troubles and intimate secrets. She was a wonderful woman, had done a great deal of good, was appreciated and treasured by the people of Belper.

Her strong personality had attracted the adoration and infatuation of Sarah Burgess. A friendship of sorts had developed. Of late Sarah had made excuses to visit the convent where she found companionship, contentment, and peace. The girl with nuns was a better girl. Saturday was to be the annual Open Day for the Convent of Cranmer, and help was needed with the floral displays. The Reverend Mother had made it clear to the other members of the small community that it was their Christian duty to make Mrs Burgess feel useful and welcome. This was relatively easy since nuns are pleasant people and tend to be tolerant, and so far, no sister had yet become a victim of her spite.

It was a stuffy and malodorous air which assailed the nostrils of the cool and detached Mavis as she entered the gloomy, untidy, brothel-like bedroom of Aubrey Pod. Treading over crumpled clothes which had been carelessly thrown down the previous night, she opened the curtains, and briefly took some comfort from the effervescent and glistening westward view over the river valley and on to the Chevin

Hills. The reflected brightness stabbed the unwholesome room, and brought a low grunt from the blobby, slobby, screwed up bundle in the bed. This was followed by a moan and slight movement, as the heedless servant made her quick exit, chamber pot in hand, at the very distant end of a fully extended arm.

A few minutes later she returned, and sharply deposited a large mug of hot sugary milky tea with a thud on his bedside table.

Her *"Mornin', Mr Pod"*, had a hard tone which sounded more like a reprimand than a greeting at the best of times, but she was still smarting from the brief unwelcome appearance of her late mistress on the day before last. The master moved, gradually opened unwilling little squinting piggy eyes, and made his third inarticulate sound by way of a groan. Mavis stood back, well back, safe from an assault of foul breath, and made a beeline to the refuge of the kitchen and the call of the frying pan.

He dragged his shapeless form to the reviving tea, and with some misery, mentally counted the last few precious days of his long holiday. The Herbert Strutt Grammar School would start the autumn term on the following Monday, and his annual high summer freedom would give way to classroom bondage, and the chronic pain of a daily assault on his dignity. Aubrey Pod was an excellent musician and good teacher to those few who were disposed to listen. The school was proud of every opportunity to show his practised competence on the piano. For the last 25 years he had been a faithful, valuable and accomplished organist at Christ Church.

Detested by the majority, but an enthusiastic few thoroughly enjoyed his boastful pomposity accompanied by exaggerated mannerisms. Most entertaining were the gloating stories he would tell in his spiteful squeaky voice, of those who had ignored or annoyed him in some way, and had gone on to meet with misfortune, such as the time when Claud Hoadley tried to dye his greying hair with disastrous results, and had to stay home for six weeks! After one service at Christ Church, a number of the congregation walked over to the River Gardens to enjoy the warm sunshine. Someone remarked on the continuing absence of Mr Hoadley, when Mr Pod joyfully recounted the failed attempt of the once handsome and ageing pretentious pedant to roll back the years. Skipping around his audience and gesticulating like an over wound toy -

*"I could have told him! You can't dye black hair, it's too stark against an ageing pale face, and **his** face gets paler every day. Mrs*

*Tonks said he looked like a crow at first - and now it's gone ginger! If the high and mighty Hoadley would deign to talk to **me**, **I** could have told him!"*

At this, the little toad-like creature broke into his 'dance of delight' which usually followed his nasty narrations.

At one time he was one of Miss Calder's Children. She first noticed this character defect when a naughty little six year old Aubrey, on one occasion, deliberately contrived to get other innocent little boys into trouble. By way of punishment he was forced to write out on his slate several times, a German proverb, followed by its English translation.

"Die reinste Freude ist die Schadenfreude." "The purest joy
is the malicious joy we take in the misfortunes of others."

But for the last few days, the gloater had become the victim, and had been darkly dwelling on the matter. Teenage girls had always been a thorn in his side, and Sarah's funny story of his discipline problem was a particularly mortifying abasement in front of so many people. An affront which demanded satisfaction. Satisfaction he intended to get today. Mr Pod had a plan - a plan which gave him pleasure. If Mavis could have seen his face at that very moment, he would have looked even uglier than usual. The already misshapen features were further contorted with menacing malice. Mr Pod intended to make Sarah suffer!

Another face not far away had a similar expression, but in this case 'hate' might be a more appropriate word. Fear of shame and being brought low was causing similar thoughts, but this man was more clever, perhaps more dangerous, but very cautious. This man was looking over a scene of rolling green hills. The silent landscape was broken with occasional trees and dotted at intervals were cows and sheep. A perfectly smooth mirrored river meandered through a soundless valley. The observer rested his eyes on a motionless rowing boat containing two ill formed dead people of oddly disturbing proportions and contortions. The river was twice crossed by a railway bridge, upon which was an inert steam locomotive pulling carriages which had come from nowhere and were going to the same place. This was the miniature, noiseless, un-stirring, private dreamscape which had been built up, little by little, since the turn of the century. This was the private world of Claud Hoadley in his large attic on Green Lane.

Julian Lawrence was cheered by the bright morning. He was thinking in terms of change. He needed a new stimulus for a new direction away from his previous mawkish work. He was hopeful. He was thinking of death.

Tatiana Lawrence needed to get out. She had always thought of her home on Long Row as charming and quaint. Now she was finding it too small and claustrophobic. The two long straight rows of neat and comfortable stone cottages were fine examples back in the 1790's, when old Jedediah Strutt built good quality accommodation for his mill workers. These historical considerations meant little to the vain lady in her mid forties, struggling to hold back the tide of time as she peered into a small mirror and skilfully applied make-up. The face which looked back at her was hard to take. A short decade before, she was still radiantly beautiful and was frequently told so, but the present daily application of the mask was now an every-morning battle. The appearance of a few extra wrinkles since Saturday evening, she put down to stress.

She had been day-dreaming of the impractical and expensive, hour-glass, chic images by Maison Dior of Paris. Her attractive, if painted looking platinum hair was now fashionably long and flowing, in stark contrast to the tight fitting helmet style of 25 years past, when it was shingled in the new permanent wave. In those past days, she was dark, the belle of Belper with a flawless complexion, smouldering eyes and carefully crafted cupid's bow lips, all neatly framed by a stylish hat. As in the precious old photograph she proudly displayed to a friend outside Christ Church, after the service, just two Sundays ago. A light tinkle of girlie laughter drifted over her shoulder from somewhere behind, accompanied by an excruciating comment involving some cruel reference to Dorian Gray. Inwardly mortified, she remained dignified, pretended not to hear, not to notice, but once again Sarah Burgess had successfully found the weak part, the open wound - and had bathed it with acid.

Mrs Lawrence long cherished the belief that Julian would become a success, and take her out of the Long Row cottage, out of Belper entirely and into a fashionable part of Mayfair. The sneering Sarah had showed her that this might not happen at all. Julian had always received good reviews, but if his work was just pleasant, and did not sell.... No! She would not think about it. It was much like the reality of the mirror. She didn't want to look. She would go to Derby and buy things. She would **do** something about Sarah Burgess!

Robin Kirkland hesitantly and lightly tapped on the private office door of his bank manager. Once within he timidly made his request which was grudgingly granted with the caveat -

*"All right, Kirkland, **if** it's important, but don't let this come too often!"*

It was very important. He needed to leave the bank one hour early today at 4.00pm to keep an urgent, but private, personal appointment.

Chapter 6

Murder

After lunch, an optimistic Sarah set out with sprightly step on her journey up to the Convent of Cranmer. Taking the north bound short way over the fields, it would be under a mile in length. She trudged up the rough Shire Oaks lane, past Jasper Wormall's craggy cottage, and took a public footpath to the left. Briefly looking back, and up at the clear blue sky and multitude of loud cawing crows above the goblin's house, she recalled the saying - 'One for sorrow, two for joy'.

"What do I get for hundreds? Or.. is that magpies?
She hopped over the wall on the right to correct her course. The younger Sarah Grindle had never been bound by existing footpaths or fears of trespass. So would Sarah Burgess press on upwards, through private field after private field, until she could see the summit of the Belper Lane hill and the strange towers of her destination.

Conceived by a pious eccentric millionaire back in 1837, this riot of ornamental octagonal turrets, projected castellated tops and oriel projected windows, was a brooding Gothic fantasy situated on the high west side of the Derwent Valley. Some had described this extraordinary flight of fancy as a monstrosity, but most observers were intrigued by the fairy tale steep pitched roofs ending in knife-edged gables and decorative finials.

It was Sarah's sixth visit, but she was studying the fearful gargoyles for the first time as they loomed closer, and eventually leaned and leered over her. Uneasily, she noticed how the individual hideous faces were all different in degrees of weather erosion, and build up of moss, and lichen, over the span of 112 summers and 112 dank sodden winters.

The sun was still shining, but in the cool shadow of the massive dark structure, Sarah felt the chill of evil as she peered into each horrible countenance. Suddenly they took on an element of familiarity! There was ugly old Jasper, rudely sticking far out an impossibly large tongue. Did the bulging toad eyes of Aubrey Pod move! Were they following her? Was that an intensity of supreme loathing, and spiteful revenge, in the stony cold fine features of Claud Hoadley? There seemed to be a strange warning in the wide-eyed, child-like, and inscrutable facade of Simple Simon. His adjacent mother grimaced with black teeth, like a furious old witch. Then at the very end,

50

unmistakable, the fixed frigid physiognomy of Miss Margaret Campbell Calder - hard and unforgiving. And of the others, she could not recognise, but they meant menace, so Sarah rushed inside to seek sanctuary.

Within the Convent of Cranmer there was more than sanctuary, there was peace. To avoid inconveniencing the sisters, Sarah had been instructed to admit herself. The mediaeval looking, thick, studded, gargantuan door moved unwillingly under her modest strength. On closure, it sent a hollow echo down the long stone cold corridor with its high vaulted ceiling. Perhaps the gargoyles had done their job well; no evil spirits here. Sarah made herself very useful and worked happily with the nuns. She had a natural eye for colour and arrangement. She did well. One of the sisters suggested that she could have helped them giving tuition to some of the slow learning children. Optional remedial classes had been provided in the recent holiday. Sunday school help was mooted by the Reverend Mother Helen. Both ideas were enthusiastically received. Sarah desperately wanted to help, and deeply needed to feel some self worth.

It had been a very long trying day for the Reverend Mother, who at a little after 4.00pm was now looking tired, complaining of feeling unwell and the onset of a cold.

"You've been so kind, my dear, and we all thank you." Several nuns smiled and nodded. *"Do stay for tea, but please excuse me, I must go and lie down."*

It was with a pang of conscience that the 'Lady of Fern Glade', and 'Lady of Leisure', realised that these committed holy women started each day at a little after 5.00am for worship and prayer. She suddenly remembered a previous appointment to be kept in less than an hour, and reluctantly declined tea with these very special and charming women. Sarah was honoured to escort her cordial and courteous friend to her private quarters, where they exchanged a few more words before the young visitor left.

Outside it had turned cooler, and, if anything, the sky was an even deeper blue. There was a nip in the air with the hint of shorter days to come. But the girl leisurely strolling down the steep Belper Lane felt a great joy and excitement at the prospect of the forthcoming unusual assignation, a little short of one mile below. She arrived at Bridgefoot and noted the time on the numberless, ornate, Jubilee Clock Tower, which indicated twenty two minutes to five - plenty of time. She crossed the river, and like most people, took a minute to enjoy the view of the cascading dancing bubbling weir and the beautiful distant hills to the east. Southbound, she passed under that most familiar Belper landmark, the quaint ivy covered Arched Gangway, with its 'never used' gun ports. Passing the Round Mill, on her left was the five storey South Mill.

At the end was Bridge House and the School where she had attended as a young girl. The wise old giant Plane Tree watched her hurry around the corner, as she turned towards the entrance of the Belper River Gardens. A few minutes later another person passed through this same entrance.

In the gloom of heavy foliage, a shaft of bright sunlight cut a spectacular figure of Percy Tinker, the old boatman. With his brilliant white shoulder length hair, honest gnarled hands supporting his weight with a hoe - an observer would have taken him for 'Old Father Time'. His old nose was unconsciously enjoying a dozen different sweet scents from nearby water loving flowers and weeds.

He looked up at the Jubilee Clock and took a few minutes to reminisce. He was a boy of five when Queen Victoria celebrated her 60 year reign in 1897, and recalled the 'big people' admiring the completed 147 foot tower, a year later. He had a little more than an hour left to finish his work around the pond and fountain. Carefully tended colourful floral displays were the delight of the town. In the 44 years since the gardens opened in 1905, Percy had proudly maintained the rocky, fragrant and leafy waterside retreat in immaculate condition.

The change had been immense. As a child in the previous century, he played in the marshy bog land which was an old osier bed, a place of wild willows used for basket making. Mr George Herbert Strutt used part of his vast inherited wealth to finance the transformation. Young Percy watched clanking, hissing and spitting steam traction engines, dredge, and remove thousands of tons of mud from the river. Solid ground was formed, upon which beautiful water and rock gardens were created. He mingled with a small army of workmen as they created a delight of glades, rock formations, alcoves, islets, avenues and terraces. The end delightful result was a wide pleasant promenade, a landing stage, boat house, a thatched picturesque Swiss tea house, lovers walk and the fountain with its fish pond.

He took little note of the two women who strolled down towards the boathouse. They looked very ordinary, but on closer inspection he recognised, with some distaste, that one was Sarah Burgess who as Sarah Grindle, had once caused him to think the unthinkable. He would resign if she and her nasty friend were not permanently banned from the River Gardens! After a campaign in the Belper News and huge public sympathy, old Percy won the day. The local 'bobby', and an official from the mill, both went to 'The Gutter' along the east end of Nottingham Road. Billy and Gladys Grindle were told in no uncertain terms, that they were to discipline, and keep Sarah away from the River Gardens so that Mr Tinker could work in peace! A similar ultimatum was delivered to a certain cottage up Cowhill.

But this was no longer Sarah Grindle, and it seemed inappropriate to run over the road to the Police Station to get her ejected. This indeed, was **the** Mrs Oliver Burgess of Fern Glade, accompanied by another adult. It seemed to him that there was still a mischievous twinkle in the eye, and a slight sneer in her tone when she asked for a boat. Somewhat grudgingly he unchained a boat called 'Mutt', and they climbed inside. He glanced at the mill clock as he passed over the oars, and said in a voice a touch sharper than usual -

"You've got joost over an hour. You'll oblige me by coomin' back before six, as that's when I'd like to go to my 'ome, thanking you very mooch!

He watched them as they floated off and passed to the left of the first island, under the railway bridge and out of sight. Old Percy scratched his white head.

"God only knows why a nice man like Mr Burgess married that!"

For the first time he gave a thought to her companion. He had not seen her before. For that matter, he had not actually seen her at all!

Kneeling by the pond, Percy lifted up his head and once again consulted the mill clock. Old bones creaked as he slowly struggled up to full height and stretched. They were overdue by five minutes. He would give them another ten, and that would be the end of it. He was hungry and wanted his tea. Sarah Grindle had always been totally inconsiderate. It was in fact at twenty minutes past six that the irritated and growling gardener locked up the boathouse and tramped out of the gardens in high dudgeon.

Thursday dawned another fine day. Mavis Fig had left her little cottage on Belper Lane as usual at 7.00am en route to Becksitch Lane to -
> *"Muck out Mr Pod".*

She too was in the habit of having a casual look at the weir, and lovely view beyond, but today she looked a little longer. One of the rowing boats was trapped in the river flow, slightly bobbing and jogging at the edge of the waterfall. In her lifetime of crossing the Derwent, Mavis had seen many odd dancing items at this same spot. All manner of floating debris, and once the appalling aspect of a bloated dead cow. Thinking no more of it, she trotted onwards to duty, to bring Mr Pod out of his deep sleep. In the next two hours, several busy people, mostly mill staff, noticed the unusual sight of Percy's escaped boat.

The man himself was none too pleased to be unnecessarily spending his gardening time dealing with the thoughtless incompetence of silly Sarah. She should, and **could** have tied up the boat properly with a little more effort. She did not appear to have much difficulty locking **him** into the maintenance shed twelve years ago! As he creakily and slowly rowed over to the helpless vessel, armed with a long ungainly grappling hook, his rumbling grumbling thoughts continued -
> *"She could've got back in time! It was the last thing I said to 'er. She can well afford a watch. **And** she didn't pay! That's arf a crown pl<u>oo</u>s the next hour. I'll 'av it off Mr Burgess if she acts awkward!"*

This last threat was followed by arrival, and a grapple to bring the boat away from the force of the fall. It was then that he noticed a large bundle under a blanket. Well balanced in his own boat, and holding both together, a brief inspection was now possible.

"Oh my God!!" In his long life, Percy's throat had only gone completely dry once before. It was many years before when he was violently threatened by rough youths. This was now the second time, as he looked at the deadly cold little white hand which stuck out of the covering. His instinct was to instantly withdraw and get help, but he mustered up enough self possession to find a head, and face, for identification, which may be needed for people wiser than himself. A simple movement revealed both. He was looking into wide open

staring bright blue eyes - eyes which seemed to be looking directly into the equally blue firmament above. The young, pale, bloodless face appeared to be appraising the expanse of the heavens - an expression which could be seen on any wondrous student. In this macabre moment, the old attendant noticed for the very first time, the pure beauty of this child with the long golden hair. It was an insect crawling across her cheek which caused a quick release in mad panic. He was rowing furiously back when the floating coffin with its putrescent contents slowly turned and, once more returned to the edge of the waterfall... to continue to gently bob, and gently jog...

Two hours later, Detective Inspector Derek Russell was sitting with Detective Sergeant John Winter on a bench in the gardens looking out over that same scene, the near river, the weir, and up high Bridge Hill beyond.

    "You were saying, sir?" Derek was aroused out of his reverie. He had been staring at the area of dark green foliage on the hillside, and the sleek low modern roof of Fern Glade. He had been thinking about Sarah and Oliver Burgess, a couple he had seen and spoken to at Christ Church on the occasions of his infrequent attendance.

    *"What exactly **did** I say, Winter?"*

    "Something about speaking to a ..'Miss Marple'...I think!"

    "Oh yes. She's not far away. I'll go and see her now. How's the old man?"

    "Bit shook up - naturally. Doctor's looking after him at the station over the road."

    "Good. We'll talk to him now. Then you can interview Commissionaire Sergeant Siddons at the Mill Office, just under the Gangway. He's nothing else to do but watch people go by. Might identify our mystery woman. Approach with caution, he's a fierce crusty old devil!"

They walked over to the Matlock Road Police Station, and stopped outside for a moment, respectfully. The late Mrs Sarah Burgess was being loaded onto an ambulance for transportation to the public mortuary, where a post- mortem examination would determine the cause of death. The Police Surgeon had attended the scene with Russell and Winter at a little after 10.30am. A cursory examination, including a rectal temperature check, suggested the young woman had been dead between 12 and 17 hours. This fitted in nicely with the initial evidence of Mr Tinker, to the effect that Mrs Burgess was last seen alive at 4.50pm, Wednesday September 7th. The doctor took into consideration that the previous high pressure cloudless night, was unusually cold for the time of year. The murder would have taken place not later than 10.00pm, presumably somewhere up the river. The girl's expression accorded with the cause of death, instantaneous, and totally unexpected. A sudden and violent blow to the back of the head - probably caused by a hammer. No help from fingerprints. On the more shiny parts of the wood, numerous smears and dabs - useless.

Percy Tinker was sipping his second cup of tea, kindly provided by Desk Sergeant Poulson, *("Good for shock")* when the two officers walked in.

"If you feel up to it, Mr Tinker, we'd like to ask you a few more questions about the second woman." He put down his cup and indicated his willingness to assist the police. DI Russell continued.

"Did you not look at her face even once?"
Percy considered.

"Looked, yes...a few times, but didn't really see."

"Why not?"

"Well...'ead scarf I suppose. It were well over 'er 'ead."
With a tinge of impatience, the senior man pressed on.

"What colour was the scarf?"

"Dark. Could be brown...or dark green? Coat same colour. Long...tweed a think. Looked nice and warm - it were a bit nippy - easterly wind."

"Please stand up, Mr Tinker."

He looked alarmed by this sudden and slightly sharp request. With the appearance of a reprimanded schoolboy, he slowly and unwillingly struggled to his feet. The inspector, who now stood directly in front of the old gardener, had decided to extract information by means of making brisk direct statements.

"Now, Mr Tinker, this woman you looked at but did not see. She was one foot shorter than me!" He studied the officer who was in fact 5ft 10 inches tall.

"Nay! No lad, she'd be... half that...or there abouts."

"So you say she was about 5ft 6" tall?"

"Yes!"

"Good, Mr Tinker!"

56

"Err...."

"Yes, Mr Tinker....something else?"

"Well she were not what you'd call straight up...sort of bent...bit of an 'oomp." Derek's mind flashed back to his school days for the second time in that hour. A fairy tale image of a humped backed, grouchy, crusty, snarling old hag floated before him.

"No!" he thought. *"Too old, too little strength, too little stamina - too Christian! Impossible!"*

After waiting a few seconds for traffic to clear, he crossed the A6, and negotiated the wide arc which enclosed the dank, shadowy, fern infested Bridge House School garden, over the low stone wall on his right. This was the shaded leafy lawn where he ran, skipped, jumped and played happily with the other boys and girls some 25 years before in the 1920's. In those days, little Derek crossed the same main Matlock Road four times a day, hardly having to look out for motorcars or carts on his way to school from his home at the Christ Church Vicarage.

Derek Russell was the much loved son of the Rev Edward Russell and his wife Jean - but not really. Right back to his very earliest memory, they were always totally honest and withheld nothing.

*"Babies come out of the tummies of their mother, but you didn't come out of **my** tummy. Your real mother and father died and gave you to Doctor Lewis, who gave you to us, to love and care for."*

Little by little, over the years, at the boy's request, this simple story was re-told acquiring more details. Baby Derek's daddy was a brave soldier killed in a foreign far off country. When he was born in a poor part of Belper called 'China', his mummy was very weak, and much too ill to live. As an 18 year old, he once had an opportunity to hear Dr Lewis's more direct and unvarnished version of the event. He looked at the earnest young man sitting before him and made up his mind.

*"It would be a dam fool thing to say 'Do you **really** want the real truth?' Of course you do, but hold tight! It's not pretty!"*

He took a moment to recollect his thoughts, and gave a faint smile.

*"It really **was** a cold dark stormy night for the middle of August...your birthday..."*

"August 15th." added Derek, helpfully.

"Oh yes, that was it. We'd been reading all about our lads roasting in the heat of Gallipoli and stubborn old 'Johnny Turk'. Terrible job that. Worst when we eventually learned all the true facts. We'd had an awful few dark days of rain, and I recall thinking we could do with some of that sun and heat here in Belper! Anyway it was late, well past 11.00 by the time I got there. Midwife had failed to show, nosy neighbours pressing up to the wide open door - and driving heavy rain! No wonder she died."

He paused respectfully, looking at the sad young face opposite.

"A mean filthy little hovel on hard trodden soil. It makes Jasper's cottage look like a palace!" Another pause. *"She was only **just** alive. You made your appearance after I arrived - she died minutes later - I'm sorry. I doubt it would have made much difference if the summons had come an hour earlier. Can't even remember her name now!"*

"Ethyl Jinks, and my father was killed in France some months before - Alfred Jinks."

"Oh yes...Jinks, that's right."

"Why did you take me to the Vicarage?"

"Best place. Edward and Jean are wonderful people. She was very depressed and desperate after her recent still birth. You were the answer to her prayers."

"I'm very grateful... thank you."

"Part of my job, young man!"

He rose briskly to signify a tactful dismissal.

*"You've made your parents very proud. We're **all** proud of you. A fine young man and a credit to the town. I've enjoyed watching you grow up."*

Doctor Lewis spoke for many in Belper. Derek Russell with his suave, smooth elegance and evocative rich voice, had that rare and precious gift of being an immensely likeable personality.

"University in September I hear? What will you read? Father's footsteps?"

But Derek assured his doctor that 'The Church' had no appeal. However he **was** interested in the footsteps of his real father and mother, and so on this particular day in 1933, he walked in the direction of 'China'. Opposite Campbell Street, standing on the south side of New Road, next to the railway line he looked down on a few miserable rows of squalid terraced houses. Several scruffy urchins were playing and chasing squawking, panicked, feather shedding chickens. Not the first time he had looked at this well known slum with its notorious inhabitants. His first teacher, whose word was law, had always warned all her pupils to keep well away from the intriguing folk in 'the depths of China'.

"*Don't behave like a cottage child.*" was one of the frequent reprimands of Miss Florence Calder when affronted by any example of crude uncouth conduct. During his privileged boyhood days in the Christ Church Vicarage, he had been fascinated by stories of 'six in a bed', ragged children walking around barefoot and of tea being drunk out of jam-jars. This last, at least seemed sensible to the tea-loving Derek who was never satisfied with the dainty size of the average teacup.

He had also heard of their kind neighbourliness and immense generosity in sharing out what little they had. Was it not a fact that on the very night of his birth, they had unselfishly joined forces to help his poor mother?

To quench a growing curiosity about his personal origins from this dark ghetto, he consulted the Belper Historical Society. They found evidence that the houses of 'China' were originally constructed sometime before 1845 by Ward, Sturt and Sharp, partners to Brettles. The small community was purpose built for their hosiery workers and probably took its name from 'China Silk'.

The pull of this forbidden part of Belper was now too great to ignore. He **had** to know more and so for the very first time, he was resolved to go in and stand in front of the place of his birth. Grey fetid faces curiously watched him walk to a tiny end cottage, which had been boarded up for 18 years. An old man with stubble and protruding glistening salivary tongue was sitting on an upturned bucket next door. With his pals from years before on their travels around Belper, he had often seen this begrimed grubby old gremlin, and speculated that he must have been sitting on that old bucket for nearly a hundred years! Derek Russell, who could nearly have been Derek Jinks, politely told the man who he was, and that he would be grateful for any information about his real parents.

The old rag-bag was flattered by unaccustomed courtesy, and the attention from such a well spoken young gentleman. Wilf Riley was keen to talk. Alfred Jinks would be in his middle twenties, the same as his wife. **If** she was his wife! Subsequent investigations in later years turned up no records.

"*Dead roough, came from Sheffield way. Got by we odd jobs, like a lot o' us. Glad at war. Arr, keen ta fight an do soommat, travel. Arr..did't coom back, like a lot on um.*" He shook his head and looked at the ground. He went on to say that Mrs Jinks "*..were always a sickly lass.*" He was surprised that Derek had survived at all. "*Doctor did marvellous, no midwife, owe took bad.*" The neighbours offered help but were strictly kept out. "*Eee, ya were a sad little boondle wen 'e took ya!*" At this point Wilf looked closely at the handsome and well proportioned youth before him. "*Arr...ya look a bit like ya dad, but yav got ya mam's nice ways. Poor lass, nowt mooch ta be doon for er, an 'e was in a 'urry ta save ya - and 'e did - grand chap Dr Lewis.*"

Six years later, Wilf Riley and his old bucket, Derek's lowly birthplace, and the decaying rat infested slum, known locally as 'China' - were all swept away leaving nothing but memories.

Chapter 7

A Question of Shadow

Forward to September 8th. 1949, Detective Inspector Russell was standing at the dark tunnel-like entrance of his old school, under the mill. The barely discernible 'Bridge House School' was still faintly proclaimed from the elderly brown board above. A slight breeze stirred up the massive foliage, which was never far away. With it was stirred up an extraordinary sensation of joy and happiness, which was part of the very fabric of this hallowed ground, and these wonderful precious women from a past age.

"No, there is no evil here!" were his rapturous thoughts. And looking up into the vast tangled green canopy -

"Hello, mighty and dear wise old friend! Do you remember me? If you could speak, I need not enter. You see all!

It was something short of a quarter hour before the children would be dismissed for lunch, and the 'past pupil' part of him was fearful to disturb the working day of Miss Florence Calder. But he was now a senior police officer, with authority, on official duty, carrying the responsibility of a murder enquiry. Emboldened, he stood to attention and marched down into the stone flagged corridor. All was silence. He began to think the autumn term had yet to start, until he gently pushed open the familiar old door on the left.

The scene inside surprised him by its very smallness in contrast to boyhood memories, but it was all there as he had left it two and a half decades back. Rows of immovable long cast iron forms with oak desk tops. Solid, reliable, tried and tested. She who must be obeyed, sat bolt upright at her high desk facing her pupils. She could see them and, even more important, **they** could see her. The smell of India rubber was combined with the sense of intelligent, firm discipline. The small sounds of boys and girls scratching on their slates stopped, as they became aware of the strange big man now framed in the doorway. For the few seconds, as much as they dared, 20 young faces turned to see the visitor, before quickly returning to work. Miss Florence Calder looked up sharply at the sudden cessation of activities, and was surprised to see Derek Russell at her door, not for a moment considering he might be on official business, here in sleepy old Belper.

"I do apologise for this intrusion, Miss Calder, but it is

important that I speak with you as soon as possible. "

At the sound of the powerful deep masculine voice, small interested faces were once again up turned. A dark, doll-like, pretty girl on the front form, with shoulder length wavy ringlets, was especially noticeable. Until, like the others, she caught the eye of her stern mistress, and re-applied her mind and grey slate pencil to the labours of 'copperplate' script. The Victorian teacher moved to the door and simply said -
"We'll talk in the parlour. "
He half expected to hear something to the effect of -
"You will continue to work in silence. " but no such instruction was given. He realised from his own personal memory, that such a command was totally unnecessary. Also in his past memory was the familiar, furious, shrill shriek which echoed down the corridor from the second classroom.
"Don't be alarmed. " said Miss Florence, *"It's only Madge. Dolly will be misbehaving again. Or it could be Philip? Most likely Dolly. "*

As the old teacher pushed open the door leading into the private quarters of the Misses Calder, Derek was surprised to hear a tuneless, common voice of uncertain gender, screeching out a popular song of the day -
*"...lets go where thee keep wearing them silks, an' satin, an' linen that shows, an' am all yours in b**oo**ttons and bows. "*

A scrawny kneeling boy, with head, happily oscillating to the irritating rhythm of this inane ditty, was busy cleaning out the grate. A welcome silence fell, when the rather sooty servant turned, and froze with fascination at the unexpected sight of the handsome and athletic figure before him. Miss Florence abruptly broke this brief but embarrassing silence with a knife-edged announcement -
*"No need to stare, Simon! You've probably seen Mr Russell before in church, but didn't know he was Detective Inspector Russell. Take away that ash and sweep the back yard, which **should** have been swept yesterday. "*
She glowered at him as he rose to his feet, with a slight bob and nod, and scuttled out with a full bucket of ash. Florence caught Derek's smile at the whimsical effect of this curious character.

62

"He's quite useful really - a good lad for the most part. Actually he's 23!"

Politely the policeman remained on his feet until his former mistress was seated.

"Well, Derek, what is all this?" In tune with the briskness of his teacher, he came directly to the point. With serious expression, she listened carefully but unemotionally to the full account of the crime. At the conclusion, she took a deep breath, exhaled, closed her eyes and sat back in the arm chair. Seconds later she opened those eyes.

"You have come to consult Miss Marple, but I am afraid all you find is an ordinary old schoolmarm of average ability!"

The Inspector laughed out loud, not only because he had told Sergeant Winter that he was visiting 'Miss Marple,' but also because he knew from his parents that the old spinster was an enthusiastic Agatha Christie fan. The little joke had relaxed the atmosphere beautifully, and his warm engaging smile had the effect of softening her features. Just for a second, he saw something of the attractive young girl she once was, more than half a century back.

*"You must admit there are parallels. You knew and taught her. You knew and taught her husband. You know her parents. You probably know and have taught some of the people we'll need to interview. You know a lot about Belper! I believe I **have** found 'Miss Marple'!*

*"As you wish, Derek. **Good Heavens!!**"*

She abruptly dashed out of the room. He heard her distant voice in another place, followed by the excited sounds of freed children, changing slippers for shoes, putting on coats and escaping, some five minutes late, into the busy streets of lunch-time Belper. She returned with some embarrassment.

"Poor things! They must have heard Madge's class go by, but of course won't move until told!"

She resumed her seat and recollected her thoughts.

"Now! Oh yes - don't be too hard on Percy. Madam X is clearly a clever woman. On a bright sunny day it is perfectly easy to arrange a substantial head scarf, giving a generous brim which will cast a strong shadow over the features. This is why Our Lord was not at first recognised by his disciples under the dazzling sun of the Holy Land. Bright light tends to make people squint, the eyes naturally take cover by looking downwards, or into shade and gloom making observation difficult. In the late afternoon the sun was well into the

*west, over the Derwent. She would have taken **great** care to look into the gardens, towards Matlock Road - away from the sun. She'd also be fully cognisant of the effect produced by the sudden appearance of Sarah Grindle. Are you aware of the stormy background?"*

Derek was an occasional visitor to the town of his birth and boyhood. His young family enjoyed their periodical Sunday calls at the bungalow down the quiet pleasant Wyver Lane to see Grandma and Granddad. It was quite natural that the retired Vicar of Christ Church and his wife, would take some small pleasure in retailing a little local gossip. Sarah Burgess nee Grindle was a name which often came up. She had been pointed out to him in the church. In the interest of obtaining as much information as possible, he gave the impression of being vague, and invited the old lady to give a full history.

It was half way through this saga that Simon, at the instruction of Miss Madge, came mincing in with sandwiches, a pot of tea for two, a pirouette and various obsequious, amusing bodily contortions which reminded Derek of the comic actress Kathleen Harrison!

*"**Did** you heat the pot, Simon?"*

*"**Oh yes,** Miss Calder."* he squeaked.

After much solicitous twitter and fuss regarding napkins, cutlery, clatter, and dancing around the Detective Inspector, Miss Florence Calder pointedly boomed -

*"Thank you, Simon - **THAT WILL BE ALL!**"*

This time Derek was positively shaking with laughter as the comical character flew out of the parlour.

"You have to admit, Miss Florence, he's brightened up your lives!"

Somewhat dubiously she murmured -

"I suppose one must be grateful for small mercies."

The chronicle of Sarah's conduct and numerous enemies was eventually concluded.

"You can see why Percy would be absorbed by Sarah, and not have paid much attention to her unknown companion. Did you ask him about smells?"

"Pardon!"

"Just an idea, any identification of a scent could be useful later."

64

It occurred to his old teacher that a number of important questions may have been un-asked, but she did not wish to put him out of countenance in any way. Indeed it had been her life long policy to praise and encourage wherever possible.

"You say Percy spoke of a stoop or hump?"

"Yes, an impression of such."

"Mmmm..." She looked at him steadily.

"Do you suspect Madge?"

The directness of this short snappish question caused a jolt! He was flustered, but before he could find a suitable diplomatic form of words for careful reply - she came to his rescue.

*"It **could** have been my sister. The described deformity and height, with help from elevated shoes, would both be correct. She **said** she was taking the dogs for their daily walk at about half past four. I didn't see her until seven when Simon was enthusiastically crashing the dinner gong! She has always hated Sarah - with good reason! She was too upset to speak to anyone all Sunday after the Saturday evening. At the dinner table, Sarah had managed to tempt Claud Hoadley to air his extensive literary knowledge. She claimed an interest in the works of Victor Hugo, particularly his novel about the deaf and dumb character Quasimodo who inhabited Notre Dame.*

'Was he really as bent and hideous as depicted by the film actor Charles Laughton?'

That sort of thing."

He was studying the Victorian pattern of the worn, old, tired carpet with concerned and sad expression. He looked up at the hurt old lady opposite.

"I'm so sorry. It's early days to be suspecting anyone yet."

This note of melancholia was cheerfully interrupted by another appearance of Simon who was **so** excited, he forgot the required preface of "Excuse me, Miss Calder..."

*"There's a man at door, Belper News 'e sez. Wants ta see t' bobby. There's bin a **MURDER!**"*

"Show him into my study, Simon."

He quickly disappeared and she turned to her former pupil.

"I don't suppose you intended the news to get around so soon?"

"It would be pointless to try and keep it quiet. There were several gawking people watching us retrieve the body this morning, and we do need the locals to help us identify the unknown furtive female."

65

He continued more slowly -

"I had considered withholding the method of death..."

She finished his thought -

"...with the hope that the guilty party will incriminate herself with a reference to 'a blow to the head'?"

"Something like that."

*"Very well, Derek. As far as I know the police have **not** said how Sarah died"*

"Thank you, Miss Marple!"

She was now briskly on her feet, and courteously, so was he, a fraction later.

"A short-list of Mrs Burgess's principal enemies would be much appreciated in the very near future."

"You'll have that this afternoon." She pulled at the bell.

"Simon will show you into my study where you'll no doubt find the local press hungry for information."

After a glance at the clock, she delivered her parting shot.

"Good. I see that there is just enough time to check that our hammer is not blood stained - or indeed missing! And just enough time to question the dogs about yesterday's walk!

Good afternoon to you, Detective Inspector Russell!"

It was a little past 4.00pm, at her high desk, when Florence finished her letter to Detective Inspector Derek Russell, which incorporated the requested short-list of names. There were just two. Tatiana Lawrence and Olive Tonks. *" A short list indeed!"* She seemed to be acting like an arbitrary executioner, and felt the need to bounce her thoughts off Madge.

"But I also need stamps and exercise." Smartly she donned her coat and brusquely stepped out to the nearby Bridge Street Post Office.

There was a pang of guilt when she bumped into the first name on her list - in person - Mrs Lawrence! The poet's mother was quite relishing the excitement.

*"Have you heard the **news**, Miss Calder? I always felt that girl would open her evil mouth once too often!"*

Hearing this commonly believed and often repeated wisdom, it occurred to Florence for the very first time that it might be prudent to consider a motive, **other** than that of pure hatred. Tatiana was waiting for a response when she noticed that the teacher's attention was

66

elsewhere. Over the road, a small boy was reaching up to the stamp vending machine.

"One moment, Mrs Lawrence!" She marched up to the child, and sharply said something which caused him to; first go pale, and then just go, swiftly, in a southerly direction.

"I'll have to follow that up tomorrow. Sorry about that, Mrs Lawrence - you were saying?"

*"Knifed I'm told! The police'll be overwhelmed with suspects who'd be only **too** happy to thrust cold steel into that Jezebel. Mr Hoadley wasn't exactly grief stricken. He was in the bank, holding court, airing his beautiful vowels, as usual. Something like -*

'She has, at long la<u>rr</u>st, made her greatest and most generous contribution to society - by leaving it'!"

"Quite, but I really must get on, and back to my sister who'll be waiting to start tea. If you'll excuse me..."

Miss Calder walked back over the road and into the small Post Office. Mrs Lawrence had enjoyed her 'dig' at Mr Claud Hoadley. The hostility had dated back to an occasion when he had honoured her small humble home, by accepting an invitation to dinner.

The Lawrence's next door neighbour was tidying up the tiny front garden when he noticed the erect and smart gentleman walk by.

"'Ow do."

A simple greeting from a peasant was always a wonderful opportunity for the snob to assert his social superiority. Late afternoon, it may have been, but here was yet another chance to roll out that highly polished and sophisticated sounding southern long 'A', so that the common man and the world at large could hear the loud and long drawn out -

"Good A<u>rr</u>fternoon."

Once inside the Lawrence's cottage, all was apparently well. Mr Hoadley silently noted, with a silent sneer - the doilies, the serviettes, editions of 'The Melody Maker', 'Picturegoer', 'The News of the World', and frequent reference to the new 'settee'.

Tatiana put on her very best accent for the special occasion, but it all went wrong when it was time for the sweet to be served -

"Any one for sugar pudding?"

Her refined and erudite guest could not resist commenting on her mispronunciation of 'sugar' and 'pudding'!

67

*"Forgive me, Mrs Lawrence, but you have incorrectly sounded an open 'U' on both words. You said 'shagger' and 'padding', when in fact it is perfectly acceptable to use a closed 'U', and say 'sh**oo**ger' and 'p**oo**ding'."*

Tatiana, who had been trying very hard all evening, felt shocked, furious and embarrassed, but the pedant continued -

*"It is a common mistake with Derbyshire people from the working cl**arr**ss such as your good self, who are, quite commendably, making an effort to improve their social station."*

He took no note of her frosty features and pressed on -

*"I'm afraid you also pronounced an open 'U' when, for my comfort, you invited me to take an extra 'c**a**shion' instead of a 'c**oo**shion'. A kind thought, but sadly you lowered yourself by uttering the word - 'c**oo**mfort', which of course, for those who move in higher circles, is pronounced - 'c**a**mfort'."*

She folded her arms, lifted her chin a fraction and moved her head to one side-

"Any further suggestions, Mr Hoadley?"

For the first time he became aware of treading on dangerous ground.

*"Please don't be offended, Mrs Lawrence, but it really is **much** better to hear it from **me,** now, than to expose yourself to being sniggered at by the more cultured and educated. Since you a**rr**sk, there was **one** more point. You went on to say that the excellent steak we've just enjoyed was from the best 'b**a**tcher' in Belper!*

She continued to stare and smoulder, contemplating tipping sugar pudding all over the pompous head of her irritating guest. He broke into this difficult moment.

"I appear to have annoyed you, Mrs Lawrence, but please do try to remember that elocution is a valuable service I offer, for which a professional fee is usually paid. Many people in Belper are grateful to have an opportunity to distance themselves from the common working classes and move up to join a small elite."

Tatiana Lawrence considered herself to be already a member of that 'elite', and was so terribly upset, that she could not at that moment compose a suitable answer, and therefore remained silent. The mood in that 'charming little house' as Mr Hoadley had described it an hour earlier, was now beyond repair. Claud Hoadley, always a gentleman, now had to find a diplomatic form of words to swiftly end the engagement.

68

"I deeply regret my words this evening, Mrs Lawrence, which were intended to be helpful." He stood up and addressed her son. *"Perhaps you will kindly get my coat, Julian."*

The silent son was tempted to defend his mother by reminding Mr Hoadley of his own local background - 'Derbyshire born, Derbyshire bred ....' But Claud Hoadley was certainly **not** 'strong in t' arm' nor 'thick in t' 'ead'!

Back to the present and in the capacious Calder parlour, Florence was looking fondly on the hot buttered toasted tea-cake which Simon had, very nicely, just placed before her. He too was enjoying the high drama of the day.

"Ooo, Miss Florence, int tit awful! Poo-er Sarah, strangled we 'er own stockin's. Not safe fa a lass ta be out...."

This time it was Miss Madge Calder who first lost patience with the fuss and flutter.

*"Thank you, Simon, **we'll ring** when we need you."* He shot out.

"Well, Florence. Stabbed and now strangled! We're surrounded by fools."

*"Indeed! One is given to wonder how the wretched girl **did** meet her death."*

"No mystery at all, big sister. Sarah Burgess was killed instantly by a single powerful blow to the head!"

In shock and alarm, Miss Florence Calder nearly choked on the tea-cake portion which was still moving around the inside of her mouth. She forced it down with a gulp, and fixed the other with a glare of suspicion and extreme consternation.

*"**Madge!** Only the police know the **true** facts. If your reckless wild guess should by any slim chance turn out to be correct, you'll be putting yourself in a perilous position!"*

"Nonsense."

*"**Nonsense?**"*

"Yes, Florence, nonsense. Look here, if that silly Lawrence woman had given any thought at all to the cutting theory, she'd have rejected it at once. Think of the difficulty we had trying to put our knives through Simon's joint the other night! If our mystery murderess is so clever, as we assume she is, she would hardly risk Sarah crying out loud and attracting the attention of all Belper as she struggles to damage the girl. You know how difficult Sarah can be! Not to mention

*spurting blood all over one's clothes. Most inconvenient to have to explain later. Throttling would be even more foolhardy, **and** require great strength. Sarah would be wrestling and thrashing around for her very life. They'd both have the boat over in no time. The police would only need look for a woman with black eyes, a thick lip, and several recently knocked out teeth."*

Florence listened to this graphic adventure with rapt attention and was wondering if Madge had missed her calling. She decided to put her sister's deductive powers to a higher test.

"Can you name the murder weapon?"

"Yes."

"Yes?"

"That's the easy part."

Miss Florence Calder sat transfixed with a cold cup of tea in her lap, and her mouth open quite expecting to hear the word 'hammer'.

"The weapon is a cheap, common, heavy object, easy to wield, and which is never far from anyone in Derbyshire." She let out the last line with a flurry of triumph. *"I speak of the ubiquitous and humble piece of rock!"* Florence closed her mouth.

"You don't think it was, by any chance, a hammer?"

Madge considered.

"No...no. No a rock tossed into the river with ten thousand other well washed rocks would be the only sensible weapon."

She sat back in contented satisfaction.

For once she had impressed her older and clever sister.

Chapter 8

"Did You Notice Her Hands?"

Detective Inspector Derek Russell was also busy earlier that afternoon. It was his duty to break the news to Oliver Burgess.

"We'll walk up the hill, Winter, do us good, and we'll get a feel for the 'scene of the crime'. What did you get out of Siddons?"

"Not a lot. Vaguely noticed several ordinary dowdy women go by. Said all Belper women looked the same!"

"Yes, our murderess would take great trouble to look just like any other plain working class woman complete with head-scarf."

"I suppose the slight 'hunch' **could** *have been affected at the gardens."*

Walking down the driveway of Fern Glade was an impressive experience.

"My stars! Wish **I'd** *knocked out a few bicycles."*

"They'd have to be 'good' bicycles, Winter."

Announcements and credentials were produced in the usual way, but the very correct butler was totally un-phased by the sudden appearance of senior police officers, and answered the question in a 'matter of fact' manner.

"I'm sorry, gentlemen. Having consumed his lunch, Mr Burgess has returned to his office at the factory down on Derwent Street." Detective Inspector Russell asked the stoic Negro if he would mind answering some important questions.

"Not at all, sir. Please come this way." The admirable, tall and stately servant, led them silently across wall to wall, thick lush carpet into the large light living room. They were invited to be seated, and in turn the butler was persuaded to join them. A few enquiries elicited the interesting non-servile background of the American, and in a short time, both men knew they were dealing with a well educated, shrewd and intelligent gentleman.

"Please excuse the intrusive nature of these questions, Mr Haigh, but you'll soon learn that they are justified. At what time did your mistress return home last night?"

"I wouldn't know, sir, but she did not attend dinner, and I discovered this morning that she had not occupied her bed."

"Had she been with her husband?"

"No, sir, they have separate en-suite rooms."

"Did Mr Burgess not comment on her absence?"

"Indeed he did, sir. I gather it is most unusual. He assumed she had stayed over-night with the sisters at the convent."

"Didn't he ask you to telephone or make enquiries? Wasn't he worried about her?"

Here the butler gave a typical butler's discreet cough, which always announced a dilemma of the need to strike a balance between truth and diplomacy. This was the moment when a loyal servant had to choose his words carefully. Both officers were entertained by the polished performance of the handsome actor opposite, thoroughly enjoying his role.

"I regret to inform you, sir, that in my fifteen months in this house, I have never seen or heard my master or mistress speak to each other. Communication was rare, and when it happened at all, it was through me."

Derek decided the time was right -

"Mr Haigh, I have to inform you that your mistress has been murdered!" For the smallest moment, less than one second, his features remained unchanged. Then his eyebrows rose before he said -

"Indeed, sir!" The Sergeant and the Inspector were astounded at this low key response. The latter said as much.

"I am not given to histrionics, sir, nor do I claim any feelings of surprise or grief. Mrs Burgess made many enemies. She was civil to me, but to be frank, I did not like her."

Russell outlined the events of the previous day and asked, first where the butler was, and did he see a hunched woman about 5ft 6" tall wearing a dark coat and dark head-scarf. Alex claimed he was in the house all afternoon. At this the detectives gave thanks and announced their departure.

"May I make a suggestion, sir, which may be of some small help."

"We need help." said Winter.

"Perhaps it is my American way, a different aspect.. but.."

"Yes, Mr Haigh?"

"You look for an unknown woman you may never find. It could be an expensive waste of time and manpower...sir!"

For the first time the smooth detached black man was becoming slightly more human. Detective Inspector Russell became suddenly interested in this novel line of foreign thought.

"What **are** *you getting at?"*

"I was thinking of the classic conjuring trick, sir, sleight of hand. My uncle made his living as a magician. Two women are seen getting into a boat. They row up river. One comes back dead. We naturally assume the unidentified lady has killed the known lady. In fact we do not **know** *that, sir. We only know what we have seen! X could be a person or persons unknown. It is entirely possible there are* **two** *dead women - sir."*

They looked at him steadily with some slight irritation.

"Thank you, Mr Haigh, we'll consider your instructive observation. Both banks of the river from Belper to Ambergate have been searched by our team. I'll ask them if a second body has been found!"

At the top of the drive, John Winter said -

"What team?"

"I'll ask for a couple of men to check."

"He may **have** *something there, sir."*

Derek Russell resorted to uncharacteristic and definitely un-Calder like language -

"That's what's so bloody aggravating!!"

They were not looking forward to the next call. The factory sounded very busy and prospering when the gatekeeper telephoned to Mr Burgess's private secretary, and then directed them to the main office. They were announced and shown inside the inner sanctum. Both men studied the rather soft creamy bespectacled face. A very ordinary face Derek had seen several times before in church, without much interest, beyond the fact that here was a wealthy man - a man who looked un-fit and was clearly unaccustomed to climbing the steep hills of Belper. Consulting his notes, Sergeant Winter was surprised by the age, and thought Burgess looked nearer to 60 than his 50 years. With consideration and tact, the news was gently broken.

He seemed to regard the information after the fashion of reading some mediocre sales results, and took out his handkerchief to clean his glasses. Something told Derek that it was important to scrutinise these carefully controlled emotions. Somehow they would be important, later, if not now. But the mask held firm, and Oliver Burgess had given away nothing. He had responded in much the same way as his butler. No shock, not even great surprise, and certainly no sorrow. He seemed more concerned about the welfare of his official visitors.

"I'm grateful you've taken the trouble to inform me. It must be very difficult to bear such appalling tidings. Having to deal with evidence...the body ..that is, it can't be very pleasant. You've been very busy today ... and I don't doubt there is a great deal of hard work ahead of you. Naturally, I'll help all I can..."

He looked at them with helpless, but dry, eyes.

Looking back at the factory gate, John Winter said to his boss -

"I'm actually beginning to feel sorry for this un-loved lass! D'you think we'll find anyone who'll shed a tear?"

DI Russell took a deep sigh -

*"Your next port of call might see some drama, **and** you'll be on your own. I've got things to do in Derby."*

*"Where am **I** going, sir?"*

"You're going into 'The Gutter', my lad! You're delivering (what should be) bad news to Billy and Gladys Grindle."

John Winter took a lonely walk along to the eastern end of Belper. Eventually he came to one of the old terraced houses in the area known as 'The Gutter'. An un-welcoming gruff man with a coal encrusted black face opened the door. *"Yes?"* John felt intimidated, but squared up to his official position as DS Winter, and was grudgingly admitted into the small house. He was led down the musty narrow dark passageway, which appeared to have the original Victorian wallpaper, complete with a hideous deep brown dado. His unpleasant duty, together with a hostile reception from the grumpy inarticulate Billy Grindle, caused the young Sergeant to resent this visit.

"It's a job for a more senior man!" he thought. He greeted the rather shabby looking woman within, who received him in complete silence. Standing rather awkward, as no one asked him to be seated, he announced the tragic news. At first the young man formed the impression that Gladys Grindle had not taken it in. She stared at him as if a half message had been received, and she was waiting for the rest. Into this embarrassing social space, he added, rather clumsily, more details of the crime, but stopped when Mr Grindle seemed to drop into an easy chair.

"This has been a terrible shock. I wouldn't dream of bothering

you now, but we'll need some information later.... I'd better go."

He made for the passageway, but was surprised to find Mrs Grindle behind him at the door. Her eyes were pleading and watery. It was the nearest he had seen to the shedding of tears for the loss of Sarah Burgess.

"Ya mustn't mind Billy. It's 'is way. She's bin a worry to us, an 'e 'asn't spoke to 'er fa .... ay .. a long time - a long time."

"I'm so sorry to have brought this awful news ...."

She closed the door and was gone.

The morning of Friday September 9th saw the high pressure area as strong as ever; brilliant sunshine, but now a touch warmer. Breakfast at Bridge House School was an introspective affair. The sisters said little to each other. Florence had a clear objective for the morning and was mentally planning.

"A shame to waste beautiful weather, we'll do the nature walk this morning, both classes."

"Both!"

*"Please bear with me, Madge. I **must** talk to Percy Tinker without delay."*

*"But **both** classes!"*

"You can cope with 40 children. Simon will go with you to help bring up the rear."

*"**Simon!** Really, Florence!"*

*"Why not? You know how the children adore him, and he's quite good with them. Yes! He'll enjoy being freed from his morning chores - which he will **do** - later!"*

After an hour of academic work, the boys and girls were excited to be lined up, hand in hand, two by two, outside the school, ready for their walk. The chatter and animation died away to total silence and stillness, as Miss Madge Calder went through the rules of good behaviour on the public streets of Belper. A loud cheer went up at the announcement of Simon being the temporary replacement of Miss Florence. She smiled at the happy throng, as her diminutive sister gave the 'Forward' command, and led the merry party towards the Mill Bridge with little Simon blithely skipping behind.

Old Percy was once again on his knees as he saw the unmistakable smart stately figure of Miss Florence Calder with a forthright and determined measured step, approaching. Totally unprepared for this unusual and sudden august presence, with some panic, he struggled up to his feet.

"Good morning, Percy. I'm sorry to interrupt your work but I would like to ask you some questions."

She sat on a bench facing the river. He stood at attention by her side.

*"**Do** have a seat. Now, Percy! Cast your mind back to Wednesday afternoon. That woman, the one we're looking for. It would seem she made some attempt to disguise herself, long coat, head-scarf, that sort of thing?"*

"Yes, Miss Calder."

"Quite! But 'would be' deceivers tend to forget to change their distinctive gait."

"Pardon?"

"The way they walk. Did her walk remind you of anybody? Did she plod? Did she skip?"

Percy Tinker made a supreme effort to re-capture the memory of the two women, but he could only see Sarah. That was the big problem, he never really looked at the other lady and regretfully had to explain this to his interrogator.

*"Never mind, Percy. Sarah had that quality of attracting attention to herself. She was both beautiful **and** notorious. Very well then, let us stick with Sarah. How was she? Was she happy or was she sad?"*

Percy was much encouraged by this question. Here he felt he could be of some use.

"Now then, Miss Calder! Now you come to mention it..."

He considered in an effort to get the right words.

"Sort of... well.. a bit excited you'd say. Err.. up to a bit a mischief. Goin' ta do a prank.."

"In other words typical Sarah!"

They both gave a short laugh - which ended abruptly as the inappropriateness of mirth quickly dawned on them.

At that instant a familiar 'toot toot' came from the bridge. She froze still! Staring over towards the road, she just caught the disappearance of an odd bulbous shaped foreign car. Percy noticed this intensity and apparent disapproval.

76

"Don't you go worrying about that silly fool, Miss! Mr Pod's up and down that 'ill like a yo-yo. Plays for the sisters. Likes everybody to know 'e's got a good 'ooter. Full a 'imself!"

She remained deep in thought for a few more seconds, before responding, as was called for by common courtesy.

"Sorry, Percy! I was just thinking..."

She turned on him with a renewed enthusiasm and fresh direction.

"Getting into a small rowing boat is rather awkward and clumsy is it not?"

He warmed to this subject in which he had considerable experience.

"Not arf, Miss! Av seen some..."

*"**Did** you form any idea as to the age or fitness of this mystery woman?"*

He reflected.

"Careful, took 'er time. 'Ard ta say age. Fit enough a suppose. Yoong un did rowin'".

Florence had to make sure her next question was not leading.

*"How well **did** she enter the boat? That is, was she uncoordinated? Was she rather ungraceful? Was she inelegant?*

The boatman knew from her tone that this was a very important question. He was perplexed, and felt like a schoolboy who had been given a difficult test. He desperately wanted to please this distinguished visitor, and give her the correct answer. The following moment saw Percy's old face in an agony of retrospective study. The result for the old teacher, when it arrived, was disappointing.

"She got in... average, I expect. Managed it all right... She coped." He scrutinised her face to find approval. She looked back at him appraisingly, and decided on one last try.

"Did you notice her hands?"

"'Ands! No, sorry.. no."

The old lady gave a deep sigh, but graciously gave her sincere thanks and prepared to depart; when Percy suddenly thought of something.

"Noticed 'er bag, Miss."

*"**Bag**! Did you indeed! What sort of bag."*

"Big, soft cloth, full o' somethin'."

"Something hard with edges. Or something soft like cloth."

"More like cloth, Miss."

"What colour was the bag, Percy?"

"Don't really recall.. dark, like rest o' er."

"Thank you, Percy."

Chapter 9

The Convent

Miss Florence Calder felt it was now urgent that she spoke with Detective Inspector Derek Russell as soon as possible. Important information had to be dispatched, so she went straight to the police station opposite the entrance to the River Gardens. The Desk Sergeant who was poring over some document stiffened to attention at this unforeseen regal entrance.

"Good morning, Miss Calder!"

She was content to leave a message and accept the slower Victorian time-scale of communication, but the Sergeant persuaded her to speak directly to her one time pupil on the telephone.

With some trepidation, and admiration for modern science, she gently picked up the black heavy instrument and spoke slowly into the mouthpiece in a loud, measured, clear voice.

"Is - that - Detective - Inspector - Russell?"

The electronic voice at her ear, responded in a more moderate and natural tone.

*"That sounds to me like Miss Marple! But quite frankly madam, if you raised your volume any further, we could dispense with the **need** for a telephone!"*

*"Really, Derek! You must remember that **my** generation are unaccustomed to the miracle of speaking directly over a distance of eight miles. It's very naughty of you to make fun!"*

"Dear venerable and cherished teacher, please accept my humble apologies, by allowing me to take you out for afternoon tea."

Underneath this light banter was a deep seated and long held love for his old mistress.

"Apology accepted, but as you say, I am a teacher, and must teach. On behalf of our quest, I've already taken off half the morning. To be absent half the afternoon, would, as Lady Bracknell said - '...expose me to comment!'"

"How about dinner? To have your charming company would be such an honour."

She thought about Madge eating alone, with Simon running circles around her. She expressed various doubts, mentioned his wife and children, but finally weakened, and succumbed to the onslaught of his unrelenting dashing enchantment. She handed the receiver back to the smiling Sergeant Poulson and fixed him with a firm forbidding look. Her sharp *"Good morning"*, was shot out with the effect of a reproof. He stopped smiling.

As she walked briskly back over the road to school, her thoughts were aimed to reconcile that part of herself which was a strict spinster, to the other part of herself; a young girl thrilled to have a date with a bewitching young man.

*"It is my **duty** to assist. **How** can we exchange, discuss and analyse information if we don't come together in a tolerable atmosphere? Surely people will realise that it is entirely reasonable for me to aid the authorities when a former pupil has been brutally murdered? After all, he's young enough to be my grandson..."*

Later that morning DI Russell decided it was time to trace and investigate the final movements of the victim. His motorcar slowed down and complained somewhat at having to scale the steep Belper Lane. The great dark bastion was looming up on his right. Taking care to apply the hand brake and firmly engage first gear, he looked up at the sinister carvings. *"Dracula's castle!"* Wielding the heavy door knocker and hearing the echoes within was fun. Eagerly he anticipated Bela Lugosi answering the door, but it turned out to be a elderly nun with a kind face. Walking down the corridor, he looked up to find a high dado of ornate large script in old biblical style, but quite readable in English -

"And forasmuch as my hand offended, writing contrary to my heart ... when I am come to the fire, it shall first be burned."

"The noble last words from the frightened servant of a ruthless king." It was the little old nun reminding him of his half forgotten history lessons. She shook her head sadly.

"They were terrible days for those of firm and unyielding faith. He made one of the 'Holy Bonfires', a victim of 'Bloody Mary'! Did you know that the original meaning of our word bonfire comes from 'bone' fire? That's all that was left of poor Thomas. It's nearly 400 years ago now."

*"Cranmer! Of course, the Archbishop of Canterbury. Something about the Book of Common Prayer. Didn't he 'confess' his wrongs to Queen Mary, and **still** she burned him?"*

"Oh yes, he was very human and flawed just like the rest of us. Fearful of the agonies of fire he tried hard to save himself. A gentle scholar, not a hero, a martyr, not a saint."

It was his first visit to the Convent of Cranmer, but, at Christ Church, he had spoken to the Reverend Mother Helen on at least two previous occasions. A remarkable woman. He had the impression that some powerful emotion was working behind the composed and pious exterior. In a sparsely furnished mediaeval looking room, he was asked to wait. During the minutes which passed, he wandered through French windows on to a balcony which gave out onto a magnificent vista of the Derwent Valley. He looked straight down the precipitous drop of the buttressed tapered masonry, far below to a kitchen, herb and physic garden which had been seriously invaded by overgrown shrubs. A difficult pathway travelled snake-like, down to an old decrepit garden door in the high wall. Barely discernible, the footpath continued down the hill into Wyver Wood where it disappeared completely. His eye travelled across Coppice Wood and over the river, before going up to the far side and reaching the church at Crich. Further along were the woods of Lea, his destination for that evening.

"Beautiful! Is it not." The voice was rich, liquid and unmistakable. He turned round to look deep into the lovely brown eyes of a handsome woman who looked a good ten years younger than her 52 years. That attractive face held an ineffable affection, and once again he sensed something behind the outward charm and majesty of this holy lady. She offered her hand which gripped too strong and too long. Was she afraid of something?

"We've been expecting you. Please sit down, Inspector."
News had travelled fast in the town, but he gave her a summary of the main facts.

*"Siddons at the mill didn't notice anyone in particular, not even Sarah herself. Of course that is just one of the four compass directions she **could** have come from. X could have walked from the north, down the Matlock Road, or south from Bridge Street, or east down Long Row."*

*"**Or** she could have simply alighted from a bus at the Triangle!"*
"A bus?"

"Yes. Sister Elizabeth saw Mrs Lawrence, a very distinctive blond owing more to art these days than nature, return from Derby at about 4.40pm. Of course you're welcome to question her, but I took the precaution of making these notes before her memory faded. Sister Elizabeth is over 70."

Derek was greatly comforted by such efficiency. She reached into her black habit and extracted a small notebook.

"Ah, here we are. Dark head-scarf and dark coat. Of course you will be fully aware, Detective Inspector, that most women in Belper will be similarly dressed during this cool sunny spell."

"Did the good sister see where she went?"

*"**Assumed** she went up Long Row to her home, but an assumption is **not** an observation."*

"Quite so."

She looked back at her little book -

"Oh yes, she had a rather large bag. Been shopping in Derby, no doubt."

Derek knew his former teacher and the head nun were close friends, so he decided to entrust her with information from the recent letter.

*"Only **two** names submitted!"*

"Yes, but one of them is Tatiana Lawrence."

*"Mmm, yes she **was** annoyed with Sarah last Saturday ... together with a few others. The other name?"*

Derek revealed more and told her about the 'bread woman' incident. The Reverend Mother Helen admitted that she had spoken to Olive Tonks and mentioned the word 'slander'.

"Perhaps it was not the best way to placate Mrs Tonks, but I intended to discuss the seriousness of the matter with Sarah."

Here she looked very sad, and perhaps tired and a little older.

"People thought I was the only person who liked her - I didn't. But I did have some small influence for good. I tried. We all tried. She liked being with us."

"I gather that the Flower Festival and Open Day will take place tomorrow as planned?"

"Of course! A lot of time and hard work has gone into the gathering and arranging of displays. Sarah's own work is very artistic, highly commendable ...."

Her voice weakened and abruptly stopped on a choke. For a moment he thought she might break down. Inside, Derek was alarmed, fearful and embarrassed. He was no good with tears. He never could cope with people in this distressed condition. In the course of his professional duty, it had happened several times. He just stood back and watched helplessly. He was not a tactile person, not even with his immediate family.

The woman in front of him rallied. The crisis was over, and he breathed a great sigh of relief. She continued -

"Please excuse me, Detective Inspector, you'll appreciate that this has been a great shock for us all."

"Of course! Perhaps a visit on another day?"

"No! Not at all...   I was just about to tell you that Sarah produced two excellent displays, which of course ... have now become ... memorials. We usually open the event with prayers. Naturally I will say a few words in reference to the work and life of Sarah Burgess. Such a waste ..."

She stared over the valley for a moment, before coming back to the point with renewed strength -

*"Olive Tonks! Don't underestimate **her**. She may not **seem** to have the intelligence to plan the crime, but she has the necessary energy, fury, determination and audacity. She's a fierce fighter for the dignity of her children. And yet it all seems so unlikely..."*

Her voice trailed away deep in thought. He waited, and eventually she bounced back with a twinkle.

*"We all suddenly appear to be in what they call a 'whodunit', Detective Inspector Russell! As the 'least likely' woman, perhaps you should be asking about **my** motives and movements."*

Derek was happy for the improved lightness of mood, and assured her that the chat was extremely useful. Sergeant Winter had spoken to the sisters the previous day, but failed to get any further with the mysterious assignation. Sarah made no further reference to her plans, according to the Reverend Mother, who was the last person to speak with her at the convent.

*"I **can** hazard a guess - but it is only a guess."*

"All help gratefully received, madam."

*"Ask Robin Kirkland what **he** was doing at that hour!"*

Back at the Belper Police Station, Sergeant Winter handed his superior a file.

"Just arrived from the Derby forensic pathologist, the full analysis. There's a bit of a jolt in that, sir."

Sure enough, it was an interesting surprise which recalled to him the final words of the Reverend Mother Helen.

"...and the victim was found to be about three months pregnant."

Detective Inspector Derek Russell did not like to eat late, so he sent a message to ask if Miss Florence Calder would be kind enough to be ready at 6.30. It was clearly a motorcar of some quality. She was agreeably impressed by the comforting rich scent of leather and polished wood. They purred along the Matlock Road, turned right at Ambergate and left at Bulbridge, under the railway line, over the River Amber, and then over the Cromford Canal. The engine toiled up the steep climb into the high craggy village of Crich. Round to the left in front of, and under the prominence of the Crich Stand tower. Magnificent landscape to the west and north, before they went through lovely woodland and into the sleepy village of Lea.

"I love this area, so remote. Time has forgotten this tiny place. Here we are, our favourite restaurant"

They stopped in front of an attractive quiet farm house with a modest sign in the front garden - 'Coach House'. Florence wondered that a living could be made at all in such an isolated, if charming corner of Derbyshire. Derek sprung out of the car and opened the door for his guest. They took a moment to enjoy the varied patchwork picturesque panorama of fields and woodland which first went down into the crevice of Lea Brook, and then up to scale the heights of Bilberry Knoll. Intrigued by the view, he noticed something in particular and walked towards the fence. Florence had an opportunity to admire the good looks of her 'beau' for the evening, noting the fine jaw line, carriage of head and the angle of neck to the shoulders. Just for a moment he reminded her of somebody else?

On a very remote top to the north west stood the familiar dark rugged and jagged Riber Castle. The former teacher broke into his thoughts -

*"It **looks** ancient, but it isn't really, and not a true castle. I was once presented to the queen of that castle."*

"Really!"

Florence smiled as she recalled herself as a shy sixteen year old.

"Yes, I shook her freezing cold hand in that draughty gritstone of watchtowers and battlements." She shuddered. *"Caroline Smedley was very ill, and died soon afterwards. It was 1892, and what an exciting day! Into the Great Hall, where a fine oak staircase took you up to the Grand Salon a 100 feet long. But she could never get warm up there, and neither could the boys a few years later when it became a prep school!"*

He looked at the woman who was often dismissed as a narrow, disapproving, Victorian, and had to remind himself that she was once a young woman, who had sailed with Mary Strutt on the family private steam yacht 'Sandra'. Florence was also accomplished in golf, photography, music and dancing.

After a moment admiring a handsome hornbeam tree, they went into a cobbled courtyard which at one time enclosed stables and harness rooms. In the dimly lit cosy bar, they sat in front of a welcome open fire. Detective Inspector Russell was greeted cheerfully by the staff who knew him well, and they were soon enjoying pre-dinner drinks, mesmerised by crackling, dancing flames.

"Thank you *so* much, Derek, this is such a treat!" But it was also work for the policeman who, at the beginning of this case had decided to share all knowledge with his very own 'Miss Marple'. She listened to his account of the convent visit, and in turn he heard what Percy had to say that morning.

"Not a great deal of enlightenment, but perhaps we can discount Sally Tonks."

"Sally! I didn't think you **had** considered her?"

"Some jealousy there. Sarah had come up in the world, Sally is still living on Cowhill. Also Sally has attended church the last four Sundays wearing four different dresses." She looked at him meaningfully.

"She **does** have a full time job at the mill... I'm not sure.."

"They were expensive dresses. She boasted that they were purchased in Friargate. Belper mill girls don't buy garments from Jeanettes in Derby."

"Her wealthy friend **could** have given her the money as a gift."

"Possibly - but unlikely. Sarah liked Sally and they were close, but there has never been any evidence of financial generosity. A poor and common Sally made Sarah look much better. She was once heard to say that Oliver should have built a splendid mansion on Cowhill, right next to Olive's cottage!"

"Your theory?"

"On my advice, Oliver denied his young wife the opportunity to overspend her allowance with a chequebook, so he gave her, in my opinion, a generous, **much** too generous, cash sum of money on the first day of each month. It would be pointless for Sarah to give Sally a loan

84

which she could never repay. It is therefore probable that Sally knew where Sarah hid her 30 day supply, and stole it!"

"And was challenged?"

"As I say they were close. Sally was often in Sarah's private room. Sarah would suspect Sally.

*What **may** have followed next is more difficult to speculate on. Sarah would not have tolerated such dishonesty and disloyalty from her best friend. She may have threatened to go to the police, and would have enjoyed her new power over a begging abject Sally. The boat trip in disguise could have been some sort of forfeit in which Sally would end up looking foolish and atone for her sin. Percy said she was excited. I merely guess. I do **not** know. But power and the ability to impose humiliation were the key features of Sarah's twisted mentality."*

"However, you did say Sally was 'discounted'?"

*"Listen, Derek, you have to be **very** careful not to lead Percy, but he inadvertently gave a clue when he said '..the young one rowed', suggesting X was the older woman."*

*"Even so, slow movement **can** be affected."*

"Absolutely. Don't forget, Sally was at the Herbert Strutt Grammar School too. A common girl, but a bright girl.."

They were interrupted with a large impressive leather menu.

"Hello, Jayne. I'm here tonight with my mistress."

"Derek!"

*"That is, my **ex**-schoolmistress."*

Introductions and jolly assurances all round. Florence was proud and admired the social skills of her former pupil. His warm brown eyes which lit up with a quick winning smile, charm, and easy manner of speaking, which was at variance with her perception of the usual manner from a police officer.

Ten minutes later they were in the harness room restaurant, and the amateur decided it was time to unveil her principal theory.

"You were telling me about the butler and conjuring tricks. Well, we may have been deceived in a different way."

"Do tell."

"You recall my questions this morning about gait, difficulty of getting into a boat, elegance and grace, etc."

"You didn't get much help."

*"No. But I could hardly have said to Percy -'Was it **really** a woman - or could it have been a **man**?'"*

The spoon full of soup which had just reached the level of Derek's mouth, was now motionless. Indeed for the next few seconds he was frozen like a photograph.

"Either drink that soup, Derek, or put it back. It's getting cold."
He put it back making a sharp clink on the plate, and stared for a few more seconds. She could 'see' the fresh implications flashing through his mind, which of course included the offended men at the party.

*"And that particular thought **never** crossed my mind."*

"A simple and effective disguise, head-scarf, long coat. It would explain her excitement and smirking to old Percy. It would also explain the necessity for a bag to allow 'her' to reappear later as a man. I expect the blanket was in the bag."

"So we want a short man." he said slowly.

*"Plenty of those, and it is '**may** want'. If X looked like a woman, she probably **was** a woman. Percy was not struck by masculinity, but in this we have a problem."*
She looked at him with great meaning.

"Cast your mind over the list of our principal candidates!"
Their eyes met with a mutual unspoken understanding. She continued -

*"Exactly! Not too many 'he-men' there, unless Mr X is a **very** gifted actor."*

"It rules out the butler." he said smiling.

"Agreed. You can build up your height, but not easily reduce it. Mr Haigh would have to bend over double..."

"Thank you, Barbara. That was the owner by the way."

"Did you notice her hands when she removed our plates?"
He was intrigued and full of admiration for this intelligent unpaid assistant.

*"No I didn't. **Do** tell me all about the hands of Mrs Hobson."*

"I've made my point. You are a regular, and have seen her hands many times, but never really observed. Percy didn't observe last Wednesday."

*"Well, what **about** her hands?"*

"The point being, nothing remarkable. They are entirely consistent with her age and gender. The proprietor has no reason to be incognito. Like the gait of a person, hands are difficult to disguise, unless of course they are gloved."

"Hands!"

*"Hands indeed. Useful in many ways, such as telling the type of work a person may do, or an indicator of age when relaxed and flat. A taut fist could be an attempt to look younger. **Had** he been observant, the boatman's evidence probably wouldn't be much use anyway..."*

The main course was placed before them.

"My goodness this looks good!"

*"They have an excellent chef - but **why**?"*

"So that people will return to eat again!"

*"No no! **Why** would Percy's evidence be of little use?"*

*"Because my dear, Derek, in alphabetical order, the hands of Claud Hoadley, Robin Kirkland, Julian Lawrence and Aubrey Pod, are **all** small, as indeed, they are also **all** short."*

She tucked into her meal while her companion absorbed this new data staring out of the window at horses frolicking in fields of fading light. Eventually he said,

*"Oliver Burgess was right, we **do** have a lot of work to do."*

"Ah yes, Mr Burgess!"

*"What **about** Mr Burgess?"*

"He too, is short with small hands."

Chapter 10

The Poet and the Princess

Driving back from Lea, Detective Inspector Derek Russell had little to say to his dinner date. His head was spinning with new information. Nearing Belper, eventually the silence was broken -

"This is going to be far more complicated than I first thought. We seem to be dealing with a first rate brain."

"Probably." replied his adopted assistant. *"But don't lose sight of Helen's advice, which she summed up in one word - audacity. Olive Tonks has always nurtured a hateful jealousy of Sarah's friendship with her daughter. I for one would like to know where she went last Wednesday afternoon, after she left us just before the children's dismissal at 4.00pm."*

*"We'll check into that. We'll also make sure that Sally really **was** at her machine in the mill until 5.30 with the rest of the girls. And that will dispose of the terrible Tonks."*

"Not quite!"

He took his eyes off the road just for a fraction to glance at the cynical profile of the wise old face.

*"You **can't** be serious!"*

"I am perfectly serious, and I don't want you to leave any stone unturned, Detective Inspector Derek Russell! As Helen said - 'do not underestimate'."

At this point they had arrived at Bridge House School, but Miss Florence Calder remained inside the motorcar and briefed him on the psychic activities and powers of Simon.

*"He looks foolish, **is** often foolish - but make **no** mistake - Simon is no fool! Personally I'm not taken in by all this nonsense, but I appreciate, and am impressed by the skills involved."*

"What skills - exactly?"

"The skills of the illusionist! The marvels of the mimic and the manipulator. The enchantment of the entertainer. Turning into that odious old ghoul Nelly Pod, without the aid of make-up or costume, was a first class performance! A pity I missed it."

"Wasn't he the dame last Christmas in the Christ Church pantomime?"

"A bizarre and pretty dame at that. Too young really, but notwithstanding, very good. We might do worse than recruit Simon on to our side. He amazes people with these, so called, card readings. What he can tell about their past, advice for the present, predictions for the future."

"I understand," mused Derek, *" that some fortune tellers have a clever technique of extracting information by asking questions, making statements, and a talent for quickly and deftly shifting their ground if they meet with a negative response."*

*"Exactly! Most people around here fail to discern Simon's acute faculties, his extreme sensitivity and keen receptivity. He reads the way you sit, facial expressions and mannerisms. He can tell **my** mood by the way I walk! Most disconcerting.*

I gather an extrasensory performance was given to the mill girls last Wednesday lunch in their dinner house. One of the older women had pretensions to being a hypnotist and decided to regress Simon to a previous existence!"

Deep into the trance, the clairvoyant started to moan

"'ot, 'ot, oow it is 'ot."

"Where are you Simon?"

"Sand, sand everywhere. Big brawny butch blokes, toiling, sweatin' cobs. Oow look at em - muscles, great strappin' studs...."

"Are you one of the workers Simon?"

"No, no, it is not for me to slog away. I am an innocent untouched young lass, bein' bathed in asses milk, bein' prepared for my dooty."

"What is that Simon?"

"To give pleasure to an ugly old priest!"

Miss Florence Calder continued -

*"An amusing performance which caused an uproar in the dinner house. No real harm done, so long as it is kept at arms length from **my** school."*

Derek himself was making the car shake with laughter.

"A nice change for the girls to be temporarily transported to the heat of ancient Egypt!" His smile faded. *"OK. Ability is agreed, but do we have sufficient motive? Sarah made fun of him, but doesn't everybody?"*

"That is the difficulty with Simon. His true feelings are well hidden behind that baby mask of half smile and wide eyed innocence. We may never know how deeply Sarah hurt him. He was a favourite target ..."

She sighed and slowly shook her head.

"Yet he's asked for permission to go up Belper Lane tomorrow afternoon to pay his respects at the Flower Festival. I'm told Helen will open it with a short memorial service. He wants to see Sarah's displays. Simon likes flowers."

Her face suddenly became less sentimental and a touch more cynical -

"No doubt Simon will enjoy the two hour break from his duties at Bridge House! And that reminds me..."

"Yes?"

"His afternoon off is on Wednesday. Oh dear look at the time!"

He hopped out of the car and opened the passenger door. Graciously, she gave profuse and final thanks before they exchanged 'goodnights'.

Inspector Ronald Marfleet of the Belper Police Station at 22 Matlock Road, had thoughtfully organised a temporary office for Detective Inspector Derek Russell and his official assistant Sergeant John Winter. On the Saturday morning of September 10th, they were arranging the little room when the latter unburdened his deliberations.

"I've been thinking, sir. It's my view that this murder's been carefully planned for months, and has a lot to do with certain weather conditions."

From a pile of papers, his superior looked up with interest.

"Fire away."

"Tinker's been at the River Gardens so long, I understand he enjoys a lot of freedom. That is, independence in his work. If it's windy and the river's a bit choppy, or it's raining - no boats, and that's final! The murderer would know this, hence good weather needed. Also Miss Calder's point about 'deep shadow' helping the disguise. On the other hand if it were too hot, X couldn't very well neatly fit into the local population by wearing a long coat and head-scarf."

The other nodded.

"Yes, good lad, that's helpful. More than this."

He was holding the report from the officers who had scoured both river banks. Other than the usual footprints of fishermen in the usual places, there were no signs of a boat being pulled to the side. No

90

obvious indications of weeds being disturbed, and no bloodstained blunt instruments were to be seen, which did not surprise him.

"I'll be damned if I'm going to drag the river for the three miles up to Ambergate looking for a very wet and useless hammer. Probably find several hammers. Could've been anything. A stone would do. No! We won't solve this mystery by crawling around, getting our knees damp and sludgy, pretending to be Sherlock Holmes."

*"How **will** we solve it sir?"*

Russell pointed in the direction of Bridge House School.

*"By keeping in with that woman over there. Everything **we** know, **she** must know. Which reminds me, she has yet to learn about the baby."* He looked slightly embarrassed. *"Couldn't quite bring myself to discuss such things in front of Miss Florence Calder! But this is a case of local knowledge. She knows them all."*

He took in a deep breath, stretched his arms up towards the ceiling, and slowly exhaled, putting his hands behind his head.

"We'll solve this murder by checking the motive, opportunity, and alibi of the principal possibilities."

*"And we'll need witnesses to come forward. It would be nice and handy to have a chat with an observant fisherman. If there **were** any fishermen who just happened to be sitting around in the right place at the right time. The Belper News isn't out until Thursday."*

"Yes, but I spoke to the Derby Evening Telegraph. Main headlines yesterday, but, as yet, it seems Miss, Mrs or Mr X was invisible!"

"Mr?"

Derek spent the next 20 minutes talking about his interesting dinner up in the wooded hills of Lea.

"It's the old story, sir, we're probably not asking the right questions. Did a man go into some bushes in the River Gardens and come out as a woman?"

"Mmm... I think it's time we paid another visit to see Mr Burgess. But first we'll have a chat with the Lawrences and then the Tonks.

It was a neat little home on Long Row, a pretty cobbled part of the town. Tatiana Lawrence was easily put at her ease by the usual patter.

"Routine questions, madam, we have to speak to everybody."
She confirmed previous information. A bus trip to Derby, returning at the Triangle at about 4.40pm. She went straight home.

"A bag?"
She looked puzzled at the two men, and slightly alarmed.

"No! I had no bag - I didn't buy anything. It was just an afternoon out."

The young poet had just descended the narrow steep stairs. With his superior air and light voice he greeted the visitors.

"Good morning, gentlemen, found our murderess yet?"
Over-riding this tinge of sardonic contempt, Derek glanced at his small white hands and maintained a firm professional optimism.

"Soon, Mr Lawrence. I detect little grief in your manner!"

"You'll have considerable difficulty finding any sadness at the removal of Sarah Burgess. The world will not miss her."

"Quite right, Julian! We're not hypocrites, Inspector. Last Saturday night, she was very nasty to my son. I've considered advertising a handsome reward to the killer in the Belper News!"
John Winter, stroked his chin.

"You will, of course, let us know who the claimant turns out to be."
Derek interrupted this growing farce.

"Mr Lawrence, will you be good enough to give us an account of your movements on the afternoon of Wednesday September 7th?"

"Me!"

"Yes you, sir, - routine." Julian pondered.

"You were at the cemetery, darling. Remember - death."

"Of course. I was there for inspiration."

*"And **were** you inspired?"*
He gave the questioner, Sergeant Winter the cold look he reserved for philistines.

"No. It didn't work. I wanted my work to undergo a sea change."

"How long were you there?"

"Oh, let's see - about three in the afternoon to about ..."

*"You came in at eight darling, **far** too late."*

"I take it we're talking about the large wooded main cemetery just up the Matlock Road, on the east side of the Derwent." said Derek.

"It's an eerie mystical place. Lots of overgrown tangle with old decaying tombstones, curious and cryptic. I should have done better, perhaps..."

*"Did you **see** anybody?"*

"Oh.. Just Robin."

"Robin Kirkland? Did you speak to him?"

"No. I was concentrating. Anyway I've not much to say to Robin."

"What time was this?"

With some impatience, Mrs Lawrence said -

"I can hardly see what..."

"We'll be the best judge of that, madam. Mr Lawrence, did you wear a watch?"

"Err.. yes, but I didn't look at it ... well I could hardly see it."

"That will help you estimate the time. Was it still light, or was the light failing, or was it completely dark?"

"How clever. Yes let me see... It was nearly dark."

*"Try again, Mr Lawrence. Nearly dark will put the time at eight or later. **If** you were home at eight, you must have concluded your meditations and left the cemetery just after half past seven! Remember that I've grown up in Belper and know how long it takes to walk from the cemetery to Long Row. These details could become very important later on."*

Julian looked rattled.

*"It was gloomy where **I** sat. Let me put it this way if it will help. When I saw Robin Kirkland climbing up the hill with that shabby rucksack of his, it would be at least half an hour before I left."*

Sergeant Winter breathed a sigh of relief and noted down - 'Robin Kirkland (with rucksack) at cemetery about 7.00pm'.

"Colour of rucksack, Mr Lawrence?"

*"So old and dirty...I suppose it originally **did** have a colour. I've seen it in church. Perhaps a very dark brown?"*

Minutes later, walking down Long Row, Sergeant Winter noted his superior's frustration and spoke his thoughts -

"I suppose we're not in a strong enough position to search that little house for a brown bag."

*"It might come to that, but, **if** she's our woman, make no mistake, it'll be long gone. I'm inclined not to doubt Sister Elizabeth."*

"Do you doubt five hours sitting on a tombstone communing with the dead?"

"With Julian I think that is entirely probable, and we have a problem with motive. He seems so indifferent. But then, you never know. Brace yourself, Winter, Cowhill next!"

Feeling a touch nostalgic, Derek decided to turn left into Cluster Road and follow one of his favourite boyhood trails to the south of Belper, along the various narrow jitties which parallel the railway line.

He fell silent thinking about his exciting early memories exploring the intriguing large Belper Cemetery. He could understand Julian's enthusiasm, since it was more like an enchanted hillside wood than a graveyard. The monkey puzzle tree fascinated, and the silver birch glistened in the sun. He recalled the comfort of touching the massive trunk of the soft and kind redwood, watching scuttling squirrels and hearing the gentle note of cooing wood pigeons.

The dense heavy foliage of beech, yew, holly, large rhododendrons and conifers, formed massive caverns sheltering shadowy graves within. Under the thick canopy, old tombstones stood quiet sentinel in the gloom. One magnificent tree could only be described as a weeping copper beech. Massive, misshapen, low twisted limbs went out - then down, forming a fat 'u' shape, before snaking out at an impossible angle. This, together with other knotted branches, bowed down under tremendous weight, made the whole look like a deformed hideous monster. The weeping, ghostly, dark foliage complemented the symbols of death below. Some were sunken and crooked. Some were finished with ornate Victorian iron railings, twisted and rusty with age. Many had sad text, telling of long lost loved ones, partially obliterated by moss, lichen, bramble and ivy struggling to survive in the poor light.

The adult Detective Inspector Derek Russell was now wondering if those same murky shadows had any connection with the present evil he was now investigating?

Chapter 11

"Owe Were a Dotty Little Sod!"

Olive Tonks was annoyed to find a few odd socks belonging to her Simon -

"Stuffed oonda t' stairs! Idle little bogga!"

Notwithstanding, she washed them out and was now hanging them up on a short blackened line suspended from the mantelpiece. In spite of the continuing bright sunshine outside, it was still cool for early autumn, and the char had brought warmth and cheer to the little room with a crackling fire. She was feeling happy. Simon now had a good position, and life in the old cottage was more cosy with just Sally and herself.

She gave one of the dangling socks a tug which sent all of Simon's socks bobbing up and down. Delighted with this minor amusement, she was prompted to break out into song -

"Dance little dolly, we ya 'ole in ya stockin' an ya
knees keep a knockin' an ya toes keep a rockin'..."

Two sudden sharp loud knocks on the door interrupted this lively ditty. She rushed over to open the door. It had been the knock of authority. It was the police!

Olive Tonks was un-welcoming, suspicious and hostile to the official visit. She reluctantly parted with details of her movements of the Wednesday afternoon.

"Left school at four, went straight 'ome, where else should a go? What of it?"

She bridled at the question of witnesses for corroboration, and began to emphasise her statements by shaking the broom in her hand -

"Ooo should see me? Why don't ya arrest 'er that's doon it?"

"We'd like to, Mrs Tonks. Do you have any ideas?"

"Ideas! All Belper knows oo did it!"

They looked with puzzlement at her furious, and at the same time incomprehensible face.

"We don't know, so perhaps you'll be kind enough to tell us!"

"Lady la-di-da, 'er as use ta be Polly Pickles. 'Er an 'er precious stuck oop Julian oop Long Row."

Further questions revealed that Olive Tonks and Tatiana Lawrence were much the same age and went to the same school.

"Nowt special about 'er. Owe wer a dotty little sod. Used ta sit be'ind 'er. Ya could 'av planted bloody taters on't back a 'er bloody neck!"

It emerged that Mrs Lawrence was indeed once a Pickles and after an early marriage, assumed her rather affected new Christian name. Olive spat it out with contempt -

*"Tatiana! Tripe! Russian princess or summat. Polly bloody Pickles, that's all **she** is. Tried ta turn t' clock back, an pretends she's younger an doont know me. Scrape that clarted make-oop off, an yav'e got more bloody lines in 'er face than a map a Belper!"*

The visitors rightly concluded that a great deal of life-long jealousy existed between the low common char and the one time Miss Pickles, who had managed to scramble out of the bottom drawer of Belper, to produce a son with some small local standing. Sergeant Winter defended Mrs Lawrence -

"Well at least she doesn't claim to be Tatiana's younger sister, The Grand Duchess Anastasia! Tell us, Mrs Tonks, considering you were supposed to be at home at the time, why are you so certain that Mrs Lawrence murdered Sarah Burgess?"

Yet again, envy and jealousy reared its ugly head. Olive painted a biased potted history which had the benefit of some credibility. Mr Lawrence, a solicitor, had died leaving his wife and baby son with no more than a tiny income. The cosseted and overly protected Julian became the frequent butt of Sarah's jokes. Tatiana Lawrence, who had suffered a financial tumble, had to endure seeing the same odious Sarah transformed from rags to riches. Naturally, Sally had told her mother about every detail relating to the evening of Saturday September 3rd, which included the fury of Tatiana Lawrence. Olive advanced the view that a dirty scruffy girl, who could change into something like a royal Russian princess, could easily disguise her identity for a short trip up the Derwent to do a spot of murder. She seemed genuinely surprised when the detectives suggested it just may have been a different woman.

When the subject came around to the departed Sarah Burgess, the char softened her tone -

"Mind ya, I'll not speak ill at t' dead. No. She could ave bin me own. Yes. A feel sorry fa Gladys Grindle, poo-er soul. Must be black ovver t' g<u>oo</u>ter nar."

She stared at the floor. Detective Sergeant John Winter suggested that Mr Grindle might also be upset, but this revived Olive's usual demeanour -

"That ignorant owd bogga! **Pig** *ignorant! Only gr<u>oo</u>nts. Never spoke a civil werd ta that gal! Mind ya she could be 'n awkward bogga s<u>oo</u>m times."*

Once more the broom was brandished at the two officers -

"A could ave bloody killed 'er when ...." But she suddenly subsided when the thought of Sarah's present condition returned to mind. More softly -

"Well ... owes in a better place nar. I'll go an' pay me respects oop at t' Convent this afternoon, n see 'er flowers. Thee say thee rate nice. Arr Simon's goowin' ya know. Them n<u>oo</u>ns a reely nice, thee say s<u>oo</u>ch l<u>oo</u>vly things to 'im! Ey oop, when's funeral?"

"Not for some time yet, the body has yet to be released, being still under examination." replied Detective Inspector Derek Russell, just before thanking Mrs Tonks for the benefit of her advice and kindly giving up her valuable time.

"When do we arrest Tatiana Lawrence?" said Sergeant Winter with a twinkle as he descended Cowhill with his senior officer.

"After all, she had been suggested by no less than two eminent ladies of Belper, and one, 'not so eminent' lady is totally **positive** *of her guilt!"*

"Oh if it were so simple! It's time for lunch at Leslie's Snack Bar, and after that we'll visit a man up Bridge Hill who, in my opinion, has gained the most from the sudden extinction of his late and un-lamented wife!"

When it came to the business, Oliver Burgess was a workaholic. He had little interest, and no time anyway for the convent annual open day, regardless of the fact that the event this year - had a tragic and personal significance. The Flower Festival, so near by, was far from his mind.

It was not at all unusual that he should be beavering away in his 'home' office on a sunny Saturday afternoon. His visitors found him cheerful.

97

"You should have eaten here, gentlemen! You'd have been most welcome. Now then ... Wednesday afternoon? Here's the diary. Of course ...Walter Kurrlie, 2.30 to 4.30. Actually he stayed a little later, I should say he left at ... about 4.45? Or there abouts."

"Who is Mr Kurrlie?"

"My gateway to the West Coast of the United States! A very important contract, finally achieved by complicated agreements dealing with economic volume and certain specifications required by American taste. But, with a little luck, by Christmas, the Beaurepairian will be on sale in California." He beamed triumphantly at his visitors.

"What time did you leave the factory last Wednesday?"

"Oh, let me see? Couldn't have been much after 5.00."

"You did drive home that day?"

"Always drive, never walk anywhere."

John Winter was irritated and moved uneasily on his chair. This last comment was niggling at a chronic point of disagreement between him, and his superior colleague. Detective Inspector Derek Russell took the view that petrol, bought from the public purse, was expensive and still on ration for the private motorist. Regular exercise in the form of brisk walking was not only wholesome, but also good for concentration and the thought process. Consequently any distance short of two miles in length should be walked. Already today they had trudged the three quarters of a mile **up** to Cowhill, and from there, a mile and a quarter **up** to Bridge Hill. He knew a half mile hike to Cheapside, and back, was imminent. This day alone would clock up a total of about three miles of foot work.

"Is Mr Kurrlie still in the area?"

"Good heavens, no!"

"Where would we find him?"

"Well... He could be sailing from Southampton - or Liverpool? He may have gone on the Continent. He represents a large American retail chain. He could be anywhere. Sorry can't be much help there."

"You'll have his address of course?"

Oliver Burgess started to look most uncomfortable, and became hesitant and vague.

"....yes...yes they may have it in the office."

"Your secretary must have it?"

"Of course. I'll see you get it on Monday."

98

"Naturally we'll need to talk with a number of your staff to verify your time of departure." He leaned over to see Winter's notes - *"5.05 shall we say?"*

Several painful seconds passed while Mr Burgess struggled to arrive at an acceptable form of words.

"I'm not at all sure that Dorothy will be of much use. I always come into the front of my office so she'll know I'm there, but most often, I leave by the back. Nobody would see me leave ... sorry."

His mood, now much changed, was more suited to dealing with the thorny subject of the un-born child. He received the news with an unhappy expression which showed no great surprise, and at the same time a hint of grim resignation. During the respectful silent seconds which passed, he seemed to slouch despairingly more into the expensive leather desk chair like a shapeless sack of potatoes. The next question was put in a very gentle manner -

"Were you aware of her condition, Mr Burgess?"

His answer, somewhat delayed coming to terms with this new information, notwithstanding, had a strong ring of truth.

"No. No ..I didn't know."

"This is very difficult for me, Mr Burgess, but you'll appreciate that in an investigation of this magnitude, it is absolutely necessary to know all personal details..."

*"It was **not** my child, if that's what you're getting at, Inspector."* He was looking Derek straight in the eye. *"And if it helps, I'll answer your next question. Most folk around here will tell you the same. If you seek the father, go and look in Cheapside."*

"Thank you, Mr Burgess. While you're being so frank, I have one last question for you. Do you have any idea who killed your wife? Even the slightest inkling, given to us in confidence of course, could be most helpful."

He took a little time to compose his answer.

"My wife alienated many women, but none of them were probable murderers. If you were to press me...., I know that she had occasional raucous rows with her closest friend Sally."

Sergeant Winter jumped in with the next question.

"Did your wife ever complain that a sum of money had gone missing?"

99

"My wife never complained to me about anything. My wife never spoke to me at all!"

As the butler showed them to the door, he was asked about the arrival time of his master on the day of the murder.

"Unfortunately, I am unable to assist you, sir. Mr Burgess is kind enough to allow me to take a nap in the late afternoon. It is a personal custom and greatly refreshes me for the evening duties. The first I actually saw of Mr Burgess, was when he came out of his office and sat down for dinner at eight o'clock."

"I'll be damned if I'm satisfied!" said Detective Inspector Derek Russell stomping down Bridge Hill.

"You mean Burgess being put off his stride about our intention of checking up? Perhaps he became nervous because he realised that his story couldn't easily be corroborated?"

*"Perhaps. But make no mistake, Winter, we **will** find that American, and book a trans-Atlantic telephone call if necessary!"*

Near the foot of the hill, they came to the intriguing and unusual Green Walk on the right. For those crossing the river, this was a useful elevated stone walkway over the field. Originally it was a private route for George Benson Strutt, which he had built in 1790 to conveniently cut the long, if pleasant, wooded corner opposite the Talbot Inn. Derek explained the Belper tradition that it could be used by the public, **provided** that Mr Strutt was not actually using it at the time. John Winter was grateful for any short cut, but his heart sank when the boss became suddenly animated and excited, speaking of an **extra** walk along the west side of the river. They turned sharp right again, away from the bridge and were now heading west.

The Sergeant took an interest in a stony sloping incline down on the left, which gave easy access to a couple of boys exploring the boulders by the river bank.

"Great fun, Winter! We used to call it 'Belper beach'."

It did indeed end in an inviting, if tiny, sandy play area. A little way along they stopped, and Derek looked up to the right at the impressive garden of Fern Glade.

"Aha! Just as I thought." His tone was triumphant.

"Do you see what I see, my good Sergeant?"

Winter could see exactly the same view, but clearly he was blind to the significance.

"I see the larger rhododendrons peeking over the stone wall."

*"And a **door**, my friend - a door in the garden wall. With the convenience of a sleeping butler, Burgess could easily emerge from that garden as your average and un-noticed Mrs Mop to keep a river rendezvous with his wife. Plenty of cover, not likely to be noticed. Well!"*

"I'm having some difficulty..."

"I know. We have a powerful motive, some opportunity, but as yet not a shred of evidence."

*"It's so far fetched. That 'Kurrlie' bloke may yet give him an alibi. He wasn't even on civil terms with his wife. Why a sudden trip on the river? And him dressed as a lass! Can **you** make sense of that?"*

*"No, but I'll try. A romantic reconciliation? Some sort of a wager? Can you walk through the Triangle and not be noticed? She may have **thought** she was meeting someone else? Whoever did it, has the excellent advantage that we are not able to question Sarah Burgess."*

He sighed and looked up to the garden again.

"We'll go the pretty way to Cheapside. Perhaps we'll have more luck there.

Especially with this interesting little letter
I have from the bank manager."

Chapter 12

Mr Toad

The walk along the overgrown, narrow, river bank path which forced them into single file, was an orgy of nostalgia for Derek Russell who recalled the sunny nature walks from his early schooldays at Bridge House. A familiar dank smell came from the exotic, tropical looking six foot tall balsam flowers, which were strangely attached and dangling from healthy succulent stems. The intriguing and complicated hooded design of the exquisite purplish-pink flowers with its odd 'thick lip' attracted the attention of John Winter -

"Policemen's Helmets." said his superior. *"Well, that's what Miss Florence called them anyway. Miss Madge used the better, more appropriate name - 'Jumping Jack'. Watch this..."*

The recent spell of dry weather had ripened the fat seed pods which gave Derek confidence of success as he approached a particularly handsome, tall and promising specimen - to give it a sharp shake. The agitation caused several of the pods to explode and send small black seeds shooting a good distance in all directions, making the greatly surprised John close his eyes for protection! The tiny missiles triggered similar explosions in neighbouring balsams which sounded like the fall of heavy rain. The chain-reaction went down the river bank like a wave scattering its offspring everywhere to the delight of Derek who, for this moment, relinquished his rank and had once again become a carefree, laughing schoolboy.

After a few seconds this extraordinary natural phenomena died down and they pressed on to cross the Pontoon Bridge and Derby Road, up the steep and narrow jitty to Becksitch Lane, up to The Fleet, down to Days Lane and a right turn into Brookside and out up to Cheapside. Standing outside, John thought it was a charming and picturesque little row of houses, in contrast to what the name had first suggested to him.

"Not grotty at all is it?"

They were both looking at the decorative roof line fascia. Derek recalled being told that it was added on the instructions of Mr Strutt to improve the view from Green Hall.

Charlie Kirkland, a good natured and gentle man, was alarmed to see the police on his doorstep, but politely invited them inside to a comfortable front 'best room'. Robin had been sent to the shop and would be back soon.

*"It's a bad job this, but I'll be straight; am **not** sorry. An a shan't be goin' ta see 'er bloody flowers this afternoon either!"*

Asked to explain he added -

"She led 'im a right dance! Teased and taunted 'im. She'd be with a group of 'er friends and shout over t' street at 'im - 'Yoo hoo little Robin'! Waving and laughing. Nasty bitch! One time she even..."

A sound at the back announcing the boy's arrival stemmed his flow. Derek had paid small attention to this young man on his previous visits to Christ Church and was struck by just how young and pale he actually looked. There was a nervous tremulous weakness in the voice, and he joined the small hands to conceal a minor shake. Apparently aware of these observations, he said that he had been very upset by the tragic loss of his friend, and ignored a low scornful snarl from Kirkland senior.

The inevitable question was put, and he claimed to be home at ten past five on the day of the murder. This was confirmed by his father who was always home from the foundry before five. After eating, they listened to the wireless for a couple of hours, but were together all the while up to bed time. This made sad listening for Detective Inspector Russell who was inclined to like the boy and his loyal parent.

"Supposing I told you we had a witness to say you were at the cemetery at 7.00pm."

The haunted eyes became even more fearful.

"He's a fibber!"

*"'He' - **I** didn't say 'he'? If you arrived here at 5.10, where were you before? The bank's only in King Street! less than five minutes away."*

The Inspector took a deep breath of despair, and produced the letter from the manager stating that Kirkland had asked to be released at 4.00pm on the afternoon of Wednesday September 7th. At the same time he turned appealing doggy eyes to the older man which seemed to say - "Can we **please** have some truth now?" The honest pattern moulder saw that his position was hopeless and crumbled in a flood of apologies and explanations.

"A was frightened fa t' lad. Didn't want 'im mixed oop we it..."

Robin jumped in -

*"I was **supposed** to meet her. She didn't turn up - as usual. I was upset and went for a long walk."*

"Where and what time where you supposed to meet her?"

This was shot out from the sergeant, who was only a few years his senior, with a tone having the hard edge of authority.

"At half past four, in the holly bushes on The Parks. Always the same place."

The boy's voice trailed off. Winter pressed his advantage -

"Secret and frequent meetings with this married woman! Was this relationship intimate? Physical?"

"Ere, 'ere! Don't you be goin'..."

*"Unfortunately it **is** necessary to get these things sorted out, Mr Kirkland."* advised the D.I. *"If Robin was close to this woman and knew her very well, he may have vital information we need to know about."*

Detective Inspector Derek Russell turned to Robin and continued in a slightly softer note -

*"On this occasion, why was it so important to get time off work. What was so urgent about **this** meeting?"*

The unacceptable delay before an answer came was agonising for the youth and embarrassing for the others.   The answer was equally unsatisfactory when it finally arrived.

"Don't know."

He stared into the grim official faces and desperately added -

"She told me to go there.... at church, last Sunday morning."

*"And you **always** did as you were told?"* - snapped the Sergeant.

No answer. The boy had seized up into an icy silence.

The next question was put by the senior officer in a natural conversational manner -

"Did you kill your friend, Robin?"   The answer came out quickly and sounded sincere, almost in a sob -

"No."

"Have you any idea at all who did?"

"No."

At this point Detective Inspector Russell made a professional judgement to the annoyance of his assistant. His soft friendly tone continued -

*"We're leaving now, Robin, but we'll be back and I must advise you to consider your position. It **is** serious."* Here the friendliness faded. *"You **must** tell us everything!"* At this point he leaned forward and looked at him with great significance.

104

*"Remember, Robin, we have **examined** her body! Think well on that. Think before we return - and we **will** return - soon!"*

Tripping down the hill back into Days Lane -

*"Yes, Winter, I know what you're going to say, but listen to the voice of experience. You could stand over that lad with an axe and he'll **still** say nothing to **us**. I've put the fear of God into him, and he might, just might, speak to others."*

"But the baby, sir! I nearly had him there! If you'd had only..."

*"The victim was married. Robin Kirkland only has to remain silent and the world will assume the father of her child was Oliver Burgess. **And** we must be careful. We don't **know** that Robin is responsible for the child. Or indeed if that gets us anywhere at all. Somehow I can't see young Robin in drag"*

John Winter looked doubtful, gloomy and now puzzled. His boss smiled.

"A big-city word. It means a man dressed as a woman."

They turned right into a road called The Fleet which adjoined The Parks. Derek pointed up to the naughty clumps of holly bushes and oaks they had just been hearing about. John, intrigued and wearing an impish grin, said -

"Good place! Nice and dark inside."

"Possibly, but we're in deep waters here. We need help. Get your notes all typed up and give a carbon copy to Miss Calder, and include all the notes on our next visit - to see Mr Toad."

"Mr Toad!"

"You're in for a treat, Winter, I think! Angela can't stand him, along with a few others. Aubrey Pod is straight out of 'Wind in the Willows'. He's the stuff of Dickens. Forward to Becksitch Lane."

On the way, Derek gave John a summary of his own personal knowledge of Aubrey Pod based on church gossip. How the indulged and spoilt little brat used to kick the maid and make her cry. Stories of his screaming tantrums in Brittain's the toy shop when he was once denied a crawling clockwork hedgehog. How the family car would be rocked with excitement when he jumped about at the first sight of Blackpool Tower.

"Nelly Pod had to shove a jam butty into his ugly little face to sedate him! Here we are - 'Crow's Hole'."

105

They were at the foot of a very steep and slightly overgrown garden. Due to poor pay, Jasper Wormall made irregular visits to this particular client. Winter had enjoyed the comparison with Kenneth Graham's funny little character and the quirky music master. As they were ascending the long flight of steps up to the old stone house, rather breathlessly, he suddenly recalled another point of similarity -

"Wasn't it Toad who dressed up as a washerwoman?"

This caused the Detective Inspector to make an abrupt but welcome stop. He gave the younger man a significant look.

"You are quite right, John Winter. He did just that."

They took a moment to rest and survey the impressive perspective before them. It included the distant green fields of the high Chevin, surmounted by the deeper green quarried woodlands of Firestone Hill. Down below, numerous water-side alders with high summer foliage obscured the river, but for a few short shimmering stretches.

The sergeant was still thinking about the beloved book of his boyhood.

"There was some talk about - 'nothing more worth doing as simply messing about in boats'".

Derek looked up the un-climbed steps ahead and deeply sighed.

*"He's such an idiot. It's impossible to believe that **our** Mr Toad has been 'messing about' with Sarah in a boat. But ..."*

They both spoke the next, often quoted line, together, with a tension breaking laugh - *"You never know!"*

Mavis took some malicious satisfaction in announcing -

*"It's the **police**, Mr Pod!"* He nearly choked on a mouthful of tea, which was only just managed to be spewed back into a large mug. Up, and skipping urgently to the front door, the organist pushed his formless face into the near personal space of Detective Inspector Derek Russell.

*"Oh it's **you**, Derek! I thought they didn't use local officers for serious crimes in case they'd be too familiar with, or partial to, folks they'd know?"*

"I've lived away from home for nearly fifteen years now. Anyway, I persuaded my boss that local knowledge could be useful in this case. Won't keep you long, Mr Pod, just a few routine questions. This is Sergeant Winter."

106

John instinctively and quickly backed away, as the foul smelling blob of flesh shot up to within inches of his nose, with an interrogative, loud and sharp -

*"**Don't** I know you?"*

The startled and disorientated young man replied -

"I don't think so. I live miles from here, in Melbourne."

"Oh well, I never get down there."

"Thank Goodness for that!" said Winter - to himself.

The officers were much more comfortable seated at a safe distance in the seedy and rather shabby front parlour.

"You've only just caught me. Not five minutes been back from playing the organ at the convent. Bit sad this year... Well, sad in a way, sad for some. I'll give her, her due, she made two nice displays. Blue and white, and red and white... Nice - sort of..."

He was clearly very uncomfortable trying to reconcile his mixed thoughts.

*"Reverend Mother spoke just a few... a **very** few appropriate words. Nice words. Wasn't easy of course... Well as much as **could** be said!"*

A large photograph of an unpleasant crusty harridan grimaced down on them from above the fireplace. Nelly Pod always hated visitors, especially any new young friend Aubrey might acquire. One day the Christ Church congregation was buzzing with gossip about a violent row in which she had actually threatened to throw her son out of Crow's Hole onto Becksitch Lane - 'bag and baggage'. Mr Claud Hoadley was heard to say -

"Which is Aubrey, the bag or the baggage?"

Derek thought that the answers to the standard questions came a little too fast, and too well rehearsed.

"I was at the pictures."

"In the afternoon?"

"That's when I concentrate best, at a matinee."

"Which cinema?"

"The Palace, 'Snow White and the Seven Dwarfs', it was good."

"What time did you go in?"

"About half past two. I didn't come out until nearly half past five."

107

On the last word he seemed to thrust out his hideous head in an act of defiance. Just for a moment, Winter saw him as a bulldog.

"A Disney feature cartoon doesn't last three hours?"

*"The little picture was **also** very good. All about our new plane the Bristol Brabazon, the largest plane in the world! It can carry a hundred passengers. It's got eight Rolls Royce engines and can fly non-stop to America."*

The head jutted out even further and little piggy eyes gloated.

"I went to the toilet during the cartoon - more tea? Shall I ring for Mavis?" Before the eager podgy little grasping hand could attack the much used and often violently shaken bell, Derek, recognising a brick wall when he saw one, decided to change his tactics.

"No thank you, Mr Pod. While we're here, I wonder if you'd be kind enough to give us the benefit of your views on this sad business. What did you think of the deceased? I believe you taught her at one time?"

The misshapen head jutted forward with wicked excitement and his hideous features moved into a hateful snarl.

*"**Poison!** A nasty piece of work! She 'ad it c<u>oo</u>min'!"*

Sudden heinous emotion had triggered a temporary reversion to his native Derbyshire accent.

"Yes I taught 'er, with considerable pain and difficulty. Good riddance!"

Keeping a professional calm in the face of these polemics, the questioner casually asked if the good music master had any particular pet theories about this puzzling crime. He puffed up with self importance and asked a surprising question.

"Was her face bashed in?"

"Why would you want to know that?"

*"Well it's not **like** Sarah to get herself murdered! More like **she'd** do the killing, and disappear down to London with Mr Burgess's money. She'd leave Sally to be found in the boat, un-recognisable and disfigured. Something like that."*

"Intriguing but incorrect. Sarah is very dead and her friend alive and well. Any other ideas?"

Unfazed, the little man leaned forward.

*"Yes. There's another probability. Only **one** other person detested Sarah Grindle more than me, and she's dangerous. She's dangerous because she's got religious mania, and thinks she'd be doing*

the Lord's work. Now then, Percy said the mystery woman had a hump!"

He paused significantly in a failed attempt to build dramatic tension. The two faces opposite were detached, stoic and sceptical, regarding their subject as one might look at something brought in by the cat. Notwithstanding, like a trooper, he pressed on to deliver his denouement.

"The person of whom I speak is none other than -
Miss Madge Calder!"

Nonchalantly, Detective Inspector Derek Russell thanked Mr Pod for his helpful ideas and assured him all relevant individuals would be interviewed in due course. He apologised for the intrusion and said they would have to be leaving - for the time being.

Walking down the steep garden, the two men were deep in thought. The Detective Inspector was still holding to his favourite theory of a desperate husband in strange attire emerging from a garden door. But now, he could not quite put out of his head, a new vision. A toad-like form in female garb, was stealthily creeping out of the Palace toilets, un-noticed, under cover of a darkened cinema, and into the relatively quiet half day closing, King Street, Belper. Perhaps his junior colleague was thinking much the same when he said -

*"It won't hurt just to check with the Palace on the times, the films, and if anybody noticed him? After all, he **is** noticeable!"*

"No, Winter, it won't hurt."

Chapter 13

A Pompous Pretentious Punctilious Pedant

The dry and sunny high pressure influence still held on the Monday of September 12th, but now it brought subtle autumnal changes. A rather thick mist had persisted in the Derwent Valley up until mid-morning, and only the hill tops had been sparklingly cool and clear. By noon the sun was pouring into the small office at the Matlock Road, Belper, Police Station, and Detective Sergeant John Winter was feeling the benefit of radiant heat for the first time that day. He had spent the whole morning typing a complete history of the case so far, on this the fifth day after the crime. He had worked with Detective Inspector Derek Russell before, and knew generous margins would be needed for the expected numerous annotations.

The sound of the door opening cheered him. It had been a lonely morning and he did enjoy the company of his superior. They worked well together. They were a good team. Derek was unusually bouncy and cheerful -

*"Good morning, my dear Watson! Put not your typewriter away - I have **news** of our mendacious and naughty Mr Toad! I've just been to the Palace, that is, the picture Palace. The projectionist tells me that Mr Pod was perfectly correct in his enthusiastic recitation of details regarding the **advertised** programme of Wednesday afternoon. However - he 'forgot' to tell us about the projector breaking down at the start of the topical documentary about the giant aeroplane! The projector running the reel developed some problem with the arc lamp. They were able to get help from the Ritz Cinema at the top of King Street, but this caused a delay, and they had to keep running on schedule as far as possible. Consequently there wasn't time to show the 'Making the Mighty Brabazon'!*

"So that means..."

*"It means Aubrey Pod could have read those details about the aircraft from any recent newspaper. It means the creepy little man **wasn't** where he said he was!"*

It was agreed Pod could be confronted at a later time. They would stick to the original schedule, and John looked wistfully at the stationary, comfortable police motor car as they started a brisk healthy walk up to Green Lane. It was opulent and leafy, certainly one of the more mature parts of Belper. In 1863, Arthur Hoadley started life in a humble but quaint cottage in a row called The Butts, once a place of archery practice. He laboured in the mills and eventually worked his way up to becoming the mill manager in 1908. To display his new status and income, he moved his wife and twenty year old son Claud, to a substantial home in this desirable part of the town. Since both parents were now dead, Claud Hoadley had been living alone in this large house for the last twenty-three years. The well tended front lawn was as carefully manicured as the master himself, not a blade of grass out of place. Nor could be seen a single fallen leaf from the beautiful copper beech, which created an attractive mottled effect in the bright midday sun.

"It looks in pretty good nick, for a single bloke on a pension."

"Good management, Winter. Hoadley's very careful and doesn't have our liabilities. No wife, no kids, no animals and no car to run. Apart from Olive Tonks twice a week - no staff. He should have a bob or two in the bank after a lifetime teaching classics down the road and nothing much more to do than sit in there for scores of years on end reading Latin and Greek!

They were enthusiastically and cheerfully greeted at the front door with a beaming, if rather mechanical smile.

"Seeing you come down the path, I had rather expected that the agents of law and order would finally descend upon me! No police motorcar? Most commendable! As I often say to Robin, 'Solvitur Ambulando!' - the Youth Hostel maxim. It means - 'Everything is solved by walking'."

John was immediately awed and impressed with the live reality of such precise and highly polished diction. Up to that moment, he had only heard such cultured tones coming from the inside of a cabinet, encasing an electric wireless set. Derek took a different view, finding the urbane, well-bred, lilting lines, like the smile, feigned and forced. The words 'cam' and 'parrrth' were particularly jarring, coming unnaturally from what he detected as a one time Derbyshire tongue.

Both visitors felt the air of authority as they were politely invited to be seated in the large, rather austere sitting room. Plain and severely neat, with just a few well chosen expensive ornaments, but lots of quality books with improving titles. The host sat bolt upright in a firm armchair, keeping trunk and legs at a precise ninety degrees. Mr

111

Hoadley, in the classroom, had always been very keen on deportment. To slouch was a sin, which encouraged sloth, leading to sloppy work.

"Straighten up there, boy! How dare you loll in front of me! Such disrespectful drooping is indicative of an indolent and disorderly mind."
The master's discipline and influence seemed to be around him constantly like an aura. Both men felt they were in the 'headmaster's study'. Even Detective Inspector Derek Russell felt he was yielding to the invisible force and power of this slight trim and prim little autocrat. As he announced the purpose of his visit, it was with some irritation that he became self-conscious of his own increasingly careful enunciation. John Winter also began to sound affected and more artificial. His respect and veneration was given more willingly, but Derek was a reluctant admirer of this, it had to be admitted - superior person.

With Claud Hoadley, he had decided to reveal more privileged information in an attempt to get a better view of the principal characters in this drama. He was an erudite gentleman with considerable local knowledge. Pompous pedant, he may be, but his personal opinion could be of some value. It was annoying that Mr Hoadley held the same view. The sergeant made the first move with a deference which continued to irk his superior.
Choosing, and pronouncing his words with care -
"We understand you know Robin Kirkland quite well. Perhaps you'd be kind enough to comment on his friendship with the deceased."
A shadow seemed to pass over the acetous grey face. The thin mean lips became white, when pressed tightly together to indicate a hard unforgiving disapproval.
*"An **unwise** friendship. Regrettably I have found it necessary to censure the boy on more than one occasion."*
They waited for more - in vain. John pressed on managing to sound even more ridiculous -
"Can you elaborate on the nature of this relationship? Is it in any way possible that it became .... carnal?"
This last word provoked the pedagogue. His dignified composure was gone, giving way to vexation, causing an unexpected avalanche of reproach upon the unprepared and unfortunate sergeant.

112

*"It is **NOT** possible! Kindly remember, young man, that Robin Kirkland is one of Miss Calder's children! Such an outrageous and lewd suggestion is totally out of order. Unheard of conduct! To be reviled with such filth in one's own home is insupportable...."*

He continued to spit and splatter several further denunciations, with occasional reference to -

"...the lascivious and salacious mind of the police!" Eventually, once again the acid lips were pressed firmly together signalling an unspoken - "Those are my last words on this subject." John Winter looked thoroughly mortified and miserable, but Detective Inspector Derek Russell was reminded of a line in Hamlet -

"The lady doth protest too much, me-thinks."

He was proud, and took satisfaction hearing the accolade 'One of Miss Calder's children', being one himself. Recently he met up with another fellow pupil called Marion Holden who said -

"We've been privileged to spend our formative years in the care of these two unique women. You've done well, Derek, and I've no doubt you now appreciate the lessons in character building, integrity, self-reliance and discipline. They've given us a code of living, a grounding in ethics and behaviour. It's common knowledge that you're a good policeman, and it's no small thanks to our little school."

This was his fourth year in the rank of Detective Inspector, and he had achieved the reputation of a courteous, gentle approach, combining fairness and sensitivity, together with getting good results.

He brought his mind back to the task in hand.

"Sorry to have upset you, Mr Hoadley, but be assured, we have good reason to ask these questions. I understand you were one of the guests at the dinner party at Fern Glade on the Saturday evening September 3rd?"

The former schoolmaster turned his angry and sullen face towards the senior man, but did not speak. Derek continued -

"One is given to wonder how such an event ever took place, in view of the atmosphere in that unhappy house? As an intelligent, well informed impartial observer, your views could be very valuable to our investigations."

It worked. Hoadley considered.

"Social events were usually favoured and organised by the lady of the house. Oliver Burgess was content to have the occasional

*distraction. It was an opportunity for him to relax with his equals. **She**, on the other hand enjoyed the entertainment. She could tease Robin, make fun of Julian and Mr Pod, and giggle along with the appalling Miss Tonks."*

"I gather Julian is a poet?"

*"**Julian** is a rhymester and a writer of mawkish drivel!"*

Yet again, Mr Hoadley became heated -

"Really, Inspector! Have you met this counterfeit creature?"

He did not wait for an answer, but resumed his spluttering.

*"**That** sort of fake makes me .... well it makes me want to be **rude** ... very rude."* He turned to vent his wrath on Winter.

*"A good stiff kick up the backside is what **he** needs to bring him down to earth!"* Again the little lips closed conveying - "I have spoken."

Not being very much for poetry, John Winter wisely stayed silent, but Derek was thinking. He was imagining Mr Hoadley looking into a mirror, and seeing the face of Julian Lawrence. Or was it perhaps his own face of many years before, as a prissy young man?

"Do you think that Mr Pod was very deeply hurt by her unkind reminiscences?"

The mention of such an odd caricature as the humorous organist, softened the features of the pedant to something approaching a smile.

"I should think so, but Pod has suffered a lifetime of cruel quips, and consequently has erected a hard barrier of self defence. One is never really sure."

At this point John felt brave enough to ask a question.

"Do you like Mr Pod?"

"Like'? It is an irrelevancy - unworthy of consideration. Pod is a vulgar little man who tends to presume we are social equals. We are not! True, he has a first class honours degree in music."

For the next line he turned his head to the senior officer and introduced a hint of condescending sneer -

*"From a northern city I gather. His thick Derbyshire accent with the common sounding closed 'U', is entirely unsatisfactory, and totally inconsistent with his professional status. The fact that we are both academics and bachelors makes him altogether much **too** familiar. Robin finds him amusing, but **I** do not, and **will** not receive him.*

Unfortunately my tactless and mischievous young student repeated an unwise comment I once made about his tasteless crumpled, baggy and shabby clothing." Mr Hoadley started to look a little

114

embarrassed, but was prompted to continue when he noticed the two very interested faces opposite.

"I had remarked something to the effect that he could not have dressed worse if he had tried, and seated, it looked like the stuffing had come out of the armchair!"

He noted the reaction of the two officers.

*"Yes, the un-diplomatic Robin was **also** most amused. But Pod, silly and immature as ever, flew to his solicitor and made his third and most spiteful will that year - leaving **ME** all his dreadful clothes!!"*

Mr Claud Hoadley allowed himself a moment of good sporting pleasure from the obvious entertainment he produced in these younger men, who were now shaking with mirth. He decided to 'ride the laugh' until -

"However, Detective Inspector, I must remind you that there are other demands upon my time, and ..."

"Indeed, Mr Hoadley, you are most patient. If you please, briefly, just a routine account of your movements of the afternoon and evening of last Wednesday."

There was just a noticeable stillness and fraction of delay, while the shrewd eyes held Derek, before a casual sounding answer was delivered.

"After lunch I read the paper.."

"The Times?"

*"I share the same taste as our gracious lady, Queen Mary - 'The Telegraph'. Wednesday? Oh yes, one of my elocution pupils failed to attend - a disappointing and weak girl anyway with a lowly habit of addressing people as 'duck' - or in her case 'd**ook**'. It does call attention to a common working class background..."*

"Your movements on..."

"Wednesday, yes, of course, sorry. I used the time well and treated myself to a little Sophocles and tried Moliere. That particular translation I found..."

*"What we **really** need to know, Mr Hoadley, is if you left the house, and did you see anyone?"*

*"You should have been more explicit, Inspector. I always eat dinner at eight of the clock prompt, and go for my evening stroll at nine. I saw no one. No, wait! I **did** see that horrible common Tonks boy."*

"Where was this?"

"He was mincing out of the top of Long Row at a minute or two after the hour. Fortunately it was convenient to dash down Joseph Street to avoid a meeting."

115

"You don't like him?"

*"Detective Sergeant! You fail to appreciate that I have my position and reputation to consider! To be **seen**, idly chatting in a public street to that illiterate, libidinous, effeminate charlatan! **It** doesn't bear thinking about!"*

Yet again, Winter was stunned into an abased silence.

*"Larrst Sunday for an exarrmple, I was appalled. He **directly** addressed me outside Christ Church, after the service, and no less than the Bishop of Derby was approaching! I was trapped! It was awful! He **insisted** on telling me how cultured he was becoming. How he was so elevated by listening to Mr Pod playing on the piano."*

A rather amusing and clever imitation followed -

"Ooo Mr 'Oadley, it were rate good. When 'e played Claire de Bloom, a could <u>joo</u>st see Claire standin' there, in 'er de Blooms!"

"An ignorant peasant of the first order! The Misses Calder have made a great mistake in ..."

*"I have just **one** more question, Mr Hoadley. Mrs Burgess made some reference to a hobby of yours which caused some distress. Can you explain that?"*

The anger and indignation collapsed like a house of cards. The cruel disapproving lips seemed to lose their tension and gained a little colour. For the first time the keen sharp eyes became watchful with fear. The seconds passed while he composed and arranged a calm answer. He spoke the next word with an airy nonchalance -

"Distress?" Savouring the sweetness of revenge, Winter bounced back -

"Yes, sir, several guests used that very word."

"Social gatherings are very demanding at my age. I suddenly felt very tired and left early."

"I see." - said Detective Inspector Derek Russell abstractedly, who was looking through the typed notes. *"Does a .... Mr Billy Grindle share your interest in model railways?"*

*"Mr Grindle? Sarah's father who lives in the Gutter! Really, Inspector Russell! You **are** a puzzle."*

"Kindly answer my question, sir."

He seemed to flounder with a mixture of amazement, impatience and indignation.

*"I have **no** idea! How am **I** to be familiar with the spare time activities of a common coal miner? One doesn't want to appear to be*

snobbish, but you could hardly expect me to move in the same circles as the Grindles."

*"But according to Sarah, he **did** once call in to see your trains?"*

"Many people have been kind enough to admire my boyhood display in the attic." A sickly smile broke out over the fine sharp features to mask obvious discomfort.

"Do you mind if we have a look?" said Detective Inspector Derek Russell.

Claud Hoadley took a deep breath as if a crisis had passed, and wearily led his visitors up two flights of steps, to a large low room entirely dedicated to a miniature landscape. They were very impressed. With the ascent, Hoadley's spirits had also lifted.

"As you see, it's a high quality large scale '0' gauge. It won't take me long to get an engine steamed up. Would you like to see it in operation?"

There was something much more attractive about this man, who was now smiling, and enthusing like a schoolboy.

"Thank you, Mr Hoadley, you're most considerate, but that won't be necessary. Are you sure that Mr Grindle never saw this excellent display?"

The boyish smile faded. The schoolmaster returned with a less genuine grin, and resumed the effort to suppress emotion and sound matter-of-fact.

*"We must be speaking of nearly forty years back, gentlemen, when young Grindle was a gardener here. I have a **vague** memory of him asking to see this lot."*

Walking south along Green Lane -

*"Well! What do you make of **that**?"*

"A very expensive and impressive toy."

"Come off it, sir! We're on to something here at last."

Derek smiled and gave his subordinate a quick affectionate hug around the shoulder.

"You're right, Watson. A visit to The Gutter, I think!"

Billy Grindle was at best inhospitable, and positively bellicose when it was suggested that he was once a teenage gardener on Green Lane.

"What's 'e bin tellin' ya?"

*"Why don't **you** tell **me** all about it, Mr Grindle? A chance to put your side of the story. Well? We're waiting."*
The gruff miner snarled, snorted and mouthed imprecations under his breath, but revealed nothing more. Derek considered the theory of bad blood passing from father to daughter. Daughter! He decided on another tack.

"You must have spoken to your late daughter about your interest in model locomotives. She was quizzing Mr Hoadley at Fern Glade."
There was an immediate cooling of his hot temper, and visible relaxation.

"Oh she did, did she. Well then, yad better talk ta 'is majesty ant ya?"

Out on the street - *"Dam! A big mistake. And I nearly had that one. With both Hoadley and Grindle, when the subject turns to toy trains, they start to feel safe. Sarah had stumbled on to something - but what?*

Was it something that cost her - her life?"

Chapter 14

The Goblin

It was a good long walk all the way along the Nottingham Road, back to the centre of town, where they enjoyed a simple but wholesome, if very late, lunch at Leslie's Snack Bar. Another long walk took them up Bridge Hill, and beyond up to Shire Oaks. After his initial visit to Miss Florence Calder, on Thursday September 8th, Derek had jotted down a considerable amount of information, now refined and typed. It included the references to old Jasper Wormall at the dinner party, and his visit to Bridge House for advice on the following Monday September 5th.

Jasper was not a favourite or serious suspect, but in view of the possible motive, an official visit was in order. Like many of the players in this drama, Derek knew Mr Wormall slightly from his occasional visits to Christ Church. As they ascended the rough track, a plume of white smoke could be seen rising and shrouding the crown of tall trees above the ancient cottage with its sunken roof. Just for a moment, the ugly hunched old man looked sinister, piling his garden rubbish upon the crackling bonfire. Derek recalled the words of the old nun back at the convent - 'A fire of bones'.

He was pleased to receive this unexpected visit, and it was no surprise that they were given a typical 'Jasper' welcome - freshly 'mashed' tea and home made cakes. No complications about Wednesday September 7th.; Jasper had no jobs that afternoon, and stayed in all the time. Instinctively, the officers were reluctant to touch on the painful subject of the departed Sarah Burgess, but when invited to make an observation, the little man surprised them -
"A woonder if there wont a mistake! It's like wrong un got killed. Yad expect t' gaffer ta be dead - not 'er. Not likely, nay, not 'er!

Conversation with this interesting charming little man was a sheer delight. He was a living link with the distant past, affectionately repeating the anecdotes of his old granddad, who could remember back to 1825 when England was ruled by George IV, and the Lord of Belper was George Benson Strutt. The nearby, imposing stone built mansion of Bridge Hill House had been demolished some 17 years earlier in 1932, but Jasper told tales of his grandfather's brothers who were

119

footmen, coachmen, grooms and gardeners to Mr Strutt. Derek and John learned about the Great Conservatory which boasted tropical palms, azaleas, melons, vines and peaches.

Approaching the Police Station, Detective Sergeant Winter was looking forward to going home to relax after a long, full day. A surprise visitor would prevent this. Desk Sergeant Poulson introduced them to Frank Blount, the landlord of the Talbot Inn at the foot of Bridge Hill.

"Suppose a should have come before now, but me an 't missus didn't think much of it at first..."

"We appreciate any information, Mr Blount. Have a seat."

"Something I saw. It may mean nothing, but...anyway - here goes. It would be about 'arf past four last Wednesday. A decided to break in me new boots we a little walk, and were lacing them oop on a barrel on t' front. A can see t' bridge an t' owd gents lavatory."

"You mean the cast iron urinal on the corner?"

"That's it. Well there's Jasper coming round 't corner, an..."

"Mr Jasper Wormall? Are you quite sure?"

"Am positive, sir! Jasper, with a sort o' carpet bag. Went inside - an didn't come out!"

"You mean he didn't come out for a long time?"

"Well.."

Detective Inspector Derek Russell smiled at the publican and suggested

"You know that old men can take a long time in such matters. How long did you actually watch the toilet?"

"Boots are such a long fiddle to do up - about ... three minutes."

"Well that's not too long." said John Winter, taking notes.

"'Ang on a bit. A started walkin' over 't bridge, an looked back, cos am curious like. No Jasper, must be still inside! Now that'll be six minutes! When a get ta t' Triangle .. eight minutes, still no Jasper - but there's this woman!!"

He paused to allow the significance to sink in.

"An she'd got this bag.."

Derek was thoughtful, and said -

"It's unlikely that the old gardener would walk down to Bridgefoot to relieve himself and then climb the hill to go back home."

"If Jasper comes down t' 'ill, is goin' ta Belper!" said Mr Blount with conviction.

"Or perhaps the River Gardens." said John with a touch of irony. The publican had only a brief look at the woman, and could give

120

no better description than in the newspaper. Derek stood up to indicate an end to the proceedings.

*"There could be any number of simple explanations for what you saw, Mr Blount. We thank you for coming forward, but please let **us** draw the conclusions and do the investigations."*

This was a depressing coincidence coming less than half an hour after leaving Shire Oaks. Neither man wanted the delightful little chap to be in the frame. They sat in silence for a few moments staring at the lino, until John Winter lifted his head -

"In all probability the old man simply took a long time and came out when Blount wasn't looking."

*"Nearing the Gangway, he wouldn't be able to see the lavatory anyway. The 'woman', at **that** time could well have been the genuine X on her murderous errand."*

They looked at each other and John let out a deep sigh.

"And yet..."

"We have a witness who is certain that Mr Wormall was at the bridge with a bag at the crucial time ... and Mr Wormall clearly stated he was in his little cottage all day long!" - said Derek, slapping his cheek in mild frustration.

It had been agreed that the two detectives would meet at Bridge House School at 8.30 the next morning of Tuesday September 13th to save time. Detective Sergeant John Winter, after a difficult drive, was the first to arrive in an unusually quiet murky and foggy Belper. It was now colder than it had been since the spring. The great Plane Tree had started to shed its leaves and as he stood at the door, John was soothed by watching two of them slowly drift and glide through the still, grey, damp air. Brown and yellow, they made a wide circle around the garden, one to fall into the road and one disappearing into the dark home of ferns.

He was admitted by Simon, the first time the two had met. They stared at each other. John had heard fragments of comment, but was not prepared for the unusual and inscrutable young man who stood before him, head on one side wearing a half enigmatic smile. The servant was comfortable with this silent probing moment, but John was grateful when Miss Madge bustled into sight and curtly dismissed the meagre little man. Madge Calder was not noted for her patience or tact.

"I thought you had come to bring news of an arrest! It's now nearly a week! What have you been doing?"

*"Give us a chance, ma'am! There's only the two of us and the victim **did** have a good many enemies. There's still a few folks to talk to."*

"With a capital offence, I should have thought a number of senior detectives would be involved."

*"More effective for all data to be co-ordinated and analysed in a small team. Anyway, we simply **do** not have an endless supply of public money or trained police offices, or for that matter..."*

The interruption of the tinkling door bell came just in time to stem his growing irritation, and the imminent danger of his being rude to the critical, squat mistress. Detective Inspector Derek Russell had arrived.

Minutes later they were chatting to Miss Florence Calder in her neat study with its scent of erudition.

"This will have to be quick gentlemen, the children will be here soon. Since your findings are now coming to me in concise, well presented sheets..." She graciously inclined her head to John Winter - *"... I must share with you the results of **my** visit to the cycle factory on Derwent Street yesterday."*

"You went to see Mr Burgess?"

*"I don't think that would be very productive. He won't tell **me** what he won't tell you. No, I went to see Dorothy, who confirmed to me personally that she's never **quite** sure when he's left the office, unless she has need to speak to him."*

On that subject, Derek interrupted her to say that, with some difficulty, a trans-Atlantic, person to person telephone call had been achieved from the Derby Police Station to a Mr Walter Kurrlie in the city of Detroit. The Victorian schoolmarm looked at him with a mixture of disbelief and admiration.

"The result doesn't look good for your friend! At best, it could be said he has a very poor sense of timing. Mr Walter Kurrlie remembers clearly, and is adamant, that he stepped into a pre-booked taxi at 4.00pm sharp, which took him to the Derby Railway Station in time for his 4.30 express to London. The Lion Hotel on Bridge Street has confirmed the taxi booking.

*This means that the American did **not** leave at 4.45pm as stated by Mr Burgess! Ergo, he could have departed his office, un-noticed at*

*4.00pm, and have **ample** time to prepare for a fancy dress trip up the river with his estranged wife!"*

She received this information in serious silence, and in the few precious minutes left, they brought her up to date with all the facts of the case.

She collected her thoughts -

"In brief you are still investigating Mr Burgess. So far, your most hopeful suspect, Derek?"

"As yet, most probable - yes."

"It's worth pointing out that Oliver could be a dozy child, occasionally late for school and therefore possibly uncertain of timing.

Her eyes seemed to get younger as she stared into the middle distance, and looked down the long passage of time at a fair haired, pleasant natured, deep thinking boy, slightly inclined to plumpness. He was very sensitive. She recalled the ugly incident when he vengefully put stinging nettles inside the slipper bag of a girl who had laughed at him when he wet himself. These dark thoughts were coupled with the more recent, increasingly frequent, embarrassing dramas on the pavement outside of Christ Church. Mortifying scenes where Oliver was horribly humiliated before other members of the dispersing congregation. All the more distressing in view of the softly spoken gentleman's futile attempt to maintain his dignity against a loutish foul-mouthed attack from his cruel backbiting bitch of a wife.

The old teacher decided **not** to mention these thoughts to the police.

*"You seem to have been lied to by Mr Pod and Mr Wormall. Innocent reasons **could** be uncovered for these deceptions."* Thoughtfully, she looked out of the window into the greyness at three playful leaves dancing down to earth. *"You are not at all happy with the accounts of Robin Kirkland, Mrs Tonks, Mrs Lawrence or that of her son."*

"To say the least!" - put in Detective Sergeant Winter, with some feeling.

"You have yet to question Simon, Sally and Dr Lewis?" Still smarting after his encounter with her sister, John was dearly tempted to add - "In view of the description, Miss Margaret Campbell Calder is well over-due for formal interrogation!" - but looking at the stern countenance opposite, only said -

123

"We'll start with Simon now."

"And good luck to you! He's been looking forward to being interviewed by police officers. Ah! I hear the children. I'll send Simon in to you. Just one thing which may help. At church, Helen told me that on the afternoon of the murder, Sister Hannah was approached in King Street by Aubrey Pod, wanting to know when Sarah Burgess was likely to leave the convent!"

Slightly stunned by this news, the two officers rose to their feet and watched her sweeping dramatic exit.

"Good morning to you, gentlemen."

Absorbing this new detail, at first they hardly noticed the funny little face which poked around the door with a light - *"Allo!"* The strange elfin creature sidled into the room in a cascade of camp, obsequious fawning and twisting gyrations, which on **this** occasion irritated Derek, who intended to have a serious interview.

*"**Sit** down, Simon!"* - he said in an abrupt, rather more formal than usual tone. Seeing that he had managed to amuse the other man, the little clown continued 'little boy like' teasing, playful smiles, faces and poses, head on one side, and then the other - until Detective Inspector Russell shot out a booming question.

*"**Where** were you on the afternoon of Wednesday, September 7th?"*

It was time to be serious. In coquettish style, he raised a single finger to the lips and, in an effort of thought, lisped out -

"Now let me see?"

*"It was your afternoon off. **Where** did you go?"*

He cogitated further, and delayed some more, as Derek menacingly and loudly tapped the desk with agitated fingers. The boy's face lit up like a little dog who had just performed a clever trick -

"A went for a walk!"

"Where?"

"Mmmm - a went ta pick blackberries."

*"**Where?**"*

"Over t' bridge on Chevin Road."

"And the Misses Calder will no doubt confirm that you returned with lots of blackberries?"

The flirtatious smile faded.

"Ooo no! A yet um!"

124

"Indeed. In that case you'll no doubt be able to produce a handkerchief or article of clothing with blackberry stains - since they **don't** *easily wash out?"*

The silly servant looked distinctly uncomfortable at this last question, and claimed he was unaware of any stained garments, washed or otherwise, and said he did not possess a handkerchief anyway! The Detective Inspector was beginning to think that this growing and annoying farce was a waste of valuable time. Such a complete idiot could not possibly ever concentrate long enough to organise a silly tea party, let alone a crime.

For the record, and as a matter of form, he put his last hopeless question.

"Do you recall where you were between about 4.00pm and 5.00pm?"

The answer was his best yet, and it came with surprising speed.

"A can tell ya where a was at quarter ta five, cos a looked at clock, at top a King Street."

They both leaned forward with interest.

"You mean the large projecting bracket clock outside John Medley's the watchmaker?"

"A bird sat on t' big finger, an a were lookin' at it joost before a went ta see Mr 'Oadley."

"Mr Hoadley never mentioned your visit?"

"E wont in!"

*"Are you **sure,** Simon, this is important. Did you knock hard enough?"*

"Rang t' bell, an thoomped on t' door for five minutes. 'E wont in."

"What did you want him for?" - asked Winter, recalling Hoadley's horror of all Tonks.

"A want ta talk right! Av got sum m<u>oo</u>ny nar!"

Derek suddenly felt a wave of compassion for the puny and lowly little fragment of humanity before him. A rough and ready ragamuffin, who was prepared to give up his pittance for elocution and self-improvement.

Chapter 15

Sexy Sally

Outside in the greyness, under the great ghostly tree, the cold fog was just as bad as ever.

"I think we're going to be stuck with this all day, sir. Can't even see the mill clock!"

But Derek was not paying much attention. His thoughts were up on Green Lane. Those thoughts were trying, and failing, to create an image of a certain proud and snooty classics master, dressed up as an unnoticeable, common woman. The fog seemed to depress his spirits and was now becoming metaphorical for the murkiness of this insoluble puzzle. John had a guess at his distraction.

*"Hoadley, isn't it? Now **he's** on the loose!"*

*"A possible motive shrouded in a mystery of toy trains. Ability? No doubt about it with **his** first class brain. And now .... opportunity. This thing gets more and more complicated!"*

Hardly five minutes later, inside the mill manager's office, it became even **more** complicated. The foreman, in the presence of his boss, was standing his ground.

*"No doubt about it, sir! Said she was poorly, an she did **look** poorly."*

*"So exactly what time **did** she leave work?"*

"Got it here ... Sally Tonks, left machine at ...3.52pm."

"Did she go straight home?"

"Should 'ave done, if she's ill - shouldn't she?"

He was cautioned not to mention this exchange when escorting her to the office which the manager had kindly made available. Winter was worried.

*"We really **should** have clarified with the mother, the time Sally returned home. They could lie for each other."*

"Too late for that now, we'll have to bluff."

It was the superficial facial resemblance which first struck the officers when Sally Tonks passed into the room. She looked like her brother, but that was all. She lacked his charm, warmth and wit. Snake-like, she slithered around and down into a chair, without being asked. In an oozing of sardonic contempt, her crafty eyes flashed, appraised, and undressed the two hunky men before her. At frequent intervals, a wanton liquid tongue appeared, and cunningly lubricated glistening red lips.

They both felt her lascivious power which she had every intention of using to influence this meeting, but the older man, the Christian family man, erected a moral shield fashioned out of his formative years in a Calder classroom, and a natural revulsion for this cheap and common tart. Not so for his younger colleague who was aroused by her erotic aura of fleshly promise and was reminded of a recent overheard obscene remark - a certain reference to 'a second hand dart board'. Catching sight of the sergeant's face, which reflected thoughts of fornication, Detective Inspector Russell crashed into the thick, silent, lewd atmosphere with a sarcastic -

*"**DO** take a seat, Miss Tonks!"*

At an initial reference to the killing, she showed not a trace of sadness for the loss of a friend, but there was some evidence of a certain thrill of drama which had come into an otherwise dull life.

Her voice was entirely consistent with the persona - loud, lowborn, coarse and crude. She gave the impression that an early departure on the previous Wednesday from the mill, had slipped her mind.

"Ooo arr! Ya right, a were took bad!"

"Where did you go?" The question seemed to surprise her.

"Went om, where'd ya think?"

*"Remember, Miss Tonks, we **have** spoken to your mother."*

A few moments passed while she considered this point, but the insolent smile on her brazen face was unaffected as the mobile mouth continued to masticate some unknown item within. Her rude impudence summoned from the darkest part of Derek, an evil lust for revenge in savage thoughts, which were better never expressed into words -

"Yes, be **very** careful you vile impertinent strumpet! A single shred of evidence is **all** I need to wipe that saucy smirk off your cheap face. A good strong rope, and old Jack Ketch will teach **you** some respect for your betters!"

His hateful fantasy was interrupted by her eventual reply.

"A thought a bit a fresh air an a walk 'd do me good."

*"Just now you said you went home! **When** exactly did you finally arrive home?"*

127

"Ooo a duno!"
Using the same 'How dark?' technique as on Julian Lawrence, it was eventually established that Sally Tonks was probably back at Cowhill at around 7.00pm.
"No doubt the three hour walk restored you to full health! Where did you go? Where had you got to at ... say ...5.00pm?"

At this last, the probing Detective Inspector took great satisfaction. For the first time a question had slowed up the irritating mouth. The challenging eyes had lost their insubordinate sparkle and the insulting face was finally fazed. She appeared to be selecting and de-selecting possible answers, until -
"Ant got far. Joost mucked abart ...down t' meadows. Sat next ta t' river." A wall of silence faced her unsatisfactory answer. Eventually with some irritation -
"Why don't ya ask Mr Toad war 'e were doin' on t' beach?"

John Winter was mystified with this question, but Derek leaned forward to clarify the words 'toad' and 'beach'. It seemed that the pupils of the Herbert Strutt Grammar School, like the detectives, had for many years noticed the similarity between Aubrey Pod, and the funny little character of Graham's book. Belper beach was the place of easy access to the Derwent, next to the bridge. Further careful questions revealed the presence of the music master, sitting on a boulder, throwing stones into the water at about 4.00pm.
"Dotty owd sod! Slobberin' be'ind them glasses!"
"Did Mr Pod have his binoculars?"
"Not that time."
*"But you **have** seen him before - 'bird watching'?*
She shrieked a raucous howl of derision, so loud above the general hum of machinery that the manager put his head up to the window in the door to check that all was well within.
"Berd watchin'!! 'Anky panky more like! Filthy oogly ..."
"Where did you get that money, Miss Tonks?"
This sudden change of subject put an abrupt stop to her titillating tirade on the squalid schoolmaster, but she remained composed and did not show the expected disorientation for which they had hoped. On the contrary, in the seconds which followed, her initial confidence returned with a slow, despising, leering smile. A smile which seemed to say -
"Tough! I've been waiting for this question and I'm ready for you!"

128

"A present."
"A present from whom?"
"From Sarah! Oow else?"
Winter had been giving way to the boss in asking all these questions. He wondered how **this** answer could be followed up, and soon found out - it could not!

Leaving the mill, Detective Inspector Derek Russell was irritated.
"She's worked it out! Sarah is dead and will never speak. That slut need only say the cash was a gift. Nobody can prove any different. A brick wall."
"Cheer up, sir! We seem to be tightening the noose around Aubrey's neck!"
Derek looked very unhappy.
*"Yes I know, **but,** all my instincts are against it. How **could** a nasty little poltroon like that ever have the guts and self control to plan, and carry out, a successful execution in broad daylight? It just doesn't add up, Winter!*
"He holds a university degree, and ..."
*"**And** he plays 'Claire de **Bloom**' beautifully! Yes I know **all** about it!"*

They both enjoyed a good laugh which nicely relieved the stress of the moment.

*"I'd rather put **my** money on a man with more intelligence, a man with both feet on the ground.*

Let's go and visit the doctor."

129

Chapter 16

Haunted Halls

They were once again at the entrance of the silent, ghostly Bridge House, still shrouded and un-focused in the mist. Entering the garden, they passed the more imposing Georgian Calder front door and went up to the dignified, if less ornate, west facing front door to the east wing. This was the overly spacious home of Paul Lewis who had lost his wife Molly, ten years before. They were childless.

A tiny maid led them to the principal reception room which, like next door, had the same solid and ancient feel of the once great house. In contrast to the more sober Calder taste, Victorian clutter and ornamentation were more noticeable. Derek wandered over to the handsome Georgian mantelpiece and saw an impressive professionally printed card in mint condition -

Claud Hoadley
At Home

Sunday afternoon on the 18th of September

Verdant View
Green Lane
Belper
Derbyshire

Derek smiled at the thought of the pompous little man carefully addressing and sending these cards out to the county notables which optimistically might include people like the Bishop of Derby, the Lord Lieutenant or even the Lord High Sheriff.

Detective Sergeant John Winter was trying to make sense of a strange looking frying pan with a long wooden handle, hanging on the wall. His superior came to the rescue -

"That's no frying pan, lad! It's what they call a 'warming-pan'. A 17th century equivalent of our hot water bottle. A servant would place hot coals in the enclosed pan at the end, and pass it inside, between the cold bed sheets. That's older than this house, and probably its most valuable antique! Miss Calder used to tell us a story about a

warming-pan. Now how did it go? Something about a miller's son being smuggled into a royal palace..."

The officers rose to their feet as the door suddenly opened and a smiling, sprightly, slim man, perhaps a touch shorter than average height, entered the room.

Doctor Paul Lewis had just finished his morning surgery and warmly welcomed his visitors. Unlike his sister, he was lighter, with sandy hair, but displayed her charm and warm courtesy. Also like his sister, Doctor Lewis was handsome and looked younger than his 60 years. He and Helen were both very popular. Beaurepairians were not looking forward to the time when he would retire and be lost to them forever.

The rich, sonorous voice was tender and sincere -

"How is it going, Derek?"

"Not too well, Doctor. Hardly a fragment of evidence. We've come to ask you who did it? Or would you care to confess on the grounds of being 'the most implausible candidate'?"

"Oh crickey! I didn't expect to hear that from the police!"

This light hearted start was relaxing, but produced little substance. Doctor Lewis said he was attending his afternoon surgery, between four and six o' clock on the afternoon of Wednesday, September 7th. He offered his records for examination if they were needed. His account of the dinner party of Saturday, September 3rd, supported all other accounts, with the single difference that he actually admitted to enjoying the various performances of the acid tongued Sarah.

"I was in tears of laughter over the 'Pod' and 'Jasper' sagas, rather to the disapproval of my sister, I'm afraid!"

The interview seemed to come to an end for want of any useful further purpose. John Winter, still intrigued by the rambling old house, said -

"I gather your family were here, even before the Calders and the school?"

"Indeed. They arrived in 1902 when I was a naughty 13 year old!"

His guests looked a question, and, in turn, he looked contrite.

"I suppose the police will have to know! In those days this was a creepy spooky old house."

Derek well remembered his cheerless and cryptic classroom in the 1920's, before the days of electric lighting. Especially the deep, dark, cold winter months, when he and the others would struggle to see their dim slate under frail flickering candles after three in the afternoon. The doctor continued -

"I loved to explore and one day found a mysterious wire in the attic. It was a remnant of the old bell pull system to summon servants from the days when this great house was one single mansion. Naturally, being a lad, I gave it a tug and was delighted to hear the distant and spectral sound of an eerie clanging, coming from somewhere in the west wing!"

The ringing bell was dangling in a small servants room which had been completely sealed up for many years, and was totally unknown to the new occupants, defying all attempts to be located. Unfortunately the phantom tinkling was disturbingly near, and audible, inside the bedroom of the young Madge Calder. She was convinced that a past spirit, after the style of 'bell, book and candle', was unable to rest and could manifest at any moment!

"Eventually I was exposed, and to this day, nearly a half century on, Miss Madge has never really forgiven me!"

"I'm afraid most of us get up to shameful mischief as youngsters." said Derek.

"Quite so. I suffered awful pangs of conscience when I heard poor Miss Jane, coughing her life away, in the stillness and silence of night."

"That would be Jane Appleyard Calder, the eldest daughter?"

"Yes, she died on my 14th birthday."

He suddenly looked his true age and sadly shook his head.

"Death was ever present in those days. Intelligent girls, but most of them sickly and deformed. Miss Polly had no neck at all, but was a kind lady and very clever. I never knew Nelly; she died when they lived at Albion House on Green Lane. Lucy was fun. The renegade! The only one to leave home and scandalise the family by marrying an Irish Roman Catholic."

In an un-enthusiastic voice, the Inspector took advantage of this pause -

"This is all very interesting, doctor, but you will have to excuse us while we move on and try to solve this case." He looked mournfully over in the direction of the Calder wing. *"A bit disappointing, I'm afraid. I had hoped that Miss Florence Calder would have been*

132

wandering around Belper asking questions, ferreting out local gossip, make brilliant deductions, and would now be in a position to invite us all into her parlour to unmask the villain!"

But in fact it was at that very moment, over lunch, that Miss Florence Calder **was** thinking about springing into action! She and Madge frequently spoke about the local drama and mystery and it was a facetious comment made by her sister which put the new idea into her head.

"What was that, Madge?"

"Forget it, Florence, I wasn't being serious. It's just that if it turned out that the butler did it after all, it would be so very convenient in the town. An outsider, a stranger of an alien country, race and colour, not to mention that he's a Catholic, and also...."

*"**Silence, Madge!** Sometimes you're such an appalling narrow parochial bigot! **Must** you advertise the fact that you've hardly put a foot outside of Belper?"*

She added more slowly and thoughtfully -

*"But you **have** given me an idea!"*

The small hunched lesser sister, who was well accustomed to being a total autocrat in her own classroom, now looked shocked, hurt and chastened.

*"Florence, really! **Most** unfair! My comments were an attempt at humour and not intended.."*

*"All right, Madge, we'll speak no more of it - but I must think ... It's worth a try. Yes I **will** interview Mr Haigh."*

Madge's squat form leaned forward in great surprise and excitement -

*"So you **do** suspect the black man!"*

This produced a disdainful look from the senior mistress.

*"No I do not - that is, no more than I would suspect **you, Madge!"***

*"**ME!!"***

"Listen. All along I've felt that the social chemistry of that embarrassing and disturbing dinner party may be able to shed light upon this dark mystery. Mr Haigh is a man of keen intelligence and was in a unique position." Madge looked very puzzled. *"He was able to move around and be free of any normal polite obligation to engage in conversation. Serving drinks before and after the meal, he was more mobile and better able to observe and listen than an ordinary guest. It's*

quite likely he hasn't been asked the right questions. He may have data, and be unaware of its true value."
She sprung to her feet with the agility of a teenager.
*"I'm going there **now**."*
*"**Florence!** The children! Your responsibilities. Not another nature walk with Simon?"*
"Not in this fog. We were down on numbers this morning and I expect we'll have even fewer this afternoon."
She peered through the window at the hanging, impenetrable deep murkiness which, now gathering industrial pollutants, seemed to be tinged with a dirty amber/grey.
"Getting worse if anything. You can double up. It won't make more than thirty."

A few minutes later she stepped out smartly towards the bridge, her footsteps, the only sound echoing against the high mill walls on the silent road, as her straight form dissolved and eventually disappeared into the spectral vapour.

Not far ahead, further up the hill, in the same dank, thick atmosphere, strode unwillingly, the two professional detectives. Unwillingly, because they were reluctant to challenge the kind and gentle little goblin who had been caught out in a lie.

Approaching the ghostly outline of the now silent rookery, again Derek had that odd feeling of menace. He recalled the sinister leathery face of the little man, the grizzled and leering eyes; a face which was entirely consistent with the contorted and knotted little stone cottages, set deep in the twisting, ancient, narrow nooks and crannies of old Belper.

Derek Russell had always respected his intuition on these matters but swept aside his superficial prejudicial feelings in the certain knowledge, that, yet again, he would soon be charmed by a gracious welcome and old fashioned courtesy. Perhaps it was Mr Pod's recent mention of the Snow White fairy tale, which caused the intrusive thoughts of an ugly old hag with evil bulbous eyes, pretending to be friendly, offering food ...? Perhaps?

Tea and cakes were refused. Jasper Wormall detected from the tone that all was not well. It was suggested that he might want to reconsider his original statement, in which he said that he was at home, all the time

134

on the afternoon of the previous Wednesday. The old eyes, now watery and worried, looked through the tiny craggy window at the gloomy darkening vapours and thick black tree trunks beyond. He slowly turned his head to Detective Inspector Derek Russell and in a low hoarse voice

"*Nay lad, a never toouched 'er!*"

"*That wasn't my question, Mr Wormall. You were **seen** going into the gentleman's urinal at 4.30pm on Bridgefoot, but didn't come out!*"

"*Am 'ere ant a!*"

"*Quite so, Mr Wormall. At some point, no doubt you **did** eventually emerge. You were close to the scene of the crime at about the time it was committed, and therefore could be an important witness. Why did you tell us lies?*"

"*It's ... personal.*"

"*Not in a case of murder it isn't! What was in that bag?*"

The old man's mouth fell open with chagrin. He stared at his questioner in an effort to find time to consider his next plan of action. Being unsure of the source, depth or scope of 'information received', Jasper decided to reveal the truth.

"*'Ang on a minute.*" Creakily, he ascended up crude steps into the top room, and seconds later, came down with a large carpet bag which he put on the roughly hewn table surface. It was opened and he took out two hand made exquisitely finished beautiful antique dolls.

The two younger men leaned forward with gasps of admiration for the skilled detail and artwork. Derek was no specialist in these matters but he saw at a glance that the style and dress clearly had the elegance of Georgian ladies, which made these toys about 140 years old.

"*May I?*" He carefully picked up the taller doll which would be a little under two foot in height. Made of wood, she had a highly varnished head, incorporating carved hair, complete with braid in front, held by a gold tiara. Beautiful fine facial features were painted below. A red brocade redingote, partially covered a (once) white silk dress, with yellow ribbon pleated around the hem. Long pantalettes from just above the knees obscured finely jointed slender legs which ended in charming painted red slippers.

Mr Wormall had brightened at the sudden display of delight and appreciation in his humble home.

"Best mooney could buy in it's day! They were a present ta me grandma from Mrs George Benson Strolt. Catherina, they called 'er."

These were expensive toys indeed, which could easily have amused a young Princess Victoria, let alone a child of the wealthy Strutt family.

A more friendly chat followed. Jasper came from a traditional male dominated family, a macho generation where it was totally unacceptable for a boy to keep, and worse, play with dolls! The walk to the local antique shop *"We a bag full a gals things!"* to have them valued, was fraught with danger to his local reputation. The embarrassing errand was made on the quieter afternoon of half-day closing, in as much stealth and secrecy as possible.

Yes, he **did** see a few women. Plain dowdy dull women with dark head-scarves. They all look the same to Jasper!

During the long, foggy walk down from the heights of Shire Oaks, little was said and John Winter was feeling broody. He could not argue with the fact that it was now actually safer to be on foot than in a motorcar, but he was dreading his own twenty mile slow drive back to Melbourne, in such a worsening 'pea souper'. It was sometime after three and he felt that his boss, who always tended to extend the day, should at least on **this** exceptional occasion, have been more considerate and dismissed him for the day.

But no; and when they arrived on Green Lane to tackle the 'great and mighty' Hoadley, Detective Sergeant John Winter was feeling aggressive and ready to attack!

"Mr Hoadley! **Why** *did you tell us that you were at home at a quarter to five, on the afternoon of Wednesday September 7th, when in* **fact** *you were - elsewhere!*
The pristine thin lips opened to speak; but -
*"**And** before you deny it - think on! Simon Tonks vigorously rang your bell and banged on your door for a full five minutes, enough to wake the dead! Well?"*

The sharp brain of Mr Claud Hoadley worked quickly in the few seconds of this unexpected and unwelcome challenge, as he stood in his doorway, neat, trim, prim and straight as a pole. He looked from one man to the other. Even before the response came, John Winter's heart sank, as he noticed a dark look of silent fury on the face of his superior.

*"Of course I didn't **arrn**swer the door! I could **see** who it was, and I knew what he wanted. I seem to recall gentlemen, that I made my position regarding the Tonks family perfectly clear yesterday. Or have you forgotten so soon? A more tidy and disciplined mind with the aid of ..."*

"Thank you, Mr Hoadley." said Derek, *"You've given us the information we require - for now. Further questions will be put, as and when, necessary. Good afternoon."*

Groping along Green Lane, through the thickening swirls of acrid cloud, which could now be tasted, Detective Winter had to endure an even worse taste - the taste of formal reprimand -

*"Well, well, well! Who's a clever boy then! Of course you **do** realise what you've just done?"* John looked miserable and waited for the rest. *"You've given that insufferable ponce the chance to say that he really **was** at home, when in fact now, **thanks to you**, we may never get another opportunity to prove he was down on the river bashing Mrs Burgess over the **NUT!"**

John was filling with emotion and tried to dissolve into the pavement, but there was more to come -

*"**Furthermore**, we can now never know if silly Tonks is really telling the truth or not. If Hoadley is lying and wasn't there anyway, **HOW** do we know that dizzy Simon is telling the truth? Perhaps **HE** was in a boat called Mutt with a hammer!"*

He looked full in the face at his abject partner, who was, by now, clearly shaken by such a severe tongue lashing. His anger subsided, just a touch, and the next line was delivered in a slightly softer, if exasperated tone -

*"I've said this before, John, but you **must** learn it. Ask your questions, but **never** give information. Hoadley should have been asked if he - 'would like to amend his account of movements last Wednesday'; especially with an intelligent chap like that. He then wonders - 'What do they know?' Did somebody see me? Who? Where? What time? Get it?"*

The two men continued their misty walk in failing light, clomping down an eerie deserted Long Row, in a sad sullen silence.

Chapter 17

A Thickening Fog

Approaching the Triangle, the thick solemnity between the two uncomfortable colleagues and the damp foggy outer world, were as one. They found the black police station which seemed to be hiding from view. After a difficult and speechless walk, it was good to get into the warmth and light. Both men were delighted to have the unfriendly atmosphere broken by the chirpy Desk Sergeant Poulson, who was wearing a big wide smile from ear to ear.

"Urgent edict from Miss Florence Calder!"

"Really!"

*"No less! You are to report to Bridge House School - **at once!**"*

Detective Inspector Derek Russell looked at his junior, who avoided eye contact, and made up his mind to repair the damage and, at the same time, answer the call of common sense.

*"John Winter, I will **not** allow you to make that terrible journey to distant Melbourne in these dangerous conditions. You may never get there! No. We'll both stay at The Lion tonight. Make the arrangements, Poulson. Ring up the hotel first and then our homes. Forward, Watson! Let's see what the Grand Dame of Belper wants with us. Perhaps she and Miss Madge have the murderer all gagged and tied up in the old schoolroom!"*

Not quite, but progress had been made. Woeful comments were exchanged about the thickening fog disrupting normal life, and the kindly concerned Madge was especially pleased that the officers had been spared a hazardous ride home.

"We were going to offer you accommodation here ..."

*"Most gracious, and very thoughtful, but we wouldn't **dream** of imposing, would we sergeant?"*

John eagerly agreed, and felt relieved that he had narrowly escaped a twittering, fussing, flapping, overly solicitous Simon, plumping up pillows and dancing around his bed with early morning tea!

*"But you **will** stay for high tea."* said Florence firmly. *"You'll be pleased to be re-acquainted with my guest **and** we have some serious matters to discuss!"*

Inside the parlour, he walked over to shake the small cold hand of Reverend Mother Helen. Against his protestations, she struggled to her feet, a lady of deep black vestments, making a statement of sobriety and the conservative renunciation of luxury. Again, the lovely brown watery eyes seemed thrilled to look out of the neat wimple, and deep into his own. Again, he tried to identify and make sense of the odd surge of affection coming from this enigmatic woman who, on this occasion, he thought, looked tired and less well.

The dining room was a sheer delight. The late Victorian great oak table with ten chairs, stood testament to a past time of many more Calders and their guests. All was of the highest quality and elegance, in an array of silver and porcelain, much of which had found its way from the once stately and pious table of Grandfather Frederick Calder, the Headmaster of Chesterfield Grammar School for 31 years from 1846 to 1877. He was also the Rector of Wingerworth from 1878 to his death at the age of 82 in 1900.

Bridge House had the benefit of electric lighting in the early years of the century, but Mrs Sara Calder had very definite views about which rooms should, and should not, enjoy this bright new technology. She told the electrician -

"My girls are ladies of good taste and breeding! When they can no longer eat by the natural light of God, their food will be illuminated by the soft and civilised light of candles."

As a place of sleep, similar reasoning was applied to all bedrooms, and no electric wire ever passed beyond the ground floor. This gentle, 'soft and civilised', simple light of the naked flame, enhanced the magnificent, wide, generous place settings, complete with old antique silver napkin rings. In normal conditions, darkness would not have descended for another two hours, but the misty dim amber glow, struggling through the canopy of the Great Tree outside, combined with a multiplicity of candles, created a cosy, comforting and magical effect.

A third source of cheery warm dancing light was from the high backed blazing fire, carefully prepared and lit by little Simon. He conscientiously took his time, (in Miss Madge's opinion too much time) to meticulously arrange the screwed up balls of old newspaper under neat rows of kindling, on top of which was placed lumps of coal of just the correct size.

After the Reverend Mother said grace in her emollient rich voice, the wholesome and well presented food was more than welcome on such a day. The service was entertaining yet still efficient. Simon, who enjoyed his work, was getting better, and congratulatory encouraging remarks seemed to wind him up all the more. Whirling around the table, he skipped and capered with faces and poses, making sure everybody had what they needed.

The conversation took twists and turns. Miss Florence Calder became heated over a recent newspaper article written by

"...that foolish and dangerous old man Bertrand Russell!"

She had always detested his left wing radical views expressed with barbed wit at the expense of the established order, and had never forgiven him for opening the notorious experimental school in 1932 at Telegraph House, near Petersfield in Hampshire.

*"Let us all give thanks that it closed at the start of the war and hope it will **remain** closed! Permissive to the point of moral bankruptcy! If **his** children break out into an unsuspecting world to vandalise sound traditional education, **my** children will still be there to say - 'there is a better way'!*

Miss Madge, who had never quite recovered from the shock of the surprise Labour victory after the war, made disparaging comments about Mr Attlee and his alarming and threatening experiments with nationalisation. Miss Florence mentioned continuing rationing, which prompted the Reverend Mother to comment -

*"Rationing doesn't seem to have any detrimental effect on **this** bountiful table. I look forward to these occasional treats."*

*"We love to entertain you, Helen, but our humble fare hardly compares to Sister Cynthia's wonderful concoctions with her home grown herbs and spices. Last month, Madge and I staggered out with over-indulgence and practically had to **roll** all the way down Belper Lane!"*

"I was admiring your well stocked kitchen and herb garden from that lofty balcony." said Derek.

A peace settled when Simon finally left them to enjoy hot tea and home made cakes. It was now possible to speak of more immediate matters, and Derek Russell gave them a summary of the days interviews with Simon, Sally and Claud Hoadley. For the most part, this information was received without comment, but for Miss Madge who was energetically warming to the idea that Aubrey Pod was the culprit.

140

*"And **why** not, Detective Inspector? It **all** points in that direction. He **lied** about being in the cinema, has been **seen** near to the River Gardens just before he could have changed clothes and met Sarah. All this together with the well known fact that Sarah drove him to the edge of a nervous breakdown!"*

"I must say that her 'entertainments' at Mr Pod's expense, up at Fern Glade, were reprehensible." added the Reverend Mother.

"Just one small point you've overlooked, Madge, and I quote you - 'Sally is a stranger to the truth'!"

Into the gap which followed, Miss Florence Calder delivered her important news.

"I've been questioning the butler! Forgive me, Derek, for covering the same ground, but it's been a great success."

"Not at all! Please carry on, Miss Marple, we're all ears."

*"We **all** saw and heard the very significant exchange between Sarah and Mr Hoadley about model trains, but **only** the correctly discreet servant, Alex Haigh, heard the questions Sarah put to Doctor Lewis, which apparently caused **him**, 'acute distress'!"*

"Paul, upset! Good heavens, why, Florence?"

"Bear with me, Helen, I'll come back to that, but perhaps now it's time to shed light on that 'Billy Grindle' train business."

"You know something about this, Miss Calder? You ought to have told us!"

"So sorry, Derek, but for Claud Hoadley's sake, I had hoped it would not be necessary to dig up all this unpleasantness after all these years."

She looked around the table and her eyes came to rest upon Miss Madge, when she spoke with some emphasis -

*"I'm confident that with us professionals, what is about to be said now, will **remain** within these four walls? It's no secret that Sarah had stumbled upon something painful and potentially damaging to Mr Hoadley. That much, I think we all gathered. I don't think that Sarah was ever interested in blackmail. No. She had enough money and a nice life style with Oliver's wealth and prestige. Sarah Grindle was cruel and wanted power over others. We had plenty of examples of that at school!"*

"Indeed!" murmured Madge. Her sister continued -

"I'm convinced that it was this same vicious sadism which has caused her final downfall. She was a searcher of dark personal secrets, and she found one - one too many."

"Are you about to tell us that Claud Hoadley killed Sarah Burgess?" said John Winter.

*"I **can** confirm a strong motive. Oh dear! This is not easy for me. The few of us who knew about it at the time are all now dead, but for me, Mr Grindle and Mr Hoadley. We all promised never to discuss it, with anybody - ever!"*

Derek moved slightly in his chair and folded his arms.

"We now have a case of murder, Miss Florence. A killer is on the loose. That in itself should supersede any previous commitments."

"How Sarah found out about it is a great mystery, but it underlines her powers. Similar powers to that of Simon Tonks. A keen sensitivity and receptivity. Ability to hear a private conversation above a general public hubbub. Ability to lip read at a distance. Ability to interpret slight facial expressions and follow a line of thought. Ability to ..."

*"Florence! For goodness sake! What **did** Claud Hoadley DO!"* cried Madge.

Her sister became philosophical and a little puzzled.

*"Frankly, I'm still not at all sure, but 'gross indecency' as they call it, has always been seen as cardinal sin, and definitely was a greater sin still back in 1910. The 16 year old Billy Grindle was very much a 'Jack the Lad' and eager to try new adventures. To this day, I'm convinced that **he** was the instigator ..."*

She sighed, and started to fold her napkin in the flickering light.

*"Poor Claud, he was in an appalling state when the police became involved, but maintained his dignity. He was as white as a sheet, and immobilised by fear. Arthur Hoadley came to the school and begged me to intercede. It was so cold, I remember trudging through several inches of snow, but, common sense prevailed, and thank God, we **were** successful. It was hushed up to save a promising teaching career.*

That September Claud started teaching at the newly built Herbert Strutt Grammar School, which had only opened its doors the previous year. Up until his retirement last year, he had given 38 full years of first class service. An excellent teacher. He may have his minor irritations, but our little town can be proud of its accomplished scholar. Claud Hoadley has set a good example and is much respected and admired by his pupils. He'll always be remembered as one of Belper's best educators."

Four faces continued to look at the senior mistress, who was staring into a candle, seemingly mesmerised. She had no more to say.

The nun spoke into this void in a meditative, measured voice.
"A few moments of ecstasy followed by a lifetime of regret. But, Florence, you were going to tell us about the questions Sarah put to my brother?"
Miss Calder rapidly brought her mind back to her investigations of the afternoon.
"Mr Haigh heard only an oddment of conversation, which he gathered, greatly disturbed the good doctor."
"About?"
"Well, this is a conundrum. You'll have to clarify this yourself, Helen, when you and Paul next meet, but the butler is certain the thorny subject was in fact ..."
Her gaze alighted upon the man whose handsome face was half in shadow, who had been seated at the top of the table.
"...something about you Derek!"
The officer was completely still for a few moments while he tried to make sense of this statement.
"Me? Sarah didn't know me? How could she be asking about me?"
"Florence! Paul hardly knows Detective Inspector Russell. Mr Haigh must be mistaken."
"I think not, Helen, he was quite sure. Anyway, Derek, you've attended our church on a number of occasions, and Sarah would hardly miss you!"
The Reverend Mother Helen smiled.
"She's quite correct there, Inspector, I do recall her once referring to you as 'that gorgeous hunk of man'! But I'll certainly speak to Paul about her sudden interest in the C.I.D! Most curious!"
"Curiouser and Curiouser! And it gets better! I have more to tell! I was not the only unexpected visitor to Fern Glade today. Mr Burgess's butler had another visitor this morning - one, Simon Tonks!"
"That boy had no permission from me to go wandering off up Bridge Hill!" said an irritated Miss Madge, who had strict Victorian views about the working classes in private service.

143

"He'll have to be reprimanded, Florence! Just as soon as our guests have gone, I'll..."

"No, Madge. Not yet. Let me finish. Simon asked Mr Haigh if he might borrow an article, any personal item which had once belonged to the late Mrs Sarah Burgess. He suggested it could be a handkerchief, or any item of jewellery, or clothing which had been near to her person - provided it was unwashed."

*"Really, Florence! I wonder if we should hear anymore. Such brazen impudence. Disgraceful! It reflects on **us**! He'll get the sharp edge of my tongue ..."*

*"**Please,** please, Madge. This is important to the problem in hand. Do **not** interrupt! Where was I ... Oh yes. Simon explained to the American gentleman that he would be better able to assist the police if he could employ his special powers of communication with the 'dearly departed'."*

At the starkly inappropriate use of these last two words, Derek gave John, a sardonic significant half smile, a useful aid to the healing process after the recent hurt of Green Lane.

"He intended to talk to Sarah and say - 'Who was in the boat with you? Who killed you?'" Madge opened her mouth to make yet another protest, but caught a forbidding look from her stern sister and decided against it.

"Of course Alex Haigh is a sensible educated man, but decided to indulge Simon, and found him a cheap ring dating back to her days as an adolescent." Madge grunted her extreme disapproval.

"Well there it is!" said Detective Inspector Derek Russell.
*"**All** we have to do is to summon the seer into this room and the case will be solved!"*

*"That, Derek, is **precisely** what I intend to do right now!"*

A collective gasp came from the assembled two women and two men. This extraordinary statement was entirely contrary to the previous strictures of the mistress of Bridge House School. The Reverend Mother Helen, made her own point in a measured and gentle fashion, before the pious and now boiling, spluttering Madge, was about to get herself into yet more trouble.

*"Florence, I'm perplexed? You've always objected to **any** dabbling with the occult?"*

"Yes, Helen, quite so, but on this particular occasion, I have my reasons, as you'll soon discover."

Detective Sergeant John Winter caught the eye of his boss and was emboldened to add -

"I think we'd be entertained, Miss Calder!"

"Yes, we're looking forward to it. It could be instructive." added Detective Inspector Derek Russell, wincing under the hard hateful grimace of Miss Madge Calder. But the sister was also looking deeply unhappy and disturbed. She abandoned the tone used for her close friend and equal, and substituted a slightly more authoritative strident note, which could have been used on a postulant.

*"Is this wise, Florence? I must ask you to consider **my** position before you start this un-holy charade. Please try to be fair!"*

The concerned headmistress reached over and warmly took her friend's hand inside both her own.

*"My dearest Helen! **Please** trust me. This is **not** for the purpose of a cheap show. A life has been brutally taken, and I am just beginning to see a way through the fog of this dark mystery. In some respects, Simon is a simple child, and this is the only way he can make his contribution. Trust me!"*

She went over to pull the bell.

145

Chapter 18

Contact with the Dead

Simon bounced into the room, still buoyed up with the recent kind comments about the high standard of the Calder household and, of course, excited by the presence of interesting guests. He quickly stopped bouncing and was stunned when Miss Florence Calder reproved him for leaving his post without permission earlier that day, but was thrilled when his specialist help was sought.

*"These are exceptional circumstances, Simon. Only this **one** time will I countenance this type of activity, but we **must** know the identity of Sarah's slayer. So if you will kindly get the ring ..."*

He was off like a shot. Being comfortable in the cosy, warm candle and fire lit room, the small assembly decided that Sarah's spirit would probably find the dining room more welcoming than that of the parlour. The inevitable jokes began.

"I hope Sarah can find her way through this terrible fog!"

"In fairness, I think we should show Simon some respect, Detective Sergeant."

"Sorry, Miss Calder."

When he slowly entered, Simon's mood was serious, serene and ethereal. Ceremonially, he held the sacred ring up high for all to see, put it on his finger, and sedately sat down before the small gathering.

Inside he was tingling. This was his big moment, the climax to leaving Cowhill, from when the quality of his existence had steadily continued to improve. Working at Bridge House School had given new meaning to his life. Contentment and fulfilment were unknown and relatively new sensations. In less than two weeks, happiness had crept up on him unawares. He had come to love these two old ladies who genuinely cared and tried to protect him.

The spiritual young man closed his eyes and began to breath deeply. Faint moans followed. The facial expressions watching this performance were different. The two men showed a trace of amusement. Madge Calder, originally the most hostile opponent to this experiment, was now holding her breath in a mixture of fascination and macabre horror. The Reverend Mother Helen's handsome features showed a degree of bored resignation and disapproval. The mistress of the house simply looked on with interest.

Eventually Simon smiled and spoke in his usual small falsetto range -
"'Allo Sarah!"
John Winter was unable to suppress an involuntary guffaw, and suffered
a sharp shush from a serious Miss Madge.
"'Allo Simon!" was the response in the soprano register. This
time Derek had to take firm control of a tendency to titter.
"Where are ya Sarah?"
*"Ooo it's grand 'ere Simon! A s<u>oo</u>ny spring day we bluebells,
blossom, n l<u>oo</u>vly coolin' breezes."*
John just could not resist, he leaned over and whispered into Derek's
ear,
"I'd have thought it might be a bit warmer where she was!"
The other smiled, but nudged him to keep quiet. Miss Florence Calder
permitted herself an amusing thought, to the effect that there seemed to
be a steep decline in the quality of Sarah's accent, since death had
parted her from the refining and improving influence of Mr Claud
Hoadley.
"Oow did ya in Sarah?"
*"Ooo Simon, yav made it dark!! The's a moon nar, an this lad,
is got a nice face, b<u>oo</u>t is soft n pl<u>oo</u>mp, oow is fat, flowin' we it! A'll gi
'im a c<u>oo</u>dle."*
Derek was now getting a touch bored and tempted to ask how
much longer they would have to listen to this nonsense.
*"Ooo Simon, a kissed 'im an 'e terned inta a gret black crow!
'Is gone, an it's rainin' nar, ch<u>oo</u>kin' it down n windy. It's 'orrible, a
grotty owd 'ouse - n this baby ... arr it's a l<u>oo</u>vly little thing, n 'is mam!
She int movin', Simon! Oh God - she's... she's **DEAD!***

*Doctor's runnin' we it int' dark an rain, tekin it t' church. Nice
warm church we candles. It's all right, Simon, it's all right nar, they'll
look after it. In't that nice!"*

Slight moans and more heavy breathing. Simon opened his eyes to see
much the same expressions, with a single exception; Detective
Inspector Derek Russell was looking grim - definitely **not** amused. Into
this strained silence, the hostess said -
*"Thank you, Simon, you may clear the table now and then serve
us fresh coffee in the parlour."*

147

He scuttled away, and the silent quintet filed into the next room. Nobody wanted to make the first comment, since **any** remark would seem ridiculously incongruous if it was not about the preceding scene.

John Winter was completely bewildered by the sudden sulk which had descended upon his superior. At the start of the seance, he had been just as mischievous as himself. They were two naughty lads larking about. Eventually Derek looked up and met the eyes of his one time school teacher. Florence saw hurt and anger in those eyes and read his thoughts.

"It's no use challenging him 'head on', Derek. He'll only claim that he can't remember anything!"

"A night in the police cell might just refresh his memory!"

*"No, Derek! Leave it to me. **Please!**"*

The voice of a mystified Miss Madge was a welcome intrusion into this thickening atmosphere.

*"Well! We're **still** in a fog. Inside as well as out. Sarah avoided the main question and left abruptly. Perhaps another item could be acquired from the butler, something more personal like ..."*

The Reverend Mother Helen began to smile, but her elder sister was both embarrassed and exasperated -

*"For goodness sake, Madge. Listen to yourself! Use your common sense. Do you **seriously** think that Simon Tonks climbed that misty hill this morning in genuine need of Sarah's personal effects?"*

A miffed Madge sharply retorted -

*"Well! If you're so very clever, what on earth **did** he trudge up there for?"*

*"For an **excuse**, little sister! Simon **needed** an excuse to be in a position to reveal the information he has managed to acquire!"*

The Reverend Mother Helen let out a deep and long sigh.

Lets face it, Madge, Sarah had very little to say to Simon Tonks in life. She seemed unusually chatty in death!"

She brusquely straightened herself up in her chair and turned to her best friend.

"Well, Florence! Shall we analyse the mystic magic, and interpret his ethereal dream? Shall we play his game?"

Her hard sardonic tone still held a touch of the original anger. Miss Madge was lost in a labyrinth of confusion -

"What game? Are you all telling me that this is all a load of rubbish."

"NOT rubbish, Madge, data, as Mr Holmes would say. For example ..."

Miss Calder was halted by the unwelcome entrance of Simon with the coffee. She kept the intrusion to an absolute minimum.

"Thank you, Simon, I will pour. That will be all."

As the door closed, Helen was about to speak - but was firmly prevented by the raising of a silent, authoritative, forbidding, wrinkled hand. Miss Florence Calder quietly went to the door and gingerly opened it just a crack for inspection. The hall was dark and empty. Softly she closed the door and returned to her seat to speak.

*"That is one of the simple methods employed by Simon and Sarah to gain information. They can produce the same astounding effect of the professional magician in the public theatre. It is amazing, **until** you learn the secret."*

*"**That boy** will get the back of my hand if **I** ever catch him listening at doors!"*

"I very much doubt he has ever done that in this house, Madge. It was just a possibility. We're dealing with deeply private sensitive issues here, and I had to be sure. Helen. You were about to say?"

"Well, the 'soft plump' boy sounds like the young Oliver Burgess." She turned to the men and explained that many years back, she and Oliver were friends as teenagers, before she was called by God.

"Yet he turned into a crow?" said the Inspector. *"Would that be some cryptic reference to old Jasper, who lives under that noisy rookery?"*

Helen gave Derek a warm smile.

*"No, Inspector, I think the evil raven was supposed to be **me**! Even sisters can be guilty of eavesdropping. In the days before our friendship developed, I once overheard Sarah referring to our community as a 'miserable bunch o' dirty black crows'."*

Detective Inspector Derek Russell took an interest in this revealing interpretation.

"So Simon clearly had knowledge of your association with Mr Burgess."

"Not a big secret, Inspector. Belper's a small town and memories go back a long way." The nun continued gently with tact and sensitivity -

149

"Simon is 23 years of age, and has never been out of our little town. In all that time he will have heard several versions of your dramatic birth. It's clearly upset you, and I'm very sorry - truly sorry!" Again the watery eyes, and a catch in the voice as if she might break down. Miss Florence Calder jumped in to help.

*"She's quite right, Derek. And, God help me, I bitterly regret the personal embarrassment resulting from this messy melodrama, but believe me, Derek, I **know** this child, and it is the **only** effective way to get out of him **all** he knows. Make no mistake, he will have put his **all** into it."* Derek lightened a little under this incisive, persuasive wisdom.

"Perhaps you're right, Miss Calder, but I think I'd have preferred the 'Nelly Pod Show'! I'd still like to ask him a few questions myself."

*"And you would get **nowhere**, Derek! Little, teasing, silly Simon has cobbled together fragments of intelligence to keep us guessing and on the hop. That's what he likes to do. That is what he is good at. There is no rhyme nor reason to his ridiculous performance. **Do not** look for great, or profound truth - it simply is **not** there! What we **must** do, is to study and try to make sense of the individual **facts** he has gleaned."* She turned to her nonplussed sister -

"Do you recall Simon's garbled dream? The one Mr Pod was all excited about when he came to see us the other day"

"I do indeed - most odd!" Miss Florence gave her guests a short account of the train accident involving a young Claud Hoadley and a young Billy Grindle, who was strangely transformed into his own future daughter.

*"**Quite** easily explained - after I had spoken to Sally. In their tiny house up Cowhill, there can be few really private conversations, as was the case after the Saturday dinner party. Olive Tonks waited up late for her daughter and insisted on a detailed account of the whole evening. Simon had been sent to bed upstairs, but was only a few feet away, **listening**, and **remembering** every detail, which, no doubt, would have included Sally's own lascivious interpretation of Sarah's cruel story. Hence the inspiration for Simon's creative allegorical dream based on his hazy notion of what actually happened. The whole thing was **intended** to puzzle and intrigue us."*

150

"Not to mention that it was yet another opportunity for Simon to reinforce his reputation of being the mystical oracle of Belper!" added the Reverend Mother Helen.

"Exactly."

*"Well, Florence, this **has** been an interesting and instructive evening, but I really must begin to think about groping my way through the ever thickening soup to see if I can locate a certain convent up Belper Lane!"*

With this she rose, and in true old fashioned style, so did the gentlemen at almost the same instant. Madge gave the bell a tug and in seconds the 'oracle of Belper' was fussing and twittering at the door, eager for instructions. As the six moved down the hall to the large Georgian front entrance, a social cheerfulness broke out in many voices, consisting of enthusiastic thanks, complimentary, appreciative comments about the pleasant company, good food, and welcome warm comfort on such a murky cold evening.

The Reverend Mother Helen was very grateful for the kind thought, but firmly refused an official police escort up the hill. At the doorstep, Derek was once again conscious of her firm hand grip and penetrating dark sad eyes. The little group gave a final wave and watched as her black form disappeared and became one with the thick dark fog.

*"Well 'good night' indeed, Miss Marple! The end of a fascinating evening. You've shed some light, but at the same time managed to **deepen** our mystery somewhat."*

Detective Inspector Derek Russell would have probably said more, had he not noticed Simon's little wide eyed, innocent face, looking up and taking **everything** in! Miss Florence Calder, also aware of curious ears, looked perplexed and simply murmured something about -

"Yes, Derek, I'll have a lot of thinking to do - so many loose ends..."

Both men made a big parting fuss of little Miss Madge. Detective Sergeant Winter generously put aside his minor brood, which had resulted from her frosty welcome, and ungracious criticism of the early morning. Miss Margaret Campbell Calder was clearly a victim of her poor health, unsightly aspect and narrow lifestyle. Under the stimulant of pleasant companionship, John had now seen a more appealing side of her nature. Not being used to good looking, mature members of the opposite sex, the small bent old spinster had blossomed a little this evening, and was now enthusiastically soaking up the pleasantries and courtesies being delivered by the two fawning gentlemen, who were smiling and leaning over her.

"Thanks again for a smashing evening, Miss Madge." said Winter.

"Not at all, we've enjoyed your company, but I'm afraid the evening's been rather more full of incident than we're normally accustomed to!"

"Well, keep your doors shut tight, locked and bolted!"

*"Yes, indeed. No entertaining any sinister strangers tonight, Miss Madge! We don't want to find **you** murdered in the morning, do we!"* added Derek with parting jocularity.

The two old sisters looked rather sad and vulnerable, as they stood in the doorway and watched their last guests walk away, eventually blending into the silent mist. Just before their footsteps had completely faded, Miss Florence Calder caught the end fragment of a response from one officer to the other -

"Just so. He's got a lot of explaining to do in the morning, has our Mr Toad!"

Chapter 19

The Thoughts of Florence

The great house of 15 rooms seemed to be empty and even larger when the two old ladies wearily closed the heavy, thick door. They were cheered to be reminded of the presence of their chirpy little servant who, politely and carefully moulding his mouth, said -

"Will there be anything more ladies?"

He had been receiving the benefit of speech correction for the last nine days. Originally he would have said -

"Is thee oat else ya'll be wantin'?"

Miss Madge simply reminded him that she expected the kitchen to be left in pristine condition ready for the functions of the following day. Simon was pleased to report that this was in fact already the case.

It was not late, a little after nine, but the Calder house usually retired early in preparation for an early start the next day. After the evening meal, when darkness had descended, it was customary to read improving books for an hour or so, by the yellowy light of a small electric light bulb. No electronic distractions in **this** house! Miss Florence Calder gathered that one of her recent pupils had the dubious benefit of access to a new electric television set. In the whole of Belper, there would be very few indeed, since they cost over a hundred guineas, or the total income from two academic terms at Bridge House School. In the opinion of the technophobic schoolmistress, such a large sum would better be spent on a sound collection of educative books -

"Then we would hear less nonsense about the inane adventures of 'Muffin the Mule'!"

Many homes were equipped with an electric wireless set, which Miss Madge once observed,

"...were turned on too often and much too loud!"

She was fond of quoting Sir Thomas Beecham who said back in 1927 -

"The wireless has become the paradise of the lowbrow and the bonehead!"

Simon's silly songs had confirmed her still further into this opinion.

Each night Simon's last order was to close doors, secure the house, and produce three lit candles. One for himself and one each for the two sisters who retired to the bedrooms on the first floor, which they had occupied for the last 47 years. They ascended the first wide flight of creaking stairs with the feeble, flickering flames, casting distorted ghastly shadows of the three odd characters, moving menacingly across the dark, ancient wallpaper. Simon made quite a performance of his nightly -

"Good night, Miss Madge. Good night, Miss Florence."

This was said in a voice slightly louder than necessary, irking the junior sister. The senior sister however, knew that it was in fact an attempt to keep at bay any ghosts which may be lurking in the quiet, dark corners, of Simon's solitary ascent to his large, lonely rooms on the second floor.

"Fear which was quite unnecessary!" thought Florence, with a twinkle of amusement, *"since Simon claims to be on familiar friendly terms with the 'other side'!"*

But now to serious, deeper matters as she closed the door and prepared for bed. After the usual short prayer, she supported her straight, athletic fit frame against a bolster together with two pillows, and stared directly ahead through the large window into the dense fog beyond. Somehow it was a comfort to be sitting in a warm, comfortable, clean bed contemplating the cold damp atmosphere outside. She breathed in deeply, slowly exhaled, and sat up straighter and even higher in the massive Victorian cast iron bed. A foreboding -

"Oh dear!" she thought. *"Not much sleep tonight I fear!"* Looking to her left, at least the candle was nearly new and had several hours of life to live. Too many thoughts and too much excitement. Such a bewilderment, so much to ponder. She knew Derek was in trouble. With the sole exception of Mr Blount, local newspaper appeals had produced no result at all. After a week the trail was beginning to go cold.

"Very little evidence. Indeed **no** *real evidence, and the child is depending on me!"*
She sighed again, stared into the candle flame and then idly contemplated a crucifix on the wall. *"I wonder who it was?"*

This, whispered into the dark, set off a series of selective considerations. She thought about Sarah, and mulled over the sinful thoughts she had shared with other Beaurepairians, to the effect that no great effort should be made to catch the killer.

"But it **was** *a sin to take a life! The murderer* **must** *be discovered and brought to justice. Is* **that** *why we are no further?*

Perhaps there were many clues. People did see Madam X, but were not prepared to come forward! Is that how it is? A murderer can murder again! They say it's easier the second time!"

Sarah. She **must** be the key to it all. The stupid child, poking around, uncovering dangerous information. What **was** she asking Dr Lewis? Why were the questions disturbing?

"A busy day tomorrow. The first thing I'll do is to go next door and find out."

The questions had concerned Derek. What did she want to know about Derek? Dear Derek! Such a kind boy. At Bridge House School a model pupil. Always thinking of others, never a thought for himself. She was so pleased he had done well in life. She shuddered to think of his real parents, and the life he would have had in that appalling slum called 'China'. The rough and rude folk of 'China'. No worse than the rough and rude folk of The Gutter!

She brought up the surly, unpleasant image of Billy Grindle, the blackened coal miner of few words who despised his acid tongued daughter. Not what you would call a tall man.

"Gross indecency!" Would he be prepared to permanently silence his daughter to protect his prized macho reputation?

Claud Hoadley. A principal Beaurepairian of good reputation and high esteem. A position the Lady of Fern Glade had obliquely threatened to destroy. Would **he** kill to protect that position? Hoadley regarded Sarah from 'The Gutter', as dirt under his feet. Would he be able to rationalise this extreme departure from accepted Christian conduct. Would he be capable of taking the life of Sarah Grindle? Was he **really** out of the house on Green Lane at about the time of the murder? Or... Or was Simon telling lies?

Simple Simon, or clever Simon? An attempt to make Mr Hoadley look guilty? Did Simon Tonks, the butt of Sally and Sarah's jokes all his life, nurse a long, deep hatred for the latter? The people of Belper saw him as a fool. Did he intend to 'show them', have 'the last longest laugh'?

At this point she permitted herself to laugh.

"The thoughts of Florence!" All these possibilities should be seated in her parlour downstairs. In turn, each one being scolded for

155

their suspicious conduct, subjected to her scrutiny and accusations, getting indignant, making hot denials! Derek would love it!

"And finally, at the end I point dramatically at .....?"

But who? This is real life. Is this not a case of the most **obvious** person? Rather than the least likely, as in books, in fact, the **most** likely?

In fact - **Oliver Burgess!**

The one person who was desperate to remove his evil wife. The only person in this drama who stood to make a long term practical gain by getting rid of the woman who was crucifying him. What did those eyes seem to be saying -

"Please help me! It's been a disaster!
She's destroying me... I can't go on."

He misled the police as to his whereabouts at the approximate time of the crime. He thought they would not, and could not possibly check his alibi with the American salesman, now thousands of miles away! He **could** have slipped quietly through the gate of Fern Glade garden. The butler **claimed** to be sleeping. Could he have been - assisting and supporting? Oliver Burgess is a rich man!!

"Well this won't do!" she said aloud. She looked again at the candle, now lower and regretted the waste.

"I can think just as well in the dark - much cheaper!" and blew it out. Even in the great black darkness some faint light emanated from the mass of thick fog hanging over Belper.

She adjusted her pillows, slid down into the bed and tried to get to sleep. Out of the great silence - a sound! What was it? There it is again! Now more familiar? She relaxed. Just the owl somewhere deep in the tangle of the old Plane Tree.

She tossed and turned and turned and tossed and turned.

She tried to think of something soothing which would gently carry her into the arms of Morpheus. A trick which had worked before was human flight. She was drifting over her beloved green valley, looking down on the meadows. She was becoming more and more drowsy. There was the pontoon bridge and, floating south and east over Wildersley Farm, a place of happy childhood memories. Sleep would come very soon... She looked north to see Cowhill and a row of neat little cottages .....

Olive Tonks! Olive Tonks had volubly and violently threatened Sarah in her own school, within her own hearing! The enraged and furious harridan would protect her Simon from public scandal at .... at **all** costs? She had **no** satisfactory alibi, and the described mystery woman was **exactly** the way Olive dressed every day of the year. Exactly like ... any ordinary working class woman in Belper.

Tatiana Lawrence did not consider herself to be a commonly spoken working class woman. Did she get off that bus to keep an engagement with Sarah Burgess - bold, brave and very simple? No one saw her. It may not have worked - but it did! She too would be protecting her young. Her young? Why did that strike a chord? A sudden old memory of a half forgotten dream came into her mind.
In this very room, a baby crying. It happened several nights ... but this was many years ago, when she was much younger. It must have been a dream. There has never been a baby in this house. A baby! Why had Simon woven a child into his vision?

"I've a good mind to march up there this very minute and have it out with him now!!"
No. She was being silly. She was over tired.

A baby. Of course Robin! Robin Kirkland may have been responsible for an unborn baby. Under the strict moral influence of the unyielding hard faced Claud Hoadley, was Robin unable to face the shame in this small community, let alone to face Mr Hoadley? Was that apparently gentle young man capable of using all his strength to crash a heavy object into the skull of a young girl who was carrying his child? He was besotted by her beauty. He was ensnared by his infatuation. Did the teasing eventually get too much for him?

Protecting the young. In Simon's trance Dr Lewis was protecting the young Derek. Did Charlie Kirkland, a kind and caring father, protect his son from the public humiliation of an unwanted pregnancy and continual taunting from a sadistic bitch? Did Charlie Kirkland extinguish the life of Sarah Burgess on Wednesday September 7th? Both men lied for each other to keep them well away from the time and scene of the crime.

How odd, that she had completely forgotten that dream of a crying baby coming out of the dark silent night - until now. A faint memory of her mother explaining in a condescending manner -

"Don't be silly, Florence! A young owl in the big tree can sound rather like a wailing child. You should have said prayers for our brave young men, who are making great sacrifices and fighting the Hun for us, and then gone back to sleep. I want to hear no more of it!"

Of course! She always hated the way her mother spoke down and patronised her. This was during the Great War, and she was no child herself. She was nearly 40! She knew the difference between a baby and a baby owl!

She sank back further into her pillow, and started to breath deeply, eyes wide open into the darkness, trying to make out the familiar cracks and ceiling decoration. Should she attempt another 'float' over Belper? No point. She would only notice Becksitch Lane below, and be reminded of Nelly Pod! A great pity **she** was no longer with us, **SHE** would be an excellent suspect. She would certainly kill for the protection of her young, even if she often came close to killing her young! What a joy to see her arrested, screaming at the police and later hauled before the court. Florence mischievously allowed herself the continuing fantasy of Nelly Pod, struggling, and being dragged down into the cells after giving the judge a mouthful of abuse!

But what **was** Aubrey doing down by the bridge? He had asked a nun the approximate time when Sarah would come down from the convent. It followed that he wanted to see her, and later, was waiting for her? Why? To commit murder? She should have asked Sally if Mr Pod had a bag with him, but no bag was mentioned. The gentleman's urinal was nearby where he could have transformed himself into.... a washerwoman? Like Mr Toad?

But Sally is a liar, who, like many others, loathed Aubrey Pod. An opportunity to get him into trouble with the police? A chance to divert their attention from those expensive dresses from 'Jeanettes' in Friargate? Did Sally steal Sarah's money? Did it become necessary for Sarah to be silenced - forever! Did jealousy take a murderous turn? Two socially equal friends - 'both alike in dignity' - at the start. One marries well, and moves from The Gutter, up to Bridge Hill to live in luxury, leaving the other on Cowhill living in poverty. Did Sally sit in her mother's primitive cottage brooding about the good fortune of her best and life-long friend?

At least Jasper is now well out of it.
She closed her eyes for a few minutes - then opened them very wide, sat up and spoke out loud to the foggy window and blackness of the great tree beyond -

"A really clever criminal can eliminate himself from enquiries by using a decoy. Did Derek actually check that those dolls were properly valued, where and what time? I doubt it! Unlike Aubrey Pod, people were disposed to like, believe and trust Jasper Wormall. Who in Belper would be competent to give such a valuation on an antique toy? Surely one would need to go to Nottingham! Who in Belper has actually suffered more extreme humiliation and hurt from the deceased, consistently, over a long period of years, more than that wronged little man up Shire Oaks?"

The dinner party stories may have been the last straw.
But she was very tired now and closed her eyes once again. The owl hooted once or twice, and finally - she drifted into a troubled sleep.

She heard something! But was not sure? Simon coming in with the early morning tea? No - it was still dark. She struggled over to see the time on the antique silver carriage clock at her bedside, once the property of her paternal grandmother, Selina Calder. No use. She fumbled for the box of matches and, with difficulty, just managed to light the candle. She groaned, it was a little before three!
Once again pillows were adjusted for the upright active position, but this time she slid out of bed, took up the candle, and with determination marched over to the heavy bookcase. This was only a fraction of the vast Calder library which was spread around the house, but even here, she had a choice from hundreds of titles, many in quality bindings. When visitors had complimented the erudite collection, she was fond of responding with -

*"You see before you, all the money I did **not** spend on unwise and idle pursuits! Such as smoking, drinking, wasting valuable time dawdling around shops, buying items I did not need. Compulsive and un-selective visits to the cinema, and worse, **much** worse - visits to the garish, cheap, loud, nasty fairground!"*

159

As bedtime reading, they were in no special order at all. She casually picked up and returned copy after copy. Ibsen, Sheridan, Euripides -
"Totally unsuitable! Much lighter matter is needed now.
Perhaps this is good time to be entertained by Miss Marple!"
But there were no Agatha Christie's to be seen. One old looking slender volume caught her eye. Gingerly she moved it close to the candle, and experienced a rush of nostalgic pleasure. It was a quintessential Victorian children's book called - "The Changeling".

The cover was an exquisite print, a delightful fantasy of fairies, looking at a baby, happily reclining on a mat of soft moss in a woodland glade. Beautifully painted with details of foxgloves, bluebells, celandines and wood anemone. Elves and pixies smiled from a perch on toadstools and other strange shaped, colourful fungi. Rabbits, squirrels and wood mice looked on. Songthrushes, robins, little wrens, butterflies and bees hovered over an unlikely tangle of ivy, bramble, bracken and hawthorn - all pleased to welcome the newcomer.

As a little girl, she loved to wander through the fields, meadows and woodlands around Belper, in the hope of discovering that very same enchanted, magical scene. It all came back; the dank scent of wild garlic and bluebells; the feel of the warm sunshine; the sound of poplar leaves gently clattering in the breeze; the sweet song of the blackbirds; the excitement of getting lost; the safe return home; the care and companionship of her big protective sisters, little Madge crawling across the lawn .... dear little Madge.

Florence looked at the child and smiled. An observer would have noticed many years falling away from her face at that moment. She noticed the delicate detail of the wood anemone, and recalled that she first knew it as 'granny's night-cap'. Having seen her own grandmother wearing her night-cap several times, she could not quite see the similarity? At that very moment she was wearing one herself! **She** was now as old as her own grandmother! Extraordinary! Suddenly she felt sad.
"But no grandchildren for me. Only my small pupils.
And ... yes, I still have dear Madge."

The book and the candle were taken back to bed. She looked at the inside front cover -
"To my dear little Florence on her seventh birthday.

We all hope you will come again soon to visit us at Makeney House.

With love,
Agnes Anne Strutt. 1883.

Once again she read this charming little story about a baby and these tiny supernatural beings, which she had so enjoyed in childhood, savouring each word until a pleasant drowsiness came upon her. She drooped, and eventually she slept.

But the brain never really sleeps - and it did not! It continued to search for the truth - a truth she would not welcome - a truth she did not want. Less than an hour later her eyes opened wide yet again - full of alarm! The candle was burned down. The candle was out. The book was on the floor, but the solution was there on the front cover of the book! It was still dark and foggy outside. But fog inside the mind of Miss Florence Calder had cleared. The threads had come together at long last.

Florence now knew who had murdered Sarah Burgess.

Chapter 20

A Scream in the Night

What to do? What to do first? So **much** to do! People would have to be seen - soon. The truth was at hand, but clarification and confirmation would be useful. Another murder **was** a possibility, therefore she must warn and advise. In a crisis Miss Florence Calder was competent and efficient. This was a crisis of the first order. The candle? Fortunately a small supply was available in the bottom drawer. Once again she groped and struggled in darkness to locate a new candle and the matches. Eventually there was light, and the clock indicated half past the dismal hour of four. She looked up to the ceiling and was mindful of the man just above her head. A great deep despair came over her as she darkly contemplated the painful duty ahead. There was no other way - it **had** to be done. The commandment had been broken, a life had been taken. There could be no justification, regardless of the intense provocation.

It could not wait. She must act. She must act **now!**

She got out of bed, picked up the candle, then the book, taking a last thoughtful look at the cover, and shook her head sadly before replacing it carefully on to the bookshelf.

Stealthily she moved down the dark passageway, past the large bedroom of the sleeping Madge Calder, past the empty, one time bedroom of her mother Sara Calder, and the further three bedrooms once occupied by her dead sisters - Lucy Hamilton, Jane Appleyard, known as 'Trotty', and Mary Agnes who was always known as 'Polly'.

Presently she came to the more narrow stairway which ascended to the rooms on the second floor. The silence and stillness of this landing was all the more profound on this very quiet black night as she crept up to the door of her sleeping servant.

But not deeply sleeping. Simon had been very excited by his own dramatic performance of the previous evening, and the slight creak of the old door brought his level of slumber near to the point of consciousness. It was a deep voice with an other-worldly, slight echo into the cavernous, black, drab room which caused his bleary eyes to open -

"Simon! Wake up, Simon!"

What Simon actually saw approaching was an appalling horror! The deep wrinkles were accentuated by the single source of eerie light from the flickering candle, held just below the chin. It gave this particular ancient, pale countenance, not helped by precious little sleep, an especially ghastly appearance! The flowing white robes, surmounted by a repellent grizzled head under a night-cap from a past century, all combined to give a picture of Simon's worst nightmare!

In dread, and extreme alarm at this ever nearing abomination, he sat bolt upright and let out a long panic stricken scream, filling the great silent mansion.

"Silence, Simon! You stupid boy! You'll wake Madge!"

Relief followed his initial impression, but an even more monstrous thought quickly took shape in the next few seconds. His mind searched and made an effort to rationalise this unexpected and inexplicable, nocturnal visit from an old spinster. Had she gone mad? Simon's murky and salacious mind grasped for, and reached, the only possible explanation he was able to fathom.

In the late autumn of her life, had this wizened virgin come to the conclusion that it was - 'now or never'? Had she panicked? In the dead of a sleepless night, was she contemplating the little time left before the long, permanent sleep? Simon was well aware that he was the nearest thing in that house to being - a man! Had she come to taste, the, heretofore - un-tasted? And here she was - now, at this very moment - wanting!!

"Oh! No, Miss Calder!! Not part o' me job! A coodn't! A shoodn't! A WON'T!!!"
"What are you blathering about, Simon? Foolish child!"

She was beginning to doubt the wisdom of this urgent errand, but swiftly returned her mind to the present crisis, and sat down on the foot of his bed; an action which caused further alarm, and the impulsive reaction of Simon sitting up several inches yet higher. Seriously she looked full into his funny little, if at the moment, worried face -

"You should be well aware that to wake you in this way, in the middle of the night, constitutes nothing less than an emergency!"

163

"Fire?"

*"No, Simon! No, a different kind of peril which I felt couldn't wait until the morning. This rude awakening will concentrate your mind. Now listen carefully to what I have to say, and you **must** promise me that you will not tell anyone else, not even Miss Madge."*

The small bemused head gave a slight nod.

*"Simon, you are in **great** danger! You have demonstrated that you have precarious knowledge."*

She looked into his seeming innocent, young, wide eyes, head slightly cocked onto one side.

"How you have obtained this information is not important at the moment..."

His head now cocked on to the other side, and the enigmatic half smile, if anything, proclaimed a greater innocence. Her expression became keen and penetrating -

*"To what extent you actually understand, and have been able to make sense of your data is - uncertain. For your own safety, I have **no** intention whatsoever of enlightening you, but; here are my instructions which must be followed - to the letter."*

"Wot!"

*"Do exactly as I say Simon, or you'll soon be having frequent and even longer conversations with Sarah Burgess! In this house you'll be safe. Do **not** leave it until further notice. Ignore any invitations to 'sit' or 'read'. If the police need to interview you, they can do so here in my study. Messages given at the door may not be what they seem. Don't go into the streets. Your mother can do the shopping, she'll appreciate the extra hours. Don't even go to Cowhill. Don't go anywhere away from this house which is now your home. Is that perfectly clear, Simon?"*

"Yes, Miss Calder!" came the sibilant camp reply, at least an octave higher than the previous voice of warning, which continued in a worried tone, as much to herself as to the listener -

*"There is not one iota of evidence, not even circumstantial evidence. This crime has been carefully planned, well executed and predicated on the fact that things are not what they seem. It has to do with forbidden knowledge and flattery. **You**, Simon, are susceptible to flattery - beware!"*

Simon's borrowed little bed-side clock showed the hour was not far off five. It was set to alarm at seven when he would have just 30 minutes to leap out of bed, make the kitchen fire, boil the kettle for two pots of tea and serve them on nicely prepared antique silver trays, complete with flowers, separately to the Misses Calder at 7.30 prompt. They expected breakfast to be served in the dining room at 8.00, not a minute later.

Under pressure of the current emergency, Miss Florence Calder outlined a new schedule just for this morning. She reached over and reset the clock to ring at 5.30. Simon was to serve her hot tea at 6.00 sharp and breakfast at 6.30 so she would be able to call on Doctor Lewis next door at 7.00. The times for her sister would remain unchanged.

She abruptly stood up, gave the child before her a last look and a momentary thought regarding his earlier curious conduct. Perhaps an inkling of understanding had been achieved, when with a twinkle in the eye, she delivered her parting remark -

"Well, a very early 'good morning' to you, Simon. It can hardly be 'good night'! I'll leave you with your insane, or at least misguided delusions - whatever they may be!"

She was gone. He stared at the door for a moment. He was easily muddled and struggled to sort out his new instructions -

"Nar wot is it? Tea fa Miss Florence at ... six, tea fa Miss Madge at ...'arf past seven. Err... breakfast fa Miss Florence at ... arf past six .. a think? Err....."

He gave up, put his head down on the pillow and closed his eyes - just for a moment. Niggling thoughts and confused figures caused him to suddenly sit up, look at the clock, and realise that there was little point in attempting to sleep at all!

It was a simple fact that the awakening bell would ring in less than 30 minutes!

165

Chapter 21

Urgent Visit to the Doctor

Extraordinary! Yet Florence was thinking that it must be more than 20 years since she had last set foot in the house of her neighbour, whose front door was only a few yards away from her own. Even more extraordinary when you considered that she had reached the age of 73, and never once consulted him professionally! Unlike her less fortunate sisters, Miss Florence Calder was a strong healthy self sufficient woman. All minor ills, she had treated herself, and her own steely determination and sound common sense spanning two centuries had made sure there were very few of these!

Visibility was better on the morning of Wednesday, September 14th, one week after the murder of Sarah Burgess. She went to the front school gate and could just about discern a few minutes past seven on the mill clock, but it was still foggy by any standard. The colour had returned to a more healthy grey-blue and the air was pleasantly tinged with the scent of fern and fallen leaves. The persistent thick fog had stopped the world. All was peace and stillness. All was quiet, so quiet that she could hear the distant tinkle of the east wing bell in response to her tug. The minuscule maid appeared without delay, startled by the sight of the formidable mistress she had never actually seen before on the doctor's doorstep. At the unexpected daunting grandeur of this event she felt grateful to be in full and correct uniform, not always the case at that early hour, and gave a deep and low respectful curtsy.

"Good morning, Ursula. Don't be alarmed, but I have urgent need to speak to Dr Lewis."

After a quick bob, she invited Miss Calder into the front parlour and speedily ascended to inform her master, who in fact was only just opening his eyes wondering if he had really heard the bell - or was it a dream? A dream would have been much better. The news of this particular visitor at this hour was unwelcome. Not once did he consider that she, or any other may be ill. It brought back the same threatening, nagging, dull fear he had experienced during the days following the dinner party of September 3rd. What did she know? What **could** she know?

"Must brave it out!" were his thoughts as he groped around to find clothing.

Five minutes later they were face to face.

"Good Heavens, Miss Calder!" he said cheerily with a winning smile to neatly balance a presentation of pleasant surprise and professional concern. *"As it is common knowledge that you're indestructible, that only leaves Miss Madge or little Simon - probably the latter."*

"We're all very well, thank you, Paul...." She looked round at a seat.

"Oh! Sorry, please do ..." They both sat down. Just for a moment, one small moment, their eyes met in a grim understanding.

"I'm the one who should be apologising, the hour is early, but I have a great deal to attend to before the children arrive at nine. It's about this wretched business of the murder, which of course is exercising all our minds ..."

"Certainly, Miss Calder. If I can help at all." came the reply, perhaps a little too eager. He sat back and beamed an avuncular smile.

"Shall I ring for coffee? Or is it morning tea in the Calder wing?" This was followed by a polite refusal and an account of her visit to Fern Glade the previous afternoon and interview with the butler, Mr Haigh. She repeated an outline of the discussion at high tea with his sister and the police, but made no mention of the seance. Inside, Doctor Paul Lewis was sick with apprehension, but maintained the mask of an interested but detached party. He thought quickly, and his response was effective and polished.

"I must confess, Miss Calder, Sarah's sudden interest in the background of Detective Inspector Derek Russell was disturbing! I suppose it's one thing to hear funny stories about a failed poet, that quaint little gardener and the idiot of an organist. Hoadley can be such a ridiculous figure... Of course, one regrets the hurt...but... Well dash it all! Derek has done us proud, a splendid lad. I just didn't like her poking around."

"Quite so. What did you tell her?"

"No more than she already knew, less, I suppose, if anything. No big secret about 'China', we just don't talk about it much - do we?"

"I suppose we don't. Have you told me everything Paul?"
For the first time he looked unnerved.

"What else were you expecting?"

"I wondered if she may have asked you more general questions about that year. The Great War, 1915, I think it was. No enquiries, for example about her husband as a young man, and his affection for your sister?"

"Ah, Helen!" He visibly relaxed and his face dissolved into a warm engaging smile. He was happy to talk about Helen. *"I should think everybody loved Helen, or Evelyn as she was in those days. Such a beguiling girl, so engaging, so winsome. It broke mum's heart when she returned from Canada to find her gone."*

"I know." said Florence softly. *"We all missed her dreadfully. But you didn't answer my question."*

"Oh. Oliver Burgess? No. No, she showed no interest in him in 1915, or for that matter 1949! That whole evening, she never once addressed him nor even looked at him!

Softly, vaguely, her eyes began wandering around the room, noting and disapproving of the excessive bric-a-brac, before coming to rest upon the worthy and valuable 17th century warming-pan. She gazed at it for some seconds creating an uncomfortable awkward silence, which at last he felt compelled to break.

"As you see - still there, safe and sound!"

"I've always admired it. Not far short of three hundred years old. Your dear mother polished it herself, wouldn't allow the servants to touch it. She suddenly looked him straight in the eye. *"Probably contemporary with the celebrated warming-pan belonging to our foolish king James II."*

Paul Lewis's throat went dry, but he continued to show a nonchalant expression. He was grateful when the old head started to turn and her bullet eyes went back to the hanging antique. She slowly and sadly shook her head -

"To think that a simple pan like that precipitated the Glorious Revolution of 1688! But his people were not stupid, as we today are not stupid." Once more her accusing eyes met his. *"You know the story of course?"*

"Naturally." He abruptly stood up. *"Miss Florence!"* She looked at him questioningly. He continued with some agitation. *"Miss Florence, I must take this opportunity to tell you something ... something you ought to know ... something you have a **right** to know. I'm under instruction not to reveal this information ... to anyone ... but you're different."*

Quietly and gently she said -

"I think it would be as well to tell me - everything, Paul."

But the information about to be disclosed was not what she was expecting.

168

"It's Helen ... she's ill, very ill." A pause followed as he wandered over to the west-facing window and peered into the unfocused foliage of the great tree. He turned round. *"You're not supposed to know. Nobody is."* He was not quite sure what sort of response he had expected from the old lady sitting before him, certainly not an emotional response. The deeply wrinkled face remained much the same, serious and competent, but perhaps now showing some concern, and just a touch of sadness.

"How long?"

"A matter of weeks. I'll be very surprised if she's still here by Christmas."

"When was this first diagnosed?"

"June. Too late of course. Quite typical. And Helen, as you well know, will not complain - just soldiers on and on; intends to get as much work done as possible in the remaining time - and make a quiet exit - no fuss."

Florence rose and was now standing at his side, also looking out of the window into the murky depths of the Plane Tree, trying to find a hidden focal point, as a gypsy staring into a crystal ball. As if addressing this nebulous spot, she said -

"Helen's made a big difference to Cranmer, and the whole town for that matter."

He responded with urgency -

"I knew you, of all people, could take this news, and of course you'll be discreet ... She'd be furious!

"Don't worry, Paul." She exhaled a deep sigh and looked at him again. *"Thank you for telling me. If you'll excuse me ..."* He reached for the bell. *"Don't bother Ursula, it'll be quicker .."*

"Of course." In a strained silence, they walked out into the hall and to the front door which he opened politely. Doctor Lewis made some fatuous comment about the continuing fog, which he immediately regretted. But his early guest, once again, made disturbing and penetrating eye contact which lent significance to her surprising, yet disquieting, optimistic reply.

"Before this day has ended, I think the fog will have lifted. Good morning, Paul."

169

Chapter 22

Confession

She was indeed sad. Miss Florence Calder had few friends, since she tended to socialise with equals who shared similar interests. Many of these were now dead. Helen was her best friend, perhaps her only true friend.

This grave news did not change the plans for the early morning. She had much to do before the start of school at nine, and now the Jubilee Clock, with a small improvement of clarity, proclaimed a little after 7.30am. The world was still asleep. Smartly she marched south along the east side of an unusually quiet Bridge Street.

Presently she arrived at the Lion Hotel which had only just opened its doors. She gave instructions to the bleary-eyed receptionist and was shown into the residents lounge. Detective Inspector Derek Russell was actually shaving at the time, and very surprised to be told that Miss Florence Calder wished to be received - immediately! He descended alone. Instinct told the senior officer not to bother Detective Sergeant John Winter for this interview.

They had the large comfortable room to themselves and sat face to face, reposited into generous snug wing chairs. Perhaps he should have been alarmed at the unexpected early appearance of his former schoolmistress but, as many times before, he could only feel a huge wave of affection and a gladdened heart to see her call upon him. His delight was expressed in humour -

"Simon Tonks has confessed?"

*"No, Derek, but **Aubrey Pod** will!"*

"Will he?" He was still smiling, but had some little difficulty in reading her, as ever, inscrutable features. Mentally he noted that the date was September 14th and not April 1st. She mused -

"King of Elves."

"Pardon?"

"Aubrey means - 'King of Elves'. In his case 'King of Fools' might be more appropriate. I have a request. If I personally guarantee that Mr Pod will come here to give you a full statement promptly at nine, will you promise not to question him at his school?"

Derek looked at her, quite bemused, with the fleeting thought that social embarrassment at the Herbert Strutt Grammar School would be the least of Pod's problems if he were to be arrested for murder. Notwithstanding he made an answer -

"*Certainly, Miss Calder!*"

"*Good! One other loose end I'd like to clear up, just for my personal satisfaction. Did you find out where Jasper actually took his antique dolls last Wednesday afternoon, and confirm that they were properly valued?*

Again his handsome face broke out into an engaging smile.

"*Could you have doubted me? Sent Winter to check-up. That musty old shop on Strutt Street, Mrs 'something-or-other'. Naturally she couldn't put a price on them herself, but told Jasper what he wanted to hear; something to the effect that they were obviously very old and valuable. But?*" A frown of perplexity replaced the smile. "*My dear, Miss Marple, surely you **must** be pulling my leg about Aubrey Pod?*"

"*A confession at nine, and ...*" she seemed to look suddenly much older and very tired. He sensed deep emotion, leaned forward and gently prompted -

"*And?*"

"*And I'm afraid it's not 'Miss Marple' anymore, Derek.*"

Bewilderment and disappointment overtook him.

"*Good Heavens! What **is** wrong, Miss Florence? Please tell me?*"

She fiddled with the hem of her coat, and, unusually for Florence Calder, avoided eye contact for a moment. Also unusual was the slight hesitation and faint tremor in her otherwise firm confident voice.

"*I told you last week that I was not Miss Marple, just an ordinary old schoolmistress.*"

These departures from normal were very distressing to her former pupil who had only ever known her as a rock of strength. Instinct warned him to press her no further on this matter. As one might humour an elderly relative, he said cheerily that he was looking forward to seeing 'the miserable Toad' throwing himself up on the mercy of the law! At this new up-beat tone she rallied.

"*Of course, as yet, he doesn't **know** he's coming to see you, but come he will. I must get off to Becksitch Lane.*"

Abruptly she was on her feet. Derek stood up and looked at her with some concern. A sleepless night of mental gymnastics followed by a devastating revelation, followed again by distressing news of the terminal illness of a dear friend; had all been painfully etched onto an already time-worn countenance.

Impulsively, Derek did something he thought he would never do. He put his lips up to her left cheek, and planted a gentle kiss.
"Go forth, dear and precious Lady. You're greater than any Miss Marple, and far better loved."
She was unable to respond to this, turned, and muttered a weak -
"Good morning."

To put the previous incident well behind her, energetically and with determination, she quick-stepped out into Bridge Street and made an instant decision to avoid the flat main road to her destination, a house called 'Crow's Hole'. A name she had always hated, but was so well suited to its obnoxious long time resident, the appalling Nelly Pod.
She turned left into Wellington Court, right into the Railway Station and out onto King Street. A sudden thought seized her -
"Which King? Probably George III."
Nearing to the hour of eight, a few people were now abroad. Graciously she inclined her head to the two gentlemen who raised their hats with a respectful -
"Good morning, Miss Calder."
Up and across King Street into the Bowling Alley which ran parallel to the railway line, set straight and deep into the cutting, a splendid feat of Victorian engineering. Out, across New Road where she gave a disapproving glance to the right at one of the new 'H' shaped electric television aerials, which in her opinion -
"...were an unnecessary and ugly blot on the visual landscape!"
Down into the quaint curved little area of Brookside. Right into Days Lane, and right again into 'The Fleet' and a firm march up the hill. A brief turn of the head to the right to note the home of a conscientious pupil, a charming girl who never broke her slate pencil. This reminded her that time was short, and she accelerated up the hill and down into Becksitch Lane. Finally arriving at the foot of the daunting steep climb on the left, up to the front door of Mr Aubrey Pod.
Sensibly she took a few minutes to catch her breath before the assault up the overgrown and mountainous garden. Happily, she noticed that the fog, ever thinning, had become brighter and was now positively glowing. An optimistic sign that the sun was not too far above her head and soon may make an appearance to shine upon what

could become a pleasant autumnal day. Neglected it may have been, but Mr Pod's garden was a joy to the slowly climbing old lady. A riot of colour, an assortment of interesting shapes and a potpourri of delicious, late season scents, all blended with the ubiquitous local fern and thick, lush moss clinging to Derbyshire grit stone.

At the sudden and unexpected appearance of the redoubtable Miss Florence Calder at the door, Mavis Fig, with a face registering stupefaction, dropped an instinctual and perfunctory curtsy. She would have given the distinguished visitor a customary greeting, but Florence was too quick -

"*Good morning, Mavis. Kindly inform Mr Pod that I wish to see him - **at once!**"*

"*Certainly, Miss Calder! Would you like to come into the front room?*"

With some relish, the under-paid and resentful servant energetically dived into the malodorous darkened interior, and gleefully delivered her excited message to the still drowsy, overweight, shapeless, music teacher. At that moment he was eagerly stuffing a third sausage, the last part of what had been a large, greasy fry-up, into his viscid, glistening, gooey, slashed mouth. The announcement of the presence of his former schoolmistress, the last thing he expected, very nearly caused him to choke and fall off his chair.

Miss Florence Calder, too wound up to be seated, was pacing up and down the modest 'best' room which still reflected the Edwardian, faded, musty taste of old Nelly Pod, whose distasteful image bore down upon her from above the mantelpiece. Exactly as Florence had always remembered her, an extraordinary, unchanging countenance of uncertain age - *"Was she ever young?"*

Then another repulsive face, with manifest family resemblance: an ugly, shamed, miserable face, peered cautiously around the door.

"***Aubrey!***"

A single word, but he knew the tone well. This was the deep voice of authority which had struck fear into, and cowed, generations of Beaurepairians. She held out her hand with commanding index finger officiously pointing to an armchair. No further speech was needed. The mortified little man scampered over to the designated place, sat down and faced his stern mistress.

Indeed the scene was very similar to that of 35 years before when he had been challenged over the 'hanging slippers incident'. At the start of each day, all pupils at Bridge House School customarily removed their shoes, and put on slippers neatly hanging in little bags on individual pegs, where they had been carefully placed the night before. To leave them untidily on the floor was a sin, certain to attract reprimand and punishment. One morning in the cold, stone flagged corridor, three, apparently careless and slovenly little boys, were at a loss to explain scattered slippers. Tearfully they protested their innocence to an angry Miss Calder. She was about to inflict verbal punishment upon her abject pupils when she heard a malicious titter from behind and turned round to see an evil, but familiar gig of joy. The sheer force of her personality drew a confession from naughty little Aubrey, just as it would do now.

"Aubrey Pod! I have come here this morning to spare you the indignity of a formal visit from the police!"

"Thank you, Miss ..." He cleared his throat to produce a better, stronger voice. *"Thank you, Miss Calder. Too kind!"*

"More than you deserve. To be called out of your class in front of goggling pupils and possibly arrested on a charge of murder..." His eyes went wide with terror *"Yes, I do mean murder!"*

"I never..."

"Silence! Let me finish. It would be an insupportable ignominy for both the Herbert Strutt Grammar School and your own professional reputation. Accordingly you will now dispatch yourself to your headmaster, Mr Ducker, and ask to be relieved of duties for the first hour. Not the full morning, an hour should be enough. If there is any difficulty, simply mention my name. At nine sharp, report to Detective Inspector Russell, who is at the Lion Hotel and - confess."

"Confess?"

"Confess." Her bullet eyes held him in a firm grip and the old wrinkled lips were pressed tight, signifying finality.

"Confess to murder?"

Was it a slight sound, or perhaps just instinct which made the old teacher slide silently to the door? A brisk opening revealed an embarrassed, flustered Mavis, undignified and unsteady, under the ferocious gaze of the morning guest. With sickly smile -

174

"Oh! Miss Calder! Err...well... I was just about to ask you and Mr Pod if you'd like a cup of tea?"

*"What we require, Mavis Fig, at this time, is **privacy!**"*

"Of course, Miss Calder."

*"You may **return** to your kitchen!"*

Her words were spat out with the hard sharpness of knives, causing the housekeeper to slink back to a pile of greasy pots and pans, the aftermath of Mr Pod's breakfast.

"Now then, where were we? Oh yes, murder. Don't be ridiculous, Aubrey! You are many things. You're a silly vindictive little man, and at the same time an excellent musician and good music master in a class where you can manage to keep order, but you are definitely not a murderer."

Just for a moment she glanced out of the window at what should have been a good view of the Chevin Hills. Her eyes came back into the room and alighted upon a pair of binoculars sitting on the mantelpiece, before they finally rested upon the pained, piteous features of Mr Aubrey Pod.

"We both know what you will be confessing to, Aubrey. let us not play games. You will acknowledge a bungled attempt at blackmail." The word jolted him. *"Of course I don't mean blackmail in the usual sense of obtaining money with threats and menaces. Money had never been **your** weakness,"* she said significantly, once again glancing at the binoculars. *"I mean blackmail in the sense of obtaining power and gaining ascendancy over another. You shared that particular scurrilous characteristic with your intended victim who **also** used scandalous knowledge to threaten and torment others. One of those victims decided to protect him or herself - permanently.*

Precious little evidence points to the perpetrator of this crime, but your spiteful lust for revenge has made sure that it points directly to you!"

He leaned forward and jutted out his head -

"What d'you mean?"

"I mean asking Sister Hannah when Sarah would be coming out of the convent, claiming to be at the cinema when in fact you were seen near the bridge an hour before the 'boat trip'. Which brings me back to my original instruction to tell Inspector Russell the truth."

The crestfallen master said -

175

"But will he believe..."

"Of course he'll believe that you were furious after the public humiliations of the previous Saturday, not to mention the years of disruption and abasements at school. These are matters of common knowledge - as is this absurd new hobby of bird-watching! Had you paid better attention to nature study at school, you might have passed as an amateur ornithologist.

*Tell the inspector what you saw - **who** you saw, and **what** they were doing!"*

The lamentable and lascivious little man seemed to get smaller in the chair and coloured up with embarrassment under the hard unflinching gaze of the old spinster, who seemed to have a clear window into his naughty rude mind. A voyeuristic mind which had been moulded by the repressive Victorian morality of Nelly Pod. He well recalled the previous Wednesday, pacing up and down the small area known as Belper beach, rehearsing what he would say to Sarah Burgess. How best to devastate her with his outspoken lewd observations: the time, the place, pink knickers clasped in a fist tight with ecstasy, the wide-open obscenity of splayed limbs, the puffing and panting, the ever quickening oscillation of upturned buttocks and all ending in the final collapse of the inert and exhausted body of Robin Kirkland upon the satisfied body of Sarah Burgess nee Grindle. All this he would threaten to reveal to her husband and enjoy seeing her squirm, apologise and beg for forgiveness. But it was never to be. Sarah marched over the bridge, ignoring his calls, intent on being on time for her important appointment.

The old mistress, more worldly than was generally thought, was brusquely on her feet and seized the binoculars. Mr Pod, a defeated man stood up more slowly.

"Thank you, Aubrey. This will be useful for our nature study. A generous gift to your old school - most kind!"

She looked at the expensive glasses, and then at the abject 'donor' who, down-cast, simply accepted this sudden fait accompli, when for the first time her expression softened to a near smile.

"You were in deep waters there, Aubrey, it wouldn't have worked; no, not on Sarah Grindle." He raised his head with curiosity. *"She would have laughed at you again! Do you seriously imagine she'd*

care what Mr Burgess, or anyone else, would think about her open air adultery? I expect Oliver was past caring at that stage. She would have spat in your face and berated you for your stupidity in not producing photographs."

She looked at her watch.

*"You have just enough time, 20 minutes, to see Mr Ducker and get to the Lion Hotel at a brisk healthy walk, but I expect you'll complete both journeys in your very odd little motorcar. Just one more item before you go, Aubrey. **Did** you see any woman, just behind or just ahead, or anywhere near Sarah as she crossed the bridge?"*

In his anxiety to distance himself from the scene of the killing, Mr Pod had never actually given thought to this vital question, and had to briefly consider.

"No, Miss Calder. I don't think so .... No!"

Chapter 23

A Brilliant White, Frosty Morning

During the next few days Detective Inspector Derek Russell and Detective Sergeant John Winter re-interviewed Oliver Burgess, Billy and Gladys Grindle, Alex Haigh, Claud Hoadley, Charlie and Robin Kirkland, Julian and Tatiana Lawrence, Doctor Paul Lewis, Percy Tinker, Olive, Sally and Simon Tonks.

Follow-up questions were put to clarify and cross-reference intelligence already obtained, but no new information came to light. Loose ends remained stubbornly loose. Local fishermen were sought out and interrogated without a satisfactory result. John Winter suspected the initial river-bank search was not as thorough as it could have been, but felt it wise to keep those thoughts to himself. The time was near when it was simply a waste of time to investigate further. They had gone as far as they could go. They had reached a brick wall.

On the Monday morning of September 19th, in the temporary office at the Belper Police Station the two officers were wearily packing up their files and notes into boxes. Inspector Russell attempted to raise the flagging spirit of his subordinate with -

"Of course we don't close the book entirely. No! It'll stay open for... well years - if necessary. Anything could happen. Tongues can be loosened by a nagging conscience, or drink. Something could spark a hidden memory. Friends can fall out, and one rush to the police. Unusual items can be found in odd places. Anything can happen!"

"Yes, sir." replied Winter, putting the last box into the boot of the motorcar. He was little cheered and had less hope.

They were briefly distracted by the excited shouts and squeals of happy children from the dank fern garden just over the road. These were the pupils of Bridge House School enjoying their mid-morning break on this fine sunny day, part of the continuing Indian summer which soldiered on.

"I'd better just go and say 'goodbye' to the Calders. Shan't be a minute, Winter."

If anything, Miss Florence Calder looked a little smaller than usual standing by a rockery of the unusual, sponge-structured tufa stone, watching her little boys and girls running around the rose beds. She was grateful and pleased to see her former pupil approaching.

"How kind of you to come!" Common pleasantries were exchanged including gratitude for the continuing unseasonable warm fine weather. It was inevitable that some comment was needed about the shared inconclusive task.

"I'm afraid Miss Marple has failed you!" But Derek responded gallantly.

"Not at all! You've been a wonderful inspiration and we did get to the bottom of several items of unfinished business, thanks to your superior local knowledge, and perspicacity with the principals involved. I was just telling Winter that we're not beaten yet."

It was clear from her expression that she did not share his optimism.

"I've a nagging feeling that Simon's seance information was not exploited to the full. Of course, Miss Florence, you were quite right: even after lengthy questioning, he claims no memory of the 'trance'."

"I must apologise for allowing that nonsense. It was just that - a muddled nonsense from a cocktail of misunderstood half truths based on fragments of overheard and lip read conversations. It all amounted to nothing."

"It seems it was enough for him to be put under 'house arrest' for his own protection!"

She looked at him sharply, and with some small annoyance -

"He wasn't supposed to tell you that." She sighed and idly stroked a large fern. *"Silly child! Yes, I did feel he was in danger - at first - but not now. I've allowed him out to 'sit' in Nelly Pod's chair again on Wednesday, Mavis's afternoon off. Mrs Pod will be able to be as abusive as she likes without causing ill feeling!"*

Derek smiled, but the smile concealed a jumble of conflicting thoughts. His innate curiosity, professional pride and duty to clear up a case, wrestled with his respect, nay fear, of his old schoolmistress. A fear which had been branded into his psyche from an early age. This adopted son of the Vicar of Christ Church, deep down, had an idea that somehow the solution to this mystery was inextricably bound up with his own personal past. He wanted to challenge, to remonstrate with her, but was stopped by some unspoken, unspecified warning. She knew something, something important. He knew it. But such inkling of her information as he perceived it, was both unfocused and dangerous to himself. He was fearful of the knowledge she chose not to reveal. They were eye to eye, but it was a case of - 'Nanny knows best'.

179

He put out his hand and she responded.

"*Well....say goodbye to Miss Madge for me. I expect to see you both in church from time to time.... Dear Lady. Must get on my way.*"

She watched him leave the garden and return to the Police Station. Minutes later the police motorcar took both officers away from Belper.

Many weeks passed. The old Plane Tree had now shed all its leaves and life went on much as before. Occasionally people referred to the murder which had become one of life's unsolved mysteries. A comfortable and popular theory evolved which suited some of the folk of Belper. Madam X was a mad woman from some other town who would probably never be seen again. A wilder still theory, which was creeping into the local folklore, involved the materialisation of Nelly Pod's vengeful ghost.

This last had recently reached the ears of, and amused, Miss Florence Calder as she set off walking early one pure white, frosty, quiet Sunday morning.

"*It's neat and tidy! If Nelly is guilty, then at least everybody else is innocent!*"

It was a glittering, dazzling morning in mid-December as she marched over the bridge. It was the ideal cold weather she loved. She felt very fit, healthy and energetic. A crisp day which made her feel it was possible to hike smartly for tens of miles. Distance would be limited only by the shortness of daylight. A light of such winter brilliance that visibility was at present unlimited, as she cast her eyes up to the most distant hills, sharply focused with perfect resolution.

Her high spirits were somewhat dampened at the end of the bridge when a choice became apparent. Most people with her destination would have walked ahead up the steep Belper Lane; but no, she hesitated. She would take the old route of her childhood days, turning right along the very pleasant Wyver Lane, past some picturesque cottages on her left. This may serve as a rough experiment. Would she be much noticed?

"*Nonsense!*" she thought. "*Not a valid experiment at all. December was hardly the same as early September. Fewer people, in fact **no** people standing outside passing the time of day. What **are** you thinking of Florence!*"

180

Pressing on, the little dwellings eventually gave way to a pleasant, narrow lane, now strewn with dead leaves, having the hill to the left and the river to the right. She almost missed it, but there it was - the old stile she remembered from childhood. Now almost hidden by bramble and weeds, this was the start of a little-used overgrown path, which wound up the hill through Wyver Wood emerging at the back-door entrance to the walled kitchen garden of the Convent of Cranmer. With interest and a keen eye, she noted that the thicker, more ancient, bramble had been cut back earlier in the year which made her thorny assault a little easier. Florence enjoyed the crisp, under-foot crunching of stiff, frosty, dead leaves and beechnuts in this mainly deciduous woodland. It was an interesting walk with shafts of sunlight illuminating the complete spectrum of early winter brown and green tints.

As the hill steepened, her old body felt the strain and she slowed down. She had set off with speed and confidence, clear about what she would say and how it 'would be played'. As the moment drew nearer and physical effort became greater, she felt less sure about the ordeal which lay ahead. Over the last fourteen weeks, Florence Calder had struggled with a conscience of myriad conflicting thoughts and emotions. She had prayed for an answer. Duty, loyalty, responsibility, practicality, morality and plain common-sense had been assessed, analysed, viewed and reviewed over and over again in her troubled mind. Often in her long life she had found that the easiest thing in the world to do - was to do nothing. Such it was in this example - she had done nothing, which included - not visiting the sick.

The last time she had seen her friend was on Tuesday, September 13th when they had shared high tea. After that evening, Helen's terminal illness took a turn for the worse and had weakened the Reverend Mother to the extent of her being permanently bedridden. A steady procession of people found it a pleasure to visit this popular lady on her 'good days' which were now becoming more and more infrequent. She always made a special effort to resume her former charming and gracious manner which had always captured the hearts and minds of Beaurepairians. A bed-side audience with the Reverend Mother Helen was both a pleasure and a spiritual experience. Some tearful returning visitors insisted she was well on the way to sainthood. This view was shared by Margaret Campbell Calder who could never understand why

181

her sister had not been to see her best friend when it became common knowledge that she had weeks, possibly now only days to live. After several abortive attempts of persuasion, only once did she dare to press the subject almost to the point of reprimand. Florence said nothing, but gave Madge a look of such ferocity and feeling that she fled into the great kitchen where she took sanctuary, shocking Simon in the process by showing unusual kindness, insisting that he looked in need of a rest!
"Sit down and I'll make you a nice cup of tea."

No two people were more delighted than Miss Madge and little Simon when, on this cold and frosty Sunday morning after breakfast, Miss Florence Calder made the surprise announcement of her sudden intention to climb up to the Convent of Cranmer and 'visit the sick'.

At last Florence came out of the wood and found the old door, the entrance of the convent kitchen and herb garden. It was never locked 60 years ago and was not locked now. She trudged through the sleeping winter specimens and approached the large back door. The heavy crashing knocker sent many calling echoes around the corridors within.

Chapter 24

"O Trespass Sweetly Urg'd!"

Sister Hannah was delighted to see Miss Florence Calder standing at the door. A warm embrace was followed by a short rest on a welcome seat for the old lady who had, after all, just scaled a small mountain. The nun provided a lively and enthusiastic escort up the great staircase and along to the private quarters of the Reverend Mother.

An emotional scene followed. Not emotional in terms of displayed or effusive emotion, but repressed emotion behind the decorous mask of common courtesy and conventional demeanour. Helen was glad to see her friend and grateful for the visit. In polite, measured tones, she said this. Florence cordially acknowledged the sentiment, but with a restraint which would have puzzled an observer who had known the two companions. She was not shocked by the pale and haggard countenance of the once attractive woman, nor the appalling emaciated body which barely made an impression under the bed clothes. She had heard this from others and was prepared for that sight, but had not reckoned with that fearful, sweet scent - the smell of approaching death. Miss Florence Calder was a very strong woman and needed all that strength in this bare medieval room for this imminent difficult interview. Even now she was not at all sure what would pass in the coming exchange, an exchange she had intended to avoid - up to this morning.

Helen was heavily supported by pillows, so positioned up to the thick stone mullioned window that her head was nicely near, and aligned to see the wonderful crisp, cold, sparkling view over the Derwent Valley; and then on for evermore - further, into the clear, deep, perfect blue. Her lovely brown eyes of September had become bulbous in the sockets of the gaunt and cadaverous skull. But these same unhealthy eyes were thankful for the respite offered by this very convenient window. During difficult intervals they could take refuge looking out onto the perfect, glistening, Derbyshire landscape, and avoid the stern accusing bullet eyes of her former teacher, now seated by her death-bed.

In spite of her physical condition her voice was the same: rich warm and liquid.

"Don't fear, Florence. I'll not embarrass you by asking for absolution."

"Only God can forgive, Helen. I have not come to judge you."

The invalid gave a weak ironic smile.

*"But you can't know everything and must be a little curious. How much **do** you know?"*

At this point the old teacher also found the window useful. She sought out, and located her sharp eyes to the north, onto the distant Crich Stand tower, took a deep breath and continued -

"Most of it, I suppose...of course... a few details..."

"Derek?"

Florence leaned forward with conviction.

"I can re-assure you there my friend. No one will ever know."

The wasted frame sank back deeper into the pillows and exhaled a long sigh of relief. For a moment the eyes closed in their skeletal reposits.

"I don't deserve your comfort, but am glad of it."

Seconds passed before the visitor spoke again in a manner of mild introspection.

"Of course I didn't know until that dreadful foggy night when we last met. Don't credit me with super-human powers, Helen! It was pure chance. I simply picked up a book. Do you recall me reading 'The Changeling' to the class?

The Reverend Mother became animated with a touch of distant joy.

"Delightful! The fairies who swapped the little baby with their own baby. That wonderful picture on the front cover. You still have it after nearly half a century?"

"Just as Paul still has that warming-pan hanging in your front room. Another clue, if it were necessary."

She wrinkled her pale brow in an effort of remembrance.

"The bed-pan baby! One of your intriguing history lessons. James II. A live healthy common baby secreted into the palace to replace a still-born prince.... But... How could you have known?"

"I heard Derek crying."

Again she breathed heavily, smiled and nodded.

"Of course you did! At the time I feared as much."

"When they divided Bridge House into two separate homes, little thought and less effort was put into sound-proofing. You were quite young at the time, but perhaps you'll recall the incident of naughty Paul and his 'ghostly bell'?"

"Oh dear, yes. Poor Madge!" She looked directly at Florence. *"You gathered that the Jinks child was born dead?"*

"I gathered. A rainy dark night: confusion and hubbub of pushing, fussing, well meaning but simple neighbours at the door wanting to help. If anyone had thought to ask the question - 'Why didn't the child cry?', someone may have said 'Don't be so dozy, of course it cried. Doctor knows what he's doing, don't interfere.' That sort of thing."

Dreamily, Helen noted that the midday winter sun was proving too powerful for the cloak of frost on the lower fields over the valley. Gradually the colour was reverting to a magnificent bright green.

"The poor little mite was properly buried. We both did it, Paul and I, in the dead of night - over there in the cemetery on top of a recent grave which of course already had newly disturbed soil."

Florence put a question.

"There appears to be no obvious resemblance but... Does Oliver Burgess know he is the father of Derek Russell?"

Helen savoured a small smug moment of superiority.

"You've made a wrong guess there, Florence. No! I was fond of young Oliver, but as one would be fond of a brother." She shuddered at the recollection of the soft plump pining teenager with his delicate small white hands. *"If all the boys repulsed me as he did..."* She shook her head. *"I wouldn't have ended up with this stain on my honour and character which has followed and haunted my whole life. No, I couldn't bear him to touch me."* She noted the puzzled expression on her visitors face and decided to satisfy the obvious curiosity. *"It's an interesting irony that when Jean Russell told her son that his real father died as a brave soldier; she was telling him the simple truth! This was the great love I thought would never be spoken of...."*

In this poignant moment, the voice faltered as her eyes closed in an agony of retrospective, passionate, long lost romance. Copious tears flowed. Up to this point Florence, who had been determined to maintain a firm detachment, now weakened, and reached out to hold the withered hand of her friend. After a few moments, she recovered and continued.

"The 'Depths of Lumb'. That's where we would meet, in that deep dark ravine just over the hill."

"A place already associated with tragedy." murmured Florence darkly.

185

"Nobody ever knew. The most magnificent creature I had ever seen. A Greek god!
'O trespass sweetly urg'd. Give me my sin again.'"

She turned her head to look at the old spinster in the faint hope of some small empathy. She saw none, save for the compassion of one woman shown for the suffering of another. Helen turned back to the safety of the window and continued in a lower tone.

"At least you would have approved of my teaching him to read. Not a suitable choice of book for a beginner. 'Wuthering Heights'! It was a little like that: he a labourer and me the daughter of a doctor. He loved the story. We'd just finished it when my Heathcliff went off to war... And like so many, died amid the stench of death, sinking in the eternal mud. I have no photograph, but you need only look at Derek."

Florence struggled with her conflicting feelings of censure and compassion in the hope of finding a few appropriate words.

"Your secret was well kept. I had no idea until this recent business, but... I should have known... That is, I should have thought about your religious background."
Helen responded quickly.

*"That **did** worry me with regard to yourself. It was easy to convince your mother and sisters, even my own parents that I'd received 'the call of God' and had always had a pious disposition. But you - you were different. You could assess the depth of my personal devotion, and I feared you'd ask awkward questions about a sudden spiritual emigration to the north."*

"It was tacitly understood that you would join us and teach in the school." said Florence, who, for the first time looked over at the dying lady and affectionately saw her as she once was, a pretty girl and bright promising student. *"You were a deeply conscientious and very clever pupil."*

*"Oh I've been **very** clever."* she responded with some bitterness and sank back exhausted. She closed her eyes and drifted into a sleep which was very close to the long final sleep. Florence noticed that she was still holding her hand, and decided to continue to hold it.

The bed-side visitor noted the shallow, rasping breathing, and sat watching over her sick friend. She sat and watched....

186

Chapter 25

The Sweet Smell of Death

"Do you think I look like my son?"

This clear rich familiar voice startled and awoke the sleeping Miss
Florence Calder. Groggy and disorientated, she roused herself up in the
bed-side seat. Just for a moment she wondered where she was. The sun
was very low, very red and almost setting. This same dying sun with its
last gasp had painted the white landscape a deep blood colour, and a big
fat orange moon stood behind Crich Stand like a giant halo.

Inside the room it was colder, and that sickening sweet smell of
death seemed to be even stronger, but the fading light improved Helen's
general appearance, which was now less alarming. She seemed to have
renewed strength and continued loquaciously -

*"Of course it wasn't just similar looks which Sarah first noticed.
Oh no, she was much more sensitive than that. Like your little Simon,
she was very perceptive on a personal and social level. She was
fascinated by the handsome policeman she saw occasionally at church,
and pointed out how popular we both were, and also that we shared the
same charming manners. The tiniest details. She commented on the
similar way we both walked, held our head, had the same jaw line.
What a coincidence she would say, over and over again...."*

She stopped for breath and sank back a little. More slowly -

*"For a while I felt safe. I'd smile and indulge her as one would
a child. 'Perhaps we shared an ancestor, my dear!' It was no good.
She had hit the target and knew it. She would look at my fingers and
see them shake. She could measure my mood exactly. As a Reverend
Mother at a major convent, I was a perfect trophy."*

Florence watched the darkness creep across the cold landscape and
spoke more to herself than to her friend -

*"These would be the conversations at the back of the church or
perhaps outside, overheard, or lip-read, by Simon."*

*"Most likely. That's why I was so terrified by his ridiculous
'seance'! Paul was seriously alarmed at the Fern Glade dinner party,
but she'd dug out the circumstances of Derek's birth weeks before. My
old friendship with her husband was common knowledge among the
older generation. She became very interested in my background and*

particularly my personal history in the year 1915. That infuriating slimy smirk when she would ask -

'What was it like to get 'the call' from God? I had no idea you had to 'up sticks' and shift so quick and so far away! It's a bit like the 'nine months 'flu' - isn't it?'

I had to keep calm and think. My first responsibility was to protect the background and integrity of my son. Second to that, the respectability of my own position and the convent needed to be kept as safe as possible.

Two things were clear: she was susceptible to flattery and she genuinely liked me. I encouraged and affected an interest in her friendship. Nothing was openly acknowledged or admitted, but I played up to her sense of cruel power.

'You do realise that these speculations could ruin the life of Detective Inspector Russell, destroy my own position, seriously damage the convent and scandalise Belper?'

I said that I had become very fond of her and had come to understand her much better.

'You're misunderstood, my dear; a victim of unfortunate circumstances and have never really experienced, or have had the benefit, of real love. Here you will find that love and be improved by the Christian fellowship of these good sisters.'

More and more I sat with her at church and frequently invited her to the convent. We had long private talks in this room. She rejoiced in her privileged position and new friendship.''

Miss Florence Calder, who was hanging on to every word of this revealing narrative interrupted to put a question -

"Considering her sensitivity and intelligent perspicacity, did she not once sense the possible danger of her position?"

*"Never once! I was always the charming, gracious and holy Reverend Mother. True, I had a dark secret to hide, but it was inconceivable to Sarah that such a kind and gentle lady would possibly take any direct action. She saw **me** as a soft target. It never entered her head that **she** might be at risk.*

*It would be one morning in June when I put her hand on a bible and made her swear on two points: that she **had** never uttered on these*

188

*threatening theories and **would** never utter them to a living soul. This
she was pleased to do; it formed a bond and I knew it bought me the
time I needed...to think...to plan.*

*Paul had no knowledge of my plans. I acted alone. It had to be that
way. It was a case of waiting for the right weather. I needed it to be
cool for a warm coat and head-scarf and sunny for deep shadow. It had
to be no later than September, my strength was already ebbing. I'd
been told I was unlikely to see the new year."*
She turned mournful eyes to Florence.

*"I'm sorry about the pillow up the back. Yes, it **was** done to
incriminate your sister, in the full and certain knowledge that it would
be seen as just that - an attempt to implicate poor old Madge. I knew
no one would take it seriously."*

"Mr Pod took it seriously."
Helen ignored this dark mutter and continued.

*"A quiet half-day closing Wednesday was ideal. Of course I
couldn't control the fishermen and hoped they'd be preoccupied. I was
lucky, they were not there at all."* She gave a faint knowing smile.
*"Hannah said you arrived by the back door, so I expect you've done
some reconnaissance?"*

*"I did notice the bramble at the bottom stile had been carefully
cut back at least once this year."* Florence looked puzzled. *"How did
you induce Sarah to join you and break her engagement with Robin?"*
Helen responded with a scornful laugh.

*"She frequently let Robin down. He was continually used as it
suited her purpose. Just before she left us that day I asked her to come
to my room, looked out of the window, sighed and said I'd never been
rowing on the river in my life. Not true of course as you know. I said it
would be totally inappropriate for a woman of my position to be seen in
a rowing boat with a girl such as herself. In private, I'd developed a
'girls together' giggly relationship with her.*

*'What fun to get in a boat with **you**, Sarah, **now**, this very
afternoon - and how thrilling if nobody would know me. If only I could
be completely relaxed and enjoy it - in disguise!'*

*Sara was excited, so I told her to walk slowly so we'd meet in
the entrance of the River Gardens in about 15 minutes. It was easy. all
the sisters were still inside tending the flowers or taking tea. The herb
garden was deserted. Nobody saw me leave. Lots of alder trees down
there. Lots of cover. It was very quick, very simple."*

189

"A hammer?"

"A hammer. I put it back in it's usual place downstairs. It's there now."

The Reverend Mother Helen sank back into her pillows and closed her eyes again, but Florence with stern expression was not disposed to permit sleep and rest. With an edge to her voice -

"You have put innocent people in danger! Several had strong motives and few had satisfactory alibis!"

She opened her eyes and slowly turned to the old woman at her bed-side.

"You'll recall what I said about 'my first responsibility'. No one was ever in danger, Florence. Poor Derek was never anywhere near to making an arrest. As you say, I've been a clever girl. Do you seriously believe that I'd remain silent if even that fool Aubrey Pod was about to face the gallows?"

At this, Miss Florence Calder abruptly stood up and looked down on her one time best friend. It was on the tip of her tongue to wish the sick woman a brief and rather formal 'good evening' and walk out of the room. But at this last moment even Florence Calder was not strong enough to leave this dying fragment of emaciated humanity in this way at this time. She knew it would be the last time she would see Helen alive. The latter, weak and pathetic, maintained a compelling eye contact.

Florence again sat down, took her hand and spoke in a gentle voice -

"I must go now, Helen, but If I may, I'll come back to visit you again - another time."

Helen smiled, a rich warm sincere engaging smile which reminded Florence of Derek.

*"No you won't, my dear friend, but I'm eternally grateful for these precious moments we've had. I will continue to love you, and I **do** understand how difficult this has been for you."*

Florence leaned over, kissed her forehead and left without another word. The gloomy, cold convent, now sparsely candle-lit, seemed strangely deserted but for her own echoing footsteps along the great corridor. She applied her full strength to the massive front door which

190

gave slowly onto the high reaches of Belper Lane, which was now as black as in the middle of the night. As frosty as the air was, she felt a great relief to be outside this great house of death. A brief upward glance, showed the weird outline of the monstrous gargoyles, keeping their secrets, so very silent, against a beautiful clear starry night.

Setting off down the hill, Miss Calder suddenly felt very happy at the prospect of returning to the cheery pre-Christmas warmth, high banked fires, comfort and conviviality of her little sister and the funny little man who now so affectionately looked after them both.

Chapter 26

Watching in Silence, Keeping Secrets

It was the following Wednesday morning, December 14th, when twenty pairs of small curious eyes turned to the door of the classroom of Miss Florence Calder. It framed the awesome, crow-black figure of Sister Hannah. The old teacher, who moved silently to the door, asked no questions because it was not necessary. Just inside the stone flagged corridor, the expected news was broken. Helen had died in the early hours of that morning. The funeral would be at the Convent of Cranmer on the following Monday, just under a week before Christmas.

Florence felt a touch guilty that her first thought had been one of practicality.

"The children break-up on Friday. At least I won't need to close the school."

When the news reached Simon, he was visibly moved and went very quiet and subdued over the following days. Miss Madge took it badly and wept openly. She loved Helen and had lost one of her few true friends. On the other hand, she was not at all surprised by the reaction of her sister, who was stoic, on this as any other tragic occasion. Florence was the strong one and her maxim had always been -

"Keep your tears in your pillow!"

Inside the chapel of the Convent of Cranmer the funeral service had gone very well. It was 'standing room only' at the back, with, as ever on these occasions, first class organ playing from Mr Pod. Mr Claud Hoadley sat near the front, as far away as possible from the three Tonks sitting in the middle, Olive, Sally and Simon. He was able to achieve the best social location sitting between Miss Bulstrode, headmistress of the prestigious Derby High School for Girls, and the tweedy Penelope DeHaviland, an occasional writer for the Derbyshire Life and Countryside Magazine. Enthusiastically, he chatted happily with forced artificial enunciation to these eminent county dames about the life and times of the late Reverend Mother Helen, presuming a close friendship which was, in fact, never the case.

A few rows behind sat, with serious face, the retired Vicar of Christ Church, Edward and his wife, Jean Russell. Next to them was a bored looking Julian Lawrence with his mother Tatiana who sat empty and expressionless. Real and genuine grief was etched on the soft kindly features of Oliver Burgess at the end of the row. In the pews behind sat the Misses Calder with Doctor Paul Lewis who was sad and very tired.

The windless high pressure of the eventful weeks of early September was duplicated now in December, but with a different effect. The brilliant, bright sunshine of the short daylight hours had been unceasing, yielding to long, bitter, cold, crystal, starry nights. Such it was on the dazzling afternoon at the top of Belper Lane, when the multitude of mourners poured out of the great entrance of the Convent of Cranmer. Miss Florence Calder over-heard fragments of commonplace conversation about the favourable weather. Someone mentioned it being just two days short of the very shortest day of the year. There were many familiar faces, but in general people tended to be reluctant to address the Calder sisters directly. The senior sister had noted the absence of Detective Inspector Derek Russell, but would never have commented, save for a passing remark from Madge.

"Nonsense, Madge! I expect he'll be busy on another case. Anyway he hardly knew Helen. Why should he be here?"

They suddenly noticed that Charlie Kirkland was at their side. With rough but well meant, kind, courtesy, he apologised for the absence of Robin who had been reluctant to ask for time off from the bank. The honest pattern moulder made a few fitting comments for the sad occasion -
"...a wonderful lady, she'll be sadly missed."
Miss Madge warmed to his efforts and responded with engaging, suitable, gentle agreements, but Miss Florence said nothing. Her silence was interpreted as grief.

Far above, nearer to the perfect blue firmament, thrusting out from the massive walls of the Convent of Cranmer were the hideous leering gargoyles. The short day grew ever shorter, and their ghastly shadows were stealthily creeping down the valley. As great, gloating birds of prey they watched, far below, the two old sisters descending the steep hill. These monsters, carved in stone, kept their secrets and watched in silence.

For like Miss Florence Calder, they had seen much,
but would say nothing.

Narvel's latest novel *Sea Change* is Available
from Amazon in paperback and on Kindle

A Mystery set in Derbyshire 1957 and 1958

Sea Change is a controversial story of transformation: a journey from despair to delight. Adolescence is the change from boy to man. In a sequel to Lost Lad, Simeon Hogg escapes from a living hell into an enchanted world of fairytale people inhabiting the nooks and crannies of deepest Derbyshire. Follow him as he transforms from a rough and miserable urchin who - 'Suffers a sea-change into something rich and strange' – as sung by Ariel, the airy spirit from The Tempest.

Narvel Annable has disclosed confidential erotic and embarrassing details which many gay boys of the 1950s have taken to their graves. In this brutally honest autobiographic novel, he goes further. He revisits his Dickensian Mundy Street Boys School ordeal of sex slavery and bullying in Heanor. Cruelty has a cost. Approaching his 70s, the author is now paying the bill. Adventures set in a shadowy gay world uncover a furtive existence. Under the secretive mainstream of homosexuals is an underclass – a taboo within a taboo.

With the help of legislation and enlightened education, the LGBT community of the 21st century hopes these horrors, which have damaged so many, have gone forever.

This novel explodes myths and challenges conventional thinking. Whilst not condoning, it does not condemn. At the brink of self destruction, Simeon's sexual abuser becomes his saviour, persuading him, giving him courage to escape and live – rather than to stay and die in a culture where a boy was esteemed by his ability to inflict humiliation, pain and suffering on others.

Another great yarn from the storyteller of gay Derbyshire, Narvel Annable. Interwoven with references to real-life events and history, he writes a terrific mystery novel. I wish we had a Narvel in every region of England to tell such tales.

Peter Tatchell

195

About the Author

Narvel Annable's Heanor Schooldays (1998) was autobiographic, covering his unhappiness in a grim, gas-lit, Dickensian, Church of England junior school from 1955 to 1958. Adolescence and the move to William Howitt Secondary Modern School, "A culture of kindness", in September, 1958, was a dramatic improvement, graphically retold in the second half of the social history.

In 1963 he emigrated to the United States and arrived in Detroit on the day before the assassination of President Kennedy. The next seven years saw him in a variety of jobs which included labourer, lathe-hand, bank messenger and camera salesman. In 1975 he graduated from Eastern Michigan University (magna cum laude) and taught African American History for a year at St Bridget High School in Detroit.

In 1976 he returned to Derbyshire to help organise and launch 'Heritage Education Year 1977' at Sudbury Hall. From 1978 to 1995 he taught history at the Valley Comprehensive School in Worksop which gradually became more progressive. Narvel criticises these changes in some detail in his first two books. Seizing retirement at the earliest opportunity, he started to write historical and educational articles for the local Press and has been interviewed several times on BBC Radio Derby and BBC Radio Nottingham. BBC Radio Manchester and Sheffield also invited Narvel to discuss his writing and campaigning. BBC Radio Leicester asked serious questions about Scruffy Chicken in 2006.

Death on the Derwent - A Murder Mystery set in Belper 1949, his third book and first novel, was published in 1999. His fourth book, A Judge Too Far - A Biography of His Honour Judge Keith Matthewman QC of the Nottingham Crown Court, was first published in 2001.

Inspired by Heanor Schooldays, Mr Annable's second 'whodunit' novel and fifth book Lost Lad A Mystery set in Derbyshire in 1960 (ISBN 0 9530419 6 4) was published in 2003. His sixth book Scruffy Chicken A Derbyshire Mystery set in 1965 (ISBN 0 9530419 4 8) was published in 2006. Secret Summer A Derbyshire Mystery set in 1966 – was published by The Nazca Plains Corporation in Las Vegas in 2010.

Sea Change (the real truth behind Lost Lad) was published in 2014.

Narvel lives with his Civil Partner Terry Durand in Belper, Derbyshire. In September 2014 they celebrated their 38 years together.

LOST LAD

In the glorious summer of 1960, six pals from William Howitt Secondary Modern School in the hilltop mining town of Heanor, decide to cycle up into the high Derbyshire hills. They have a great time. Everything goes well - until they cycle out of the village of Litton, along a narrow country lane and speedily descend the 550ft steep drop into a deep, wooded ravine which is called Water-cum-Jolly-Dale. Six boys were happily racing down the hill, but only five reach the bottom!

In the following hours, the boys make a thorough search for their friend - in vain. Eventually the police are called in and make a careful professional search - in vain. Where is the lost lad?

Forty-three years pass and one of the original pals who has spent most of his adult life in the United States returns to England to re-open the search. An odyssey develops which takes many twists and turns around the lives of different men, some of whom can hardly recognise each other four decades on. An investigation which turns lives upside-down. A quest which eventually comes to a dramatic and stunning conclusion when we finally learn the devastating truth about - the 'Lost Lad'.

This is an autobiographic, sometimes comic, sometimes erotic psychological thriller; a 'rollercoaster of emotions' from the depths of despair to the heights of happiness. Along the way, Narvel Annable skilfully blending fact and fiction, reveals a secret history and vividly recreates the gritty realities of his youth on both sides of the Atlantic. A local story of long-lost friendship and a Derbyshire travelogue which combines elements of folklore, legend and quirky, crooked old men who inhabit the murky depths of a sleazy underworld. It is all set against the magnificent moody backdrop of a 'howling wilderness', spectacular ravines and lush green valleys. This entertaining and ingenious whodunit will take you through the recesses, nooks and crannies of a life, which, for many years, lay hidden behind the mask of a stern and respectable schoolmaster.

Lost Lad Reviews

"Intriguing. We are made to wait nearly half a century before Narvel finally reveals to us the secret of his devilishly clever conjuring trick. Lost Lad is an entertaining, interesting and well constructed novel. It'll be a real eye opener to the folk of Derbyshire.
    "I've never featured in a mystery thriller before. I've enjoyed every minute of it."

John Holmes, BBC Radio Nottingham

"Written by a guy who so obviously loves this county of ours, the novel's Derbyshire backdrop is spectacular. It is a blend of fact with fiction and is packed with characters and events which many of you may find familiar.

"Lost Lad is a fantastic read. We at the Cash Project have no hesitation in recommending it to you."

Gary Woodhouse, The Bent Spire, Chesterfield. Easter 2005

"Lost Lad is written with conviction. In its way, it works quite well, and canters along at a reasonable pace. It's just that, the world unlidded for us here strikes an innocent like me as loathsomely tacky. But that at least underscores Narvel Annable's competence in bringing the more revolting characters so horribly to life! All in all, it is an odd book, and, for all I know, epoch-making for its genre."

Maxwell Craven, Derby Evening Telegraph, 13.02.04

"Here's a thriller for the fireside. Narvel Annable's easy style, coupled with local knowledge, makes this an entertaining read and will have the reader determined to find out what happened to the lost lad."

Judith Halliday, Derbyshire Today, December 2003

"Annable's prose is generally excellent - evocative without being torturous. It is sharp and witty. His characters are well observed and the story - on the whole - unfolds well. Narvel Annable is undoubtedly a talented author."

Mark Michalowski, SHOUT! March 2004

"The narrative seamlessly blends fact and fantasy, vividly recreating scenes from a tough and sometimes sleazy youth. The story follows the fates of six friends and the investigation which lays bare their fears and weaknesses, building to a dramatic final twist."

Ian Soutar Sheffield Telegraph 10.09.04

"An interesting tale in which truth and fiction are cleverly blurred."

Derbyshire Life and Countryside December 2003

"Some very strange 'goings on'. Narvel Annable weaves his narrative, carefully travelling from the Derbyshire Dales to the urban landscapes of America, and back, through a minefield of intrigue and mystery before the story reaches the final conclusion."

Keith How, Peak Advertiser 03.11.03

"It offers a unique insight into the former history teacher's life. The story takes us back to a Dickensian style school which almost drove Mr Annable to suicide. A word of warning: some of the action is not for the fainthearted and is more suitable for adults than children."

James Mitchinson, Worksop Guardian 17.10.03

"Compulsive reading for those who have grown up in Derbyshire, but also for anyone who enjoys a good mystery."

Emily Davies, Ilkeston Advertiser 30.10.03

"Lost Lad reveals Narvel's lifelong passion for cycling along leafy lanes and his appreciation of natural beauty. The spirit and atmosphere of the novel is cleverly captured by the Shipley Park artist Lesley Robinson."

Pauline Oldrini, Belper News and the Ripley and Heanor News 30.10.03

"An entertaining and gritty mystery of a missing cyclist."

Jonathan Dodds, Buxton Advertiser 19.12.03

Lost Lad is available on kindle at Amazon. It can be ordered from bookshops or directly from the author by sending a cheque for £8.00 to - 44 Dovedale Crescent, Belper, Derbyshire DE56 1HJ.

Scruffy Chicken

A Mystery set in Derbyshire 1965

The year is 1965. Outside, it is dull, wet and cold. Inside the steam room of the Derby Turkish Baths, it is a hissing haze of hot, gurgling, boiling anger, a chamber of pea soup where visibility is down to an arm's length. Dimly seen, a man is resting in the corner, head lolling back, eyes closed, pleasantly soaking up the heat - or so it seems. Various bathers come and go. All regulars, they all know this ugly, effeminate man who frequently secludes himself in his usual corner. They all know the outrageous, the common Becksitch Betty, the local drag act, the acid queen who has inflamed so many passions in the nervous, closeted, gay communities of Derby and Nottingham. Nobody wants to bother this infamous bitch, left to doze in swirls of vapour, left to doze in a miasma of his twisted hate and jealousy.

It was the very last time this hated old hag was ever seen. Nobody saw him dress and nobody saw him leave the building. Becksitch Betty never returned to his mean little cottage in Belper and was never, ever heard of again ... until ... On July 12th in the year 2005, Simeon Hogg is celebrating his 60th birthday. By a fluke, he stumbles upon the truth and solves the old mystery of the disappearance of the infamous, the long-past Becksitch Betty. That same ugly old queen Simeon once knew when he was a scruffy chicken forty years before.

Narvel Annable delivers yet another cracking autobiographic whodunit, which begins in Detroit on the day before the assassination of President Kennedy. Eventually, it takes us into deepest Derbyshire, into a bitchy underworld of crones, queens, toads, goblins, gnomes, feral boys and social-climbing snobs of the mid-1960's - finally concluding just days after the appalling London bombings of '7/7'.

Follow the candid teenage Simeon as he cycles. Meander with him around the leafy lanes of Derbyshire and discovers a labyrinth; a secret, subterranean, fairytale world which could have been penned by Grimm. Meet his unique collection of curious characters, all taking shelter in their twilight existence; monsters, clowns, the high and the low, the pretentious and the pompous, the scented and the sneering, the common and the crude. They are all here, all inspired by real people, all warped by the vicious homophobic cruelty and bigotry of 1965.

Scruffy Chicken Reviews

"A rare pleasure I never thought I'd see: a gay thriller set in Derbyshire."

Matthew Parris of The Times

"An excellent book by Narvel Annable! This novel is superb in that it describes the somewhat 'hidden' Gay history of the 1960s. I believe we should not forget what, for many of us, our forefathers experienced. Scruffy Chicken documents both the attitudes of the times and the experience of living in a society which derided and negated the lives of Gay men. Annable has created a masterpiece documenting much of our non recorded Gay history.

"It is his second Gay semi-autobiographical novel, and captures life in the mid 1960s, not only here in the UK but also in the USA, a definite first for this type of novel.

"Set in both Detroit and Derbyshire it chronicles the very 'misspent' youth of a Gay young man as he stumbles towards adulthood. The journey, which is essentially what it is, features some rather strange people in extremely bizarre situations. Annable manages to interweave an ingenious mystery as part of the plot, the disappearance of 'Becksitch Betty' a rather nasty drag Queen cum washed up stage act. Not surprisingly, most of the bizarre characters come under some form of suspicion!

"To describe the book as 'a novel' is somewhat disingenuous, it brilliantly documents the homophobia, fear and clear hatred faced by Gay men in the early to mid sixties and cleverly manages to transport the reader to those less tolerant times.

"The journey of Simeon Hogg – the book's central character, and Annable's alter ego – begins in Detroit in 1963, and beautifully describes Simeon's observations – of both Gay life here and 'stateside'.

204

"The encounters with the 60s Gay underworld will be enlightening for anyone under forty yet very real to those for whom Queer life was so different to today. The Derbyshire, Detroit and Nottinghamshire 'scenes' are vividly portrayed together with the local dialect and it hard to imagine that some of the bizarre characters in the story ever really existed – thankfully, they did!

"Scruffy Chicken depicts a time when homosexuality was illegal and as such this alone makes for a darker story. If you are looking for titillation this is not the book for you, although the life experiences, sexual and other are well documented.

"I can truly say this is one of the best books I have ever read and a must for all Gay men, whatever age.

"Scruffy Chicken is a real tour de force of a read!"

Paul Hunt, Chief Features Writer - Shout! - Yorkshire's Gay Paper, March 2007

"In a quaint old library deep in middle England, a coming of age story is unfolding, casting light in some dark corners of the gay world. The tale being told is sad, sometimes cruel and oftentimes laughing-out loud funny. Local author Narvel Annable, a retired schoolteacher, is creatively portraying characters from his most recent novel, Scruffy Chicken, which is inspired by his own story.

"The big picture is about a wide-eyed teenager guided on an erotic adventure tour of Turkish baths and active toilets by a series of unlikely hosts, discovering along the way how discriminatory attitudes have driven some gays to despair and isolation.

"Annable also chronicles discriminatory traits within the gay community itself, including gay on gay abuse in which elderly and unattractive gays are targeted. It is a study of contrasts, old verses young, pristine countryside beauty versus smelly toilet-side fixations and beautiful bodies versus stooped, toothless, lopsided forms.

"Tonight the audience in Derby Central Library is mesmerised by Annable's acting ability. By turns he is an adventurous chicken, ugly troll, vicious queen and arrogant, upper-class pretender. But the most interesting characters are the tormented, unattractive gays Annable encounters during his travels.

"The talk concludes with enthusiastic applause and a very civilised serving of wine amidst introductions and handshakes."

Brad Teeter was writing about his evening at the Derby Central Library on February 21st 2007. It was printed on May 9th 2007 in Vancouver's Lesbian and Gay Biweekly EXTRA! West www.xtra.ca British Columbia, Canada.

Scruffy Chicken is available on Kindle at Amazon. It can be ordered from bookshops or directly from the author. Send a cheque for £8 to Narvel Annable - 44 Dovedale Crescent Belper Derby DE56 1HJ. Or phone 01 773 82 44 83.

Secret Summer
A Mystery set in Derbyshire 1966

Here is a heartrending tale of young love. Narvel Annable reaches down into the joys and sorrows of his past to produce an autobiographic account of adventure, passion and pain. A cracking whodunit; it features a missing person and contract killers from the unforgiving criminal underworld of Detroit. Barely out of his teens, Simeon is homesick for his beloved Derbyshire, but falls in love with a mysterious tough-guy called Ahmed. The storyline explores a mixture of magic and menace following two incompatible personalities, desperately trying to make their relationship work in the homophobic landscape of Detroit, January 1966.

Why secret? Because when you are young, when you are in love and if you are gay in 1966 - it must be secret. You lust in secret, hunt in secret and love in secret. See Simeon in love; a rollercoaster, a frantic mixture of agony and ecstasy spanning the Atlantic Ocean. He has no support save for that which was available from the frequently unreliable world of gay men who were riddled with all their own personal problems, repressions and hang-ups.

Signed copies of Secret Summer are available directly from the author.

To include P&P, please send a £8 cheque payable to Narvel Annable at 44 Dovedale Crescent, Belper, Derby DE56 1HJ. Phone: 01 773 82 44 83.

"Another quirky corker in the Derbyshire mystery series from the irrepressible Narvel Annable. A Boy's Own story from 1966; it is a most entertaining read."

Peter Tatchell

Secret Summer Reviews

Review from Bradford's Telegraph & Argus printed on April 16th 2011

Inspired by a cycling holiday, this is a moving portrayal of a young gay man on the run and ostracised in the 1960s.

Bullied as a child and an adult, Narvel Annable has endured the agony of being treated as an outsider simply because he is gay. He was a guest speaker at an International Day Against Homophobia event in Bradford in 2009 and was nominated for an Equity Partnership award last year. Narvel describes writing his novel as a cathartic experience helping him to deal with painful memories.

Partly set in Bradford, the townscape and terrain of the metropolis is described as –
*   'A splendid panorama of pinnacles and finials. Most notable was the distinctive Italianate clock tower of the City Hall and the ornate Venetian Gothic parapets and pinnacles of the Wool Exchange. They reminded Simeon [Narvel's alter ego] of an ancient fairytale castle.'*

Simeon also discovers Bradford Cathedral and is delighted by its tranquil, peaceful 'secret garden'.

At its heart, Secret Summer is a touching story of young love, laced with a well-paced thriller involving a missing person and a gay criminal underworld. It is also a love letter to Narvel's native Derbyshire with beautifully written passages devoted to its natural landscape.

Emma Clayton

Five Star www.amazon.com Review of Secret Summer from the Chief Features Writer of Shout! Magazine – Paul Hunt – December 31st 2010

Superb - A Must Read!!!

This book really does have it all; joy, pain, sadness and comedy, not to mention true pathos.

I found the characters very 'real' although I do appreciate it is a semi-autobiographical novel.

The book takes you on a historical journey to life before the decriminalisation of homosexuality. The author manages, very skilfully, to explore and convey the sexual, emotional and psychological awakening of Simeon, the central character, and relates in superb narrative those who shape his future.

This book is an excellent read – you may laugh, you may cry, but you will undoubtedly want to explore Narvel Annable's other books!

Nottinghamshire's Queer Bulletin - Number 57 – December 2010 / January 2011 – page 5.

See the original on Nottinghamshire's Rainbow Heritage website - www.nottsrainbowheritage.org.uk

Detroit to Derbyshire via the Mafia, Freaks and Young Love

This is the third semi-autobiographical novel to feature young Simeon Hogg. Firstly set in Detroit where he gets involved in a complex, somewhat abusive relationship with a young man linked to a pink mafia. He literally escapes back to his native Derbyshire. Fearful for his life, Simeon goes on the run (well, actually on the pedal) as he cycles through Derbyshire and Yorkshire.

The hidden, secretive, often furtive world is reflected in encounters with some oddball characters who appear in Narvel's previous books, but also with others who anticipated the era of Gay Liberation. We meet – amongst others – Mr Toad, Droopy the Vesuvius vacuum cleaner, Fluff and Nobby the Gnome.

It's history, it's travelogue, it's crime, it's sex (quite a lot of), it's a love story and it's another good read.

If you want a signed copy of Secret Summer, you can get one directly from the author by going to his website at – **www.narvelannable.co.uk**

Review / feature from the Belper News - October 6th 2010 – www.belpernews.co.uk

Gay author's book published in the USA

Literature can be appreciated by so many different people. It can bring them together, make them laugh and make them cry. In many instances it can even serve to break down negative views and stereotypes.

A book written by a retired man from Belper, quite easily accomplishes all of the above – and more.

Not only is Secret Summer the first of Narvel Annable's novels to be professionally published, it is the first to reach audiences in America.

Narvel has achieved what so many British celebrities have tried to do and failed - he has made it in America. The book was snapped up by The Nazca Plains Corporation situated in the bright lights of Las Vegas.

Although this book has more than enough exciting twists and turns to stand alone as a truly gripping fictional read, it also has a very important message – that people's lives can be ruined by the attitudes of others.

Secret Summer is not just a must for the gay community – it also celebrates the beautiful Belper countryside and the surrounding towns and villages are given several mentions. It celebrates Narvel's love of the area.

Katy Hallam

Review of Secret Summer from Tony Fenwick Co-Chair of LGBT History Month – www.lgbthistorymonth.org - and Schools OUT – www.schools-out.org – January 12th 2011.

In many ways, Narvel Annable's Secret Summer is a very different novel. It follows the fortunes and misfortunes of a young Simeon Hogg in the 1960s.

Born and bred in the mining towns of industrial Derbyshire, Simeon moves to Detroit, where he is swept off his feet and taken into a whole new world by the sinister Ahmed, who has abducted the boy and shows his love by taking possessiveness to a whole new level.

Simeon is waited upon and lavished upon and given a complete new life and identity, but he is homesick for Belper and he knows that if he ever crosses Ahmed his life might be in danger. So he plans his escape and the physically repulsive but well-endowed Mr Toad becomes his temporary saviour in the Derbyshire countryside.

There's no cocaine fuelled evenings in the bars and clubs in Secret Summer. The novel is a mystery, but the beauty of it is that it gives us a rich insight into what it was like to be a young gay man in the US and in the East Midlands in 1966. Simeon is based on Narvel himself. The colourful and often grotesque locals he describes are real people from his past; only the names have been changed. Moreover, it shows us how people in these times coped with being outcasts and outlaws just because of whom they loved.

Review / feature from the Derby Telegraph - September 24th 2010 –
www.thisisderbyshire.co.uk

A celebration of Derbyshire as 'pink mafia' go on the rampage

When it comes to gay thrillers set in Derbyshire, author Narvel Annable seems to have cornered the market.

Secret Summer begins in Detroit in 1966. Simeon Hogg is imprisoned by his lover Ahmed, in a luxurious apartment funded by a gay criminal underworld described as a 'pink mafia'. Eventually he manages to escape with a friend, Gary, and the pair return to Simeon's native Derbyshire, where he discovers a thriving gay scene in Matlock's caves. But the mafia are hot on their heels and Gary disappears. Simeon goes on the run cycling around youth hostels under an assumed name.
Narvel is a committed campaigner and his latest book is part of that campaign. Secret Summer teaches the heterosexual majority what it is like to be an ostracized minority. His books and campaigns are Narvel's way of assuaging the guilt he feels for keeping quiet for so long. But Secret Summer will not just appeal to gay readers; it's a celebration of Derbyshire too.

Helen Meynell

Review from the Sheffield Star printed on March 14th 2011

Next time you're browsing a book shop looking for a gay thriller based in Derbyshire, you could do worse that think of Narvel Annable.

The former Worksop Valley Comprehensive teacher's third novel in his 'pink whodunit' trilogy released in the UK by The Nazca Plains Corporation in Las Vegas.

Depicting a flourishing gay scene in Matlock caves and a homosexual Mafia, Secret Summer follows on from Narvel's previous efforts Lost Lad and Scruffy Chicken.

Colin Drury

Review from the Harrogate Advertiser printed on May 6th 2011

This dramatic story crosses the Atlantic. It follows Annable's own experiences, eventually bringing his lead character, Simeon, to Harrogate. He meets Big Bill Bulman, an obese American based on Bill Silvey, whom Annable met in 1966.

Bill was living at the Old Swan Hotel and was a regular visitor to the Royal Baths. Annable describes him as a colourful character who enthused about the town in a roaring Deep South accent and thinks many other people who were in the area at the time will probably remember him.

Vicky Carr

Review / feature from *Shout!* November 2010 www.shoutweb.co.uk

The secret of summer

Shout!'s favourite author, has finally arrived. The Nazca Plains Corporation of Las Vegas, a major American publishing house, is hoping to have Narvel Annable's latest novel, Secret Summer, on bookshelves around the world.

Paul Hunt

Comments about Secret Summer from Councillor Robin Wood – November 3rd 2010

Robin is a former Mayor of the City of Derby. His partner was the venerable Jeffery Tillett [1927-2008] also a former Mayor in 1977 when the Queen granted Derby city status. During their 37 years together, Robin and Jeffery made a huge contribution, cautiously yet bravely improving the quality of life for the Derby LGBT community.

"I thoroughly enjoyed reading Secret Summer. It brought back some memories and, curiously, memories of things Jeff used to tell me decades ago. He used to talk about the 'Mansfield Case'. As far as I recall, this was a court case in the 1950s//60s when a lot of gay men were prosecuted. The implications spread far and wide making the gay crowd in Derby and Nottingham very nervous indeed - as exemplified in this novel.

"Perhaps we are all becoming gargoyles and gnomes!"

LGBT History Month Bulletin 76 – October 2010
www.lgbthistorymonth.org.uk

New Novel from Narvel

There aren't many people called Narvel Annable and there aren't many gay men who have spent half their youth in a Derbyshire mining community and the other half in Detroit.

LGBT History Month Co-Chair Tony Fenwick said –

*"Our SCHOOLS **OUT** member is an accomplished author with a wealth of experience and knowledge about gay life on both sides of the pond. His characters – heroes, villains, Adonises and monsters – are inspired by real people in real places which are still there. After enjoying Lost Lad, I'm looking forward to reading Secret Summer immensely."*

Comment from Terry Ladlow of Terivison Productions, Hunmanby, Filey, North Yorkshire – November 12th 2010

"Secret Summer is so perfect! It is sensitive, erotic, poignant, tender and so human. I've been reading it and re-reading chapters to get the full feeling and power of the interplay of characters, feelings and emotions Narvel Annable has created. I felt for Simeon and his tenderness, stimuli, aberrations, and the unenviable intolerance he suffered as a boy. Congratulations on writing such a fine book."

To obtain a personally signed copy of Secret Summer for £8 inclusive of P&P – send a cheque payable to Narvel Annable at 44 Dovedale Crescent, Belper, Derbyshire DE56 1HJ. Or phone - 01 773 824483

Heanor Schooldays
A Social History

ISBN 0 9530419 1 3

This book deals with the last hundred years but majors on the author's personal experience of the 1950's and 1960's in which he recreates the optimistic social atmosphere of teenagers enjoying the popular culture of the day. You will also gain insights into the gritty, unpretentious, honest character of Heanor folk.

It is a graphic, colourful and emotional journey from the depths of despair to the heights of happiness. Along the way, Narvel Annable honours the memory of teachers, headmasters and headmistresses who have shaped the lives of countless Heanorians. Disquiet is expressed, as discredited modern teaching methods are contrasted to the successful tried and trusted methods of past years.

Forty-five photographs and fifteen documents will rekindle memories. The work is supported by a foreword from His Honour Judge Keith Matthewman QC and contains first-hand accounts from many contributors, including the one-time local lad, The Rt. Hon. Kenneth Clarke QC, MP, the former Chancellor of the Exchequer from 1993 to 1997. 205 pages.

"I was enthralled. A cracking collection of tales."

John Holmes, BBC Radio Derby.

Reviews of Heanor Schooldays

Vivid and detailed memories of a 1950's childhood. Sensitively written, Narvel explores the vagaries of the educational system which helped to develop his character and prepare him for adulthood. This is an important snapshot of social history, and the author brings it to life with recollections of strict discipline, bullying and extreme forms of punishment. A rollercoaster of emotions."

Pauline Oldrini, Ripley and Heanor News and Belper News 05.11.98

Mr Annable mixes anecdote with comment to provide an important record of changes made in education as seen from the sides of both pupil and teacher."

Geoff Hammerton, Derby Evening Telegraph 04.12.98

"This autobiographic book charts a gritty history and weaves a graphic tapestry of Derbyshire school life 40 years ago. It is littered with colourful characters, interesting facts and first-hand accounts."

David Mark, Nottingham Evening Post 27.10.98

"Narvel Annable has managed to do what most authors never could; that is, to make a book about his schooldays a thoroughly enjoyable read.

"In his unique style he gives us a history of people and institutions. He gives us his views on education, past and present, and we are treated to a fascinating glimpse of a school-life in the fifties and sixties, complete with all its sorrows and joys. You do not have to remember those days to enjoy this book: you do not have to be an educationalist to enjoy this book: but if you are in either group, or both, you will enjoy it all the more - and so will your children."

His Honour Judge Keith Matthewman QC November 1998

Reviews of Death on the Derwent

"A remarkable murder mystery novel ... gives a new twist to the whodunit genre ... a skilful mixture of fact and fiction ... strong historical interest ... complications and twists, red herrings and false trails. Mr Annable has got himself a real-life, ready-made character in Miss Florence Calder. This could be - should be - the start of a series of Miss Calder novels."

Geoff Hammerton, Derby Evening Telegraph 17.12.99

"Peopled with distinctive characters ... meritorious for the descriptive detail. A well-produced book. Worth reading a second time or more to fully appreciate the construction of this ingenious novel."

Margaret Beardsley, Belper News 23.02.00

"Great characters!" **Bob Attewell, Belper Express 13.01.00**

"I loved the rich and qualitative language, the machinations, twists and turns of the plot. I was empathetic with the characters as they desperately tried to unravel the mystery Mr Annable has so brilliantly created."

Terry Ladlow, 'Terivision Productions', Wetwang, Driffield, East Yorkshire 22.03.00

"Simon Tonks is the village fool who ends up as a servant to the Calders, Claud Hoadley is the pompous Belper man-turned-snob who teaches elocution so that the townspeople can 'better themselves' and Aubrey Pod is a pushy 'Mr Toad' character always full of himself."

Paul Imrie, 'Talk of the Town', Derby Evening Telegraph 23.11.99

Hello Readers,

The next novel after *Sea Change* will receive inspiration from the period 1978 to 1995. I was a history master at the Valley Comprehensive School in Worksop, north Nottinghamshire. I taught as I was taught in the 1950s - too strict, too formal, too unwilling to modernise and reluctant to embrace progressive trends in state education which arrived in the 1980s. This 'Mr Chips' mindset was a cloak to conceal the continuing anxiety of leading a double life. Inside, a frightened homosexual was trying to look like a confident heterosexual on the outside. It had to look like a teacher easily fitting in with pupils and staff.

For about 16 years, for the most part, Mr Annable succeeded in dodging disapproval and maintained a mask of po-faced respectability hiding inside a small bungalow in the ultra conservative colliery village of Clowne in north-east Derbyshire. Like most isolated, closeted gay men, I spoke little of myself and was constantly on guard. It became a way of life.

From time to time there were alarming incidents at school. Our history staffroom, predominately macho male, was a hotbed of football fanaticism, strong language and raucous crude humour.

One afternoon, a colleague lazily leaned back in his seat and insouciantly yawned out –
     'Nothing much to do. I suppose we could go out and beat up a queer.'

Probably disappointed at a lack of response, he repeated the bait several times over the following weeks. Others took notice. One of them gave advice -
     'You know, Narvel. You really should make more effort to socialise. Try to fit in. Come to the pub with us after school once in a while.' He lowered his voice in earnest. 'Get yourself a girlfriend. Talk about her. Better still, get yourself married. If the boss [headmaster] thought you were queer, he'd have you out of this place so fast your feet wouldn't touch the ground!'

The final two years saw gay hate terminating a teaching career. Although my private life continued to remain very private, some pupils began to speculate on Mr Annable's sexuality. They turned him into an object of fun inflicting humiliating hurtful episodes. I might have survived a few, but there were too many. A steady torturous drip destroyed my credibility and confidence. At the edge of a breakdown, a shell of my former self, there came a point when my position was untenable. I was unable to discharge professional duties. These appalling disrespectful attacks were never taken seriously by senior management. One culprit was told –
'That was a silly thing to say.'

On Thursday, April 6th 1995, a colleague commented on continuing melancholy, my appearance and exhaustion. She earnestly advised 'a few days off'. I walked out of that classroom and never returned.

So much for reality. The fiction for Simeon Hogg detailed in a new book will be a return to work after a period of recuperation and counselling. In a halfway house between several months of lesson preparations and actual teaching, he is installed in a small classroom adjacent to his old classroom where the daily life of a busy school down a long corridor can be observed. This is the vehicle for a novel which explores all the above issues. Mr Hogg will be reflecting back on his years at the Valley Comprehensive School. His story will be told in back flashes and forward flashes as he tries to make sense of a repressed and difficult career.

When to be published? Don't hold your breath! My track record is one book every five years. If I live long enough, perhaps it will see the light of day sometime before Christmas 2019. Could be sooner.

Narvel Annable

7480067R00123

Printed in Great Britain
by Amazon.co.uk, Ltd.,
Marston Gate.